Dumpster Dying

OTHER BOOKS BY LESLEY A. DIEHL

Dumpster Dying

Book 1 in the Big Lake murder mystery series

Lesley A. Diehl

This work is dedicated to the horses, cows, and dancing cowboys of the Big Lake country.

ACKNOWLEDGMENTS

My appreciation to my critique partner, Jan Day Fehrman, who makes me write better than I think I can.

As ever, I am grateful for his support, love, and patience—my cowboy, Glenn.

CHAPTER 1

Emily Rhodes, the new bartender at the Big Lake Country Club, blew damp tendrils of sun-bleached hair out of her face as she kicked and dragged three plastic trash bags across the sunbaked asphalt lot behind the clubhouse. A full moon illuminated the area's lone palm tree under which sat a metal beast waiting for its nightly feeding.

"Here you go, big boy," she said. She let go of the bags and, with one hand, lifted the dumpster's lid on the side closest to her. The usual stench of rotting garbage assaulted her nostrils. She ignored the smell and tried to heave the bag into the container, but it tumbled back out. She shoved back the lid on the other side, and mentally crossed her fingers she wouldn't have to hop in there and stomp around on that stuff to make room like she did the other night.

By the glow of the security light she spotted a white object lying at the far end of the dumpster, a cowboy hat, a very special cowboy hat, a Silver Belly, expensive and worn by very few men. She'd encountered just such a man earlier in the evening. The circumstances of their meeting were not pleasant.

What the hell was that doing here, she wondered? Emily leaned in as far as she could. Her feet left the ground, and she teetered on the rim of the dumpster. She struggled to reach the hat, tugged at it and almost went head first into the bin, head first onto the man's face hidden beneath the hat.

Ugh! She fell back and dropped the metal lid, the clang reverberating off the side of the building in the still night. She covered her mouth with her hand, and leaned against the dumpster. *That can't be. I didn't see that, did I?*

She turned, opened the lid once more, gingerly pushed a garbage bag to one side and peered in for another look. She remembered him from earlier in the evening when he had grabbed her blouse and tried to pull her across the bar. He had worn a brilliant white cowboy shirt with roses appliquéd on the front yoke. Now the shirt front was as dark as the blood-red flowers.

She gulped hard to hold back the bile working its way up from her stomach and looked around the lot. It was empty. She needed help.

She ran for the door of the clubhouse. The knob wouldn't turn.

Oh, damn. I did it again, left the door on auto lock. Now I can't get back in. She felt in her pocket for her cell phone, then remembered she had left it along with her keys lying on the bar counter. But she had hidden a spare car key in the wheel well. *I'll have to drive for help, and the sooner the better.*

⬧

She gripped the steering wheel with sweaty hands and hunched over it, the tension in her neck sending shooting pains up the back of her head. As she turned out of the country club grounds and punched the accelerator, she saw the flashing lights of a police car heading toward her. She sat back in the seat and dropped her shoulders. *Oh, good. Help was on its way.*

As the cruiser's lights caught hers, its driver slammed to a halt and did a controlled skid blocking her lane. She stood on her brake, and stopped the car, then jumped out and ran toward the police vehicle. Tears of relief poured down her face and onto her chin.

Two officers with drawn guns greeted her.

"Stop right there, on the ground, hands out," said the officer who had been driving.

"But officer, there's a man there. I think he's dead."

"On the ground, on the ground." His voice chilled the hot, still night.

Emily raised her shaking hands and dropped on rubbery knees. *This can't be happening.*

The other member of the duo placed his knee in her back, cuffed her, pulled her to her feet, and searched her.

"Why are you doing this to me? I was trying to help. The man back there, someone killed him, I think," Emily said. The officer walked her to the police car.

"We know all about that. Got a call a few minutes ago, and we're responding. Now we'd like to find out what you know about it."

She began to hiccup, her usual reaction when she was frightened. "Me? (hic) Me? I found him (hic) when I took out the garbage. I would have called it in, but I locked myself out of the bar, and I left my cell phone inside." Her explanation sounded lame even to her ears.

"Sure you weren't running?" asked Officer Handcuffs.

They shoved her into the back seat and headed toward the clubhouse.

"Sure I was running. I was trying to get help."

"Looks like you're the one who needs it," said the driver. The other officer turned in his seat and looked at her. There was hardness in his eyes that she knew he reserved for the guilty.

"My car. It's in the middle of the road," hiccupped Emily. She twisted her head around to look out of the back window. If anything happened to that car, she wouldn't be able to afford another, and her insurance rates would go sky high. There was little point in telling the officers her financial concerns. They were after a criminal, and they thought they'd found her.

At the clubhouse, the driver shone his high-powered flashlight into the dumpster, confirming their report.

"Shot in the chest. Gotta be dead. Lotta blood."

She tried to shut out her memory of the body, but the officer's words brought it back to her in IMAX and Technicolor. It was just the reminder she needed to experience the gory scene yet again.

"Dispatcher alerted an ambulance when the call came in. Too late for this guy," said the driver. Emily could hear the siren on the main road. He walked over to the large trash bags Emily had dropped by the side of the dumpster.

"These yours?" he asked.

"From the bar," she said. "I put them down, then I..." He held up his hand signaling he wasn't interested in her explanations, walked to the back door and turned the knob. To Emily's surprise, the door opened.

"I thought you said it was locked."

"It was. I swear. It locked behind me." *This was crazy.*

As she struggled to keep herself calm, the other officer played his light around the dumpster area. The beam illuminated two objects at the edge of the employee parking area.

"What have we here?" he said. He stooped and, with forefinger and thumb, he picked up a set of keys. In the other hand he held a cell phone.

"Yours?" he asked.

Oh, Oh. Get a grip, she told herself. This is the law, and you're innocent of any wrong doing. Well, pretty innocent. "I'm not saying another thing. I want a lawyer."

Well, truth be told, she already had a lawyer, but her attorney didn't handle criminal cases. She'd have to hire someone else. And pay him. *Let's see. How can I divide my first paycheck in two? Half of three hundred dollars minus social security and FICA. Was that sufficient to retain two attorneys?* Emily didn't think so. Now she really was in trouble. *Hiccup.*

Once at the station, her escorts walked her into an office at the rear of the building. The lettering on the glass door read, "Detective Myers."

"Don't I get a phone call?" Her voice was high-pitched and shaky.

She repeated her question, this time trying to put more assertion and less fear into her tone. They undid her cuffs and pushed her into a wooden chair in front of a battered gray metal desk. The window air conditioner was valiantly trying to cool and dehumidify the tiny room, but to little effect. The space smelled like dirty socks.

Another man entered the room, but didn't answer her question. This must be Detective Myers, surmised Emily. He looked kind of like William Conrad, short, round, but without the award-winning Matt Dillon voice. He was wearing cowboy boots, but then everyone who was male in these parts wore them. When she and Fred, both retired teachers, first settled in rural south Florida to spend their winters, Emily was shocked to find that real cowboys even wore their spurs into the post office. What fun, she had told her friends back north.

But her William Conrad look-alike cop was no real cowboy, and he probably wouldn't prove to be much fun either. He pulled his pants up under his ample belly and strode across the room to his desk chair.

"Sum kinda nerdin," he said.

"What?" Emily's teeth began to chatter despite the warm, sticky room.

"Ja minom," he said. He bent to one side in his chair. Emily leaned over to follow his movements. On the floor beside his desk sat a large, rusty coffee can. He spit tobacco juice into it, then sat back up. Emily felt her empty stomach do a cartwheel of nausea.

"I said, you seem kinda nervous, but then I guess I'd be too if I'd killed someone."

Emily opened her mouth to reply, then stopped herself. "I don't want to talk to you. I don't have to talk to you. Charge me with something so I can call my lawyer."

Emily clapped her hand over her mouth, surprised at her audacity. This wasn't like her. Well, correction, it wasn't the way Emily used to behave, but since Fred, the rat, had died on her and left her without a cent to her name, Emily found she was developing a lot of backbone she didn't even know she had.

"You think you're some kind of lawyer?" Detective Spittoon asked.

"I watch a lot of TV, crime TV, and I read. I know my rights." She probably shouldn't have said that because the detective rolled his eyes and winked at the officers still standing behind her in the office.

"A regular *Law and Order* buff here. Guess you got me on that one. I'll back off and offer you a cup of coffee then."

"I don't want any coffee. I know you'll try to use the cup to get a sample of my DNA and then you'll match it to something at the crime scene, and soon I'll be heading north to the Lakewood Women's Correctional Facility, and all over bad coffee. No thanks. I'd rather die of thirst in your office and have the Civil Liberties Union take on my case." Emily folded her arms across her chest to stop her hands from trembling.

The door swung open and a tall, broad-shouldered man with wavy brown hair entered the room. Emily's gaze traveled from the full moustache riding his top lip down over his slim hips to his feet. Yep. He was wearing cowboy boots and from his tanned face and hands, he could have ridden the range.

"Toby," he said, "get out of my desk chair and go find yourself something to do. This is not your case. It's mine."

The fat man jumped from the chair and scurried out of the room, the two officers in tow.

"And, Toby," the man said, "take your damn spit bucket with you."

"Yes sir." Toby, now-no-longer-Detective-Myers-nor-William-Conrad, hustled back into the office. He grabbed the rusty can and hurried back out.

"Sorry about that," the real Detective Myers said. "I'm Detective Stanton Lewis."

"The door says 'Myers'," Emily said. She wondered if this was some kind of a police scam to confuse her into a confession.

Detective Lewis slid into the desk chair. "Myers retired years ago. We never got around to changing the lettering. Sorry about that."

"So far you've been sorry about two things, but neither of them includes apologizing for hauling me out of my car and dragging me into the station. I found a dead man. It's not something I do every day, you know."

Lewis cleared his throat and directed his attention to the file he was carrying when he entered the room. He opened the folder, and Emily looked across the desk at its contents. The goods on her.

"It says here that you were fleeing the scene of a murder."

"It does not say that. You're reading off the take-out menu for *Charlie's Grill*." Emily prided herself on being able to read print upside down.

"I want in there," said a familiar voice from the other side of the door.

"I'm here, Clara. Help me." Bravado be damned, Emily decided. She began to cry again, and her hiccups returned.

The door swung open and Clara Rogers, manager of the bar and restaurant at Big Lake Country Club, stood there, towering over Toby. Emily had seen that look on her face before. It was the one Clara used when she was about to give the boot to some cowboy misbehaving at the club. The officers who had arrested Emily flanked Toby, whose expression said he welcomed the protection. Clara was one big woman.

"Call off your terriers," Clara said. She nodded her head in the direction of the officers who looked amused at the sight of Toby fearfully peering up into Clara's angry eyes. "And take this troll outa here and get him a good mouthwash." She strode into the room.

Detective Lewis got up from his chair. "Give us a minute here," he said. He gestured his comrades out of the room and closed the door. "You know, Clara, you may be the manager at the club, but you're not the bouncer here."

Clara ignored Lewis. "I'm her lawyer," she said. Emily's mouth fell open in surprise.

"I was told a witness was being brought in," Lewis said.

"That would be me, too." Clara plopped into the chair next to Emily's and crossed her denim-clad legs, nodding her head of curly red hair up and down.

"Let's cut to the chase here. Emily is my bartender, but she's a little absent-minded at times."

"I'm what?" Sure she let the door lock her out once, well, maybe more than that, but Clara had no right....

Clara placed her hand on Emily's arm. "Shut up, Emily," she said. Clara pulled a tissue out of her jeans pocket and handed it to Emily. "You're a sight, Emily. Anyway, she's locked that door behind her five nights out of the three weeks she's worked for me. Tonight she probably had good reason for forgetting the lock and her keys. Marcus Davey was in earlier, drunk as usual, and she refused to serve him. He took offense. That's what happened."

"That's it?" asked Lewis.

"That's it." Clara set her lips together in a firm line.

"And then I found him in the dumpster with the rest of the garbage," Emily said. She hiccupped and blew her nose.

CHAPTER 2

Detective Lewis' eyebrows lifted in curious anticipation at what this pair would have to offer next. Clara he'd known for years. When he got time off work, which wasn't often, he played a little golf with some of his friends, and he'd run into Clara at the course. He knew no one messed with her, not only because of her size and attitude, but because everyone knew Clara was a straight shooter. She treated her employees right and treated the members the same. Now the other one, the one not much bigger than one of Santa's elves, Emily Rhodes, had to be "a winter visitor," worse yet, a northerner, and Lewis wasn't crazy about them. They added to the aggravation of his job, and he had enough difficulty with the locals to fill a twelve-hour workday.

Snowbirds meant more of everything he dealt with: traffic, shoplifting, theft, spousal abuse, and an occasional murder. Those were crimes, and he could do something about them, but what burned him was the snowbirds' inclination to treat the place as if it were a playground. Whether from the United States or Canada, they fed wildlife they shouldn't, raced their boats up and down the canals at top speed, and overfished the lake for catch they wouldn't eat. This one had a real attitude too, coming on like Ms. CSI expert.

"Why don't you tell me what else there was between you and Mr. Davey?" Lewis said.

"Don't say a word more," said Clara. She pulled Emily out of the chair and shoved her toward the door.

Clara was being a pain in the butt, thought Lewis, reconsidering his earlier positive assessment of her. Maybe if he played nice with them.... It was late. He looked at his watch. No, it was early, too early—three in the morning. He hated confrontations, especially those before sunup when everyone's nerves were on edge, so he revised his approach.

"Can I get anyone a cup of coffee?" he asked.

"The other one asked me that too." Emily spoke in a whisper to Clara. "He was trying to get a sample of my DNA."

"Toby?" Clara snorted in disgust. "He wouldn't know DNA from a BMW." She opened the door and pushed Emily through it. "You can talk with her tomorrow after we've all gotten some sleep," and added to Emily, " I'll give you a ride to pick up your car."

Emily sat at the kitchen table picking toast crumbs from yesterday's breakfast off the place mat. She was getting her cup of coffee, but it was in her own little park model trailer with Clara doing all the work. Clara had given her a lift back to her car, which remained, as she had left it when the officers took her in, abandoned in the middle of the country club's lane.

Because the authorities considered the keys found outside the club evidence of some sort and kept them, she had to turn over her plastic turtle in the yard to extract her extra set of house keys. Fred told her never to hide keys in the yard or under her car, but she had ignored him. She was left with no keys to open the clubhouse. Or maybe she wouldn't need those keys if the police arrested her before she could return to work.

"I don't think it was a good idea to lie to the cops, especially that Detective Myers-Lewis guy. He didn't like me. I could tell."

"He's an okay cop. He does his job well. He's a little serious about his work. Besides, he knows he needs to walk carefully on this one. The Davey family is big stuff in these parts."

"Because they have money, right?" Emily raised a large crumb to her lips and realized she hadn't eaten any dinner the night before. She placed the stale, toasted bread on her tongue and savored the bit of sweetness it brought to her mouth.

Clara caught her movement. "Got anything to eat around here?" she asked.

Emily gestured toward the cupboard over the sink. Clara pulled out a package of crackers, scrounged in the fridge for peanut butter and placed the snack makings in front of Emily.

"Money. It's always money," Emily said.

Clara nodded her mop of Raggedy Ann curls. "And I didn't lie. I am a lawyer, or I was once upon a time. I practiced on the coast. I didn't like it. Too cutthroat, too many hours, too much testosterone circulating in that office." She smiled an impish smile at Emily. "I like the country. And the cowboys."

"So tell me. You know my situation. Do I have a case?"

Clara knew Emily wasn't referring to the murder of Marcus Davey. "Maybe. How long did the two of you live together?"

"Ten years."

"There was a will?" Clara picked up the coffee pot and poured more of the strong brew into her mug.

"Yeah, written years ago, and he left everything to her," Emily said.

About to offer Emily another cup, Clara almost dropped the coffee pot.

"Fred left everything to his ex-wife?"

"He never got around to making out another will, that's all."

"And you never saw to it? What's wrong with you?"

"I talked to him about it, but he said not to worry. That I'd be taken care of. Fred was the picture of health. A jogger, played golf three times a week, worked out. Up north we backpacked and hiked. He even did most of the Adirondack peaks. We both thought we had all the time in the world. Who knew he'd keel over like that?" Emily's eyes filled with tears, and she reached into her sweater pocket for a tissue.

"Sorry, honey," Clara said. "I didn't mean to be so hard on you, but I hate it when women don't take care of themselves."

"You didn't know Fred. I tried. I really tried. Now I think I should have been more forceful, but every time I brought up the issue of a will, he got upset. I think it reminded him of his mortality, and he was plain scared of dealing with his death. So I backed off. Besides, his ex was a real nag, and I didn't think bugging him would help if he thought of her every time we talked about a will. But now I'm left with nothing but a whole lot of questions about Fred's intentions." Emily's eyes no longer held tears.

"What kind of work did you say you did before you retired?" asked Clara.

"I taught preschool. Why?" A note of defensiveness crept into Emily's voice.

"Figures."

"What's that supposed to mean?"

"You are one naïve woman, and death followed by murder is a hell of a way to get smart," said Clara. She rose from the table, took her cup to the sink and washed it out. "I gotta go."

"You didn't really answer me. Do you think I've got any chance of keeping this place and getting some money out of his estate?"

"Depends," Clara said. She paused at the door, thought for a moment, then turned back to Emily. "Got yourself a good lawyer?"

"Palatier."

"Good, and expensive, but you'll need more than him to get you through this mess."

"Like?"

"Lose the rage at Fred."

The storm in Emily's eyes sent a bolt of lightning toward Clara, and she was about to deny the accusation, but Clara was too fast for her.

"Behind the tears, the depression, and an occasional flash of resentment, I can read bone-deep anger at Fred, not that you don't have a right to be furious with him, but you've got to set all that resentment to one side. The sorry-for-yourself stuff, too. Get over it and quick. You're going to need all your emotional resources to fight the ex-wife and her lawyers. And try to keep your nose clean. Don't bump off any more upstanding citizens in this community. The court system won't look at you kindly if you do."

Emily jumped out of her chair. "Hey, I didn't touch that slimy bastard, although I had plenty of reason to."

"That's more like it," said Clara. "Anger where it belongs. Now you don't seem like such a pushover." She closed the door behind her, and Emily watched through the side window as she drove off.

"Spend thirty years around three-and four-year olds and you learn a thing or two about fighting for your toys," said Emily to herself. She flopped onto her bed, punched her pillow into submission and dreamed Fred was still alive and throwing hundred-dollar bills out their car window.

‑‑‑

She awoke to the sound of a phone ringing. Fred was still dead and there were no hundred-dollar bills anywhere in sight. Her mouth had a gummy feel to it, and she licked salt off her lips. Crackers from last night's snack.

"Hello."

"Is this Mrs. Costa?" the voice on the other end of the line asked. Emily recognized it. The company had called several times since Fred's death looking for money.

Emily groaned, hung up, and headed into the bathroom. *No, this is not Mrs. Costa. We never got around to marrying, and he never got around to putting my name on anything.* She looked at her face in the mirror and saw defeat there, then remembered Clara's words from earlier this morning. She gritted her teeth, threw her toothbrush into the sink and stalked into the bedroom where she picked up the phone.

"Arnold Mortgage? I think you called me a moment ago looking for Mrs. Costa. I'm Ms.

Rhodes, Mr. Costa's life partner. The mortgage due on our park model trailer will be a little late this month. And yes, I'm aware that you haven't received last month's yet either, but you see I had to use my pension check to pay my lawyer, but I got a job, so I can get a partial payment to you this week."

She spent several more minutes on the phone with the company, assuring them she could meet the payment schedule they were willing to lay out for her. She saw no reason to tell them she might lose her new job because she was the prime suspect in a murder or that Fred was dead and she was making payments on a house that now legally belonged to Fred's ex-wife.

The phone rang again.

"Ms. Rhodes?" This time it was for her, but any relief she might have felt at the call evaporated when the caller reminded her that the insurance on her old, red sedan was overdue and would be cancelled tomorrow unless she made a payment today.

Another payment schedule to be arranged. Another twenty minutes out of her life to remind her how Fred had failed her.

At least she wouldn't have to deal with the car people any longer, she thought as she scooped coffee grounds into the pot and punched the brew light. The loan company holding Fred's note on the Chrysler Sebring convertible, the one Fred assured her they could afford, picked up the car several weeks ago. Like so many things Emily had depended upon, it was in his name.

In Emily's imagination the car had been towed off to Fred so that he could drive it around in heaven. No. Correction. He was driving it through flames. Didn't she wish. Again remembering Clara's advice, she adjusted her attitude. *Time to put a little steel in my backbone. I've got a roof over my head and my car to drive to work. The maneuvering on the house probably constitutes some form of fraud, so I won't tell my lawyer about it for a while.*

The thought of her lawyer must have sent a negative ripple throughout the cosmos because, when the phone rang this time, it was Mr. Palatier.

"Ms. Rhodes," he said. His voice came across smooth as a weasel's.

"Mr. Palatier. I was thinking about you."

"Thinking about that retainer, no doubt."

"No doubt."

She got him off the phone by promising a three-hundred-dollar check in the mail. She figured he might continue on the case if she sent him a hundred, no fifty, perhaps.

She glanced at the clock and realized it was after ten. She felt too tired to play golf with the ladies today, but she didn't have time to find a substitute. She'd have to go, even though the last thing she wanted was to revisit the scene of the crime. But not her crime, she reminded herself.

She thought it damn silly that detective thought she was involved in the murder. How could she take him seriously?

It was her turn to ferry the gals to the course. She worried they'd be disappointed at having to ride in Stan the Sedan and not the convertible. But they weren't at all unhappy. They were too excited about the news in the morning paper announcing the murder of Marcus Davey.

"Wasn't he your mixology instructor?" asked Vicki.

Vicki was her next-door neighbor and the friend responsible for first helping Emily pick up the pieces of her life after Fred's death.

Emily thought back to Fred's memorial service and her conversation with Vicki. She had finally admitted to her friend that she and Fred weren't married. Most of the folks in the condominium RV park where they wintered were Midwesterners—conservative, church-going types who wouldn't have accepted the couple if they'd known there'd been no minister to bless their union. Emily also told Vicki of her financial plight. Everything except for Stan the Sedan, her old car, was in Fred's name only.

"I'm terrified I'll get thrown out of the house," she had told Vicki. All this was before Emily knew the worst of it. First, no will could be located and then, when it was, it left the ex-wife all his property.

Vicki had come up with a great idea. "Every time we have a neighborhood party here, you're the one who makes the drinks. You're a better bartender than most of the ones at the restaurants, bars and clubs around here. Why don't you take a bartending course? There certainly are enough places in the area where you could get a job."

Vicki had expressed her appreciation of Emily's mixology skills on numerous occasions, and she was hard to please. A tall, Nordic blonde, she liked her drinks as big as she was, but done right.

Marie Jordan's voice brought Emily's thoughts back to the present. "The dead man was your instructor, wasn't he, and he almost flunked you, didn't he? Sure you didn't bump him off because he was so mean to you?"

Emily gave a wan smile while her friends hooted at the notion of retired preschool teacher, tiny Emily Rhodes, killing anybody. *A good thing they can't read my mind when it comes to what I'd like to do to Fred, except, of course, he's already dead. I hope they never find out where I spent most of last night either.*

As if reading Emily's mind, Vicki spoke. "You came home pretty late last night. I got up around four to pee and your car wasn't in the drive. Where were you? The bar can't stay open that late, can it?"

"No. I was in jail," Emily said. She made it sound like a joke.

The friends whooped and hollered with laughter once more, and Emily joined them. They'd soon find out the truth anyway. She pressed down harder on the accelerator so they wouldn't be late for their tee time.

Detective Lewis unfolded his body from the police cruiser. It had been a long night, and the morning after the murder felt more like a week had passed than half a day. He ached in every joint. It couldn't be he was getting older, could it? He dismissed the thought. He'd spent the past two hours checking the alibi the victim's widow had given for the time Davey had been killed. It was one of the best he'd run across in years, and it stood up. Mrs. Davey had been at a bible study class.

He'd sent Toby, that worthless pile of gator poop, to look at all of Davey's enemies. It was a job that would take days, provided Toby worked at it and didn't park in the shade of some palm tree and nap away the afternoon. Marcus Davey was a man not many in the community liked.

Lewis ran his hand over his face. He should have stopped at the station and taken a minute to shave. He moved his shoulders up and down and stretched his back. *Where was that little gal?*

A beat-up red car pulled into the club parking lot, and Lewis recognized the person with the blonde hair driving it as the woman he'd questioned or tried to question last night. That little five-foot bundle of attitude had eluded him with the help of Clara. Now he had her.

He spotted Clara at the side door of the club-house. She saw him at the same time.

"Detective." She yelled loud enough to announce his presence to all in the parking lot. Emily ducked into the side entrance of the club. By the time Lewis entered the building he glimpsed Emily's Kelly green golfing outfit as she turned the corner and ran into the women's room. A taller Valkyrie-like woman followed her into the bathroom. My God, she's being guarded by Amazons, Lewis thought.

"Looking for someone?" asked Clara. She joined Lewis in the hallway.

"You know damn well I am, and you know who. You warned her off. But I can wait here until she comes out."

"Suit yourself, detective," said Clara. She covered the smile forming on her lips with her hand, then turned and walked down the hallway into the bar. Through the window she watched as Emily and the other three women in her four-some exited the rear door of the women's lounge. They grabbed the two carts waiting for them and drove off to the first tee.

"Ha," said Clara to no one in particular. She rinsed off some bar glasses and placed them on a towel to dry. "You've got a mighty long wait ahead of you, Detective Lewis."

CHAPTER 3

Lewis knew he was an expert when it came to interviewing witnesses. He could make even the coldest of criminals uncomfortable, pinning them with his steely gaze and trapping them in their own lies. One meeting with him and the thought of another confrontation sent suspects running for a pen and a confession form. So when Emily Rhodes did not reappear from the bathroom, Lewis was surprised his appearance at the club hadn't shaken her up enough to spring her from her place of refuge. Instead, here he was hanging out in the hallway with tanned, chattering ladies in golf garb toting Big Berthas and Ping putters pushing him out of the way to get to their carts.

He worked his jaw in anger and embarrassment when he realized she'd slipped past him. Worse, he knew she had eluded him intentionally. No fear in her. No respect either, he added to himself.

"Are they playing nine or eighteen?" he asked. He slid onto a bar stool.

"Eighteen." Clara's eyes locked with his and held. "The bar doesn't open for another hour," she said. She returned to wiping bar glasses.

"I'm not here to drink. You know that." He hesitated a moment, then tapped his knuckles on the bar. "Maybe you can tell me a little about her. You hired her and must have thought well of her background for the job."

Clara raised one of her auburn eyebrows in a look of skepticism, and put down the glass she'd been polishing. Then she shrugged and walked around the bar to take a seat beside the detective.

"Okay. But only because I like you."

Lewis smiled at her remark.

"Some. I like you some, even though you're a cop."

Lewis' smile disappeared.

"Emily needed a job, and I thought she'd be the right person for the clientele here. Young bartenders tend to move from one job to another, and I wanted someone with staying power. Emily's the age of most of our members, and she knows how to treat people. Customers feel they can talk to her. She's a hard worker and strong for her build. She's worked out well except for a few snags."

"Like?"

"Like locking herself out when she empties the garbage. I think she's got a lot on her mind right now, and she forgets."

"That's one."

"The other will never be repeated now that Davey is dead. And it wasn't her doing. It was his."

"I can't ask him about that, can I? So tell me what the issue was between them."

"I told you. He came in here that night, drunk. She refused to serve him, and I backed her on that. Sent him out the door."

Lewis thought there was more to it than that, but he let it go for now and shifted his attention from Clara to the scene outside the window.

A young woman in a bright pink golf outfit was hitting balls from a driving range tee box. The golf pro, Lenny Sharples, stood behind her, smiling and nodding his head. As mediocre a player as Lewis was, he could tell a promising young golfer when he saw one.

"She's damn good," said Lewis. Then he turned his attention back to Clara.

"Yeah, she's Lenny's newest project," said Clara. She rolled her eyes.

"You don't like Lenny much?"

"That's not my area of the operation. He teaches, and I feed and water 'em. Now, if there are no more questions, I've got a bar to set up." Clara reached for her bar rag, but Lewis put his hand on hers to stop her. She gave him a warning look.

"One more thing. When does Ms. Rhodes get off the course?"

"About three. She's due in here to work around then. I can't stop you from talking to her when she's on duty, but try not to frighten away my customers, will you? Make your interrogation when there's no one in here."

"Why so mean? I thought you and I were friends." Lewis removed his hand from hers and put it on her shoulder and squeezed.

"We are. Friends. And you're a rolling stone. When you find out Emily is not your killer, leave her alone. She's got enough problems right now. She sure doesn't need a randy detective adding to them."

"Problems? Like what?"

"If she wants you to know, she'll tell you. If not, don't try to get it out of me."

Clara walked around the bar and pushed through the swinging door to the kitchen, leaving Lewis alone. He swiveled around on the stool to watch out the window as the young woman hit a drive over two hundred yards down the range. Lenny came up to her and hugged her. Lenny certainly was supportive of his students, observed Lewis.

⚬

Clara caught Emily as she came through the kitchen on her way to the bar and warned her the detective was waiting.

"Doesn't he have other work he should be attending to?" asked Emily.

"He's been doing it. You can count on that. There's no sense trying to avoid him forever.

Answer his questions truthfully, but don't volunteer anything."

"Your advice as a lawyer?" Emily asked.

"I don't practice any longer. My advice as your friend," Clara said.

She grabbed her purse out of the back room and made for the door. "I'll be home if you need help."

Emily wondered if Clara meant help with the bar or help with the police. I might as well get this over, she decided. She took a deep breath, stood as tall as her five feet plus and an eyelash could offer her, and marched into the bar.

"What'll you have?" Emily asked. She tied the bar apron around her middle, businesslike.

"A few answers," he said. He patted the bar stool next to his.

It wasn't an invitation to join him. It was a command. Emily emerged from behind the bar feeling vulnerable without the polished wood between her and the detective. The corners of his mouth lifted in what Emily took to be a smile, but it did not extend to his eyes, which remained a feral shade of gold, like a wolf's.

She looked around the empty lounge knowing that most of the male league players wouldn't be off the course for another hour. No one was here to rescue her today.

"Fine, but if someone comes in, I'll be busy."

"Taking lessons on how to avoid police questions from Clara?" he asked.

"Yeah, well, Clara told me you were in this morning."

"As if you didn't see me."

Before Emily could reply, a woman with more brassy blonde hair than head to hold it all rushed through the door. Buried beneath that big "do" were small features, her mouth accentuated by bright coral lipstick. Blue eye shadow painted her lids, and black eyeliner outlined her closely set eyes, so small that Emily couldn't determine their color. Her appearance evoked reminiscences of the late seventies. She was like someone caught in a time warp.

She walked up to where Emily sat beside Lewis and poked her bat-like face into Emily's space.

"Are you the bitch who was after my Marcus?"

"Huh?" It was all Emily could think to say.

"Mrs. Davey," said Detective Lewis, "you look upset. Maybe Ms. Rhodes here can get you something to drink. A glass of water or something."

Emily nodded, anxious to put a barrier between her and the woman, but Blondie blocked her path.

"You are the bitch!" She pulled back her arm and let a fist fly at Emily's face.

What was this crazy woman doing? Emily ducked to one side and the woman fell on the bar's floor like a soufflé too long out of the oven.

"She killed him," said Mrs. Davey. Detective Lewis helped her off the floor. He handed her one of her platform shoes, which had slipped off her foot in the fall, and helped her onto a barstool.

"And why would that be?" he asked.

"Why, it's as clear as the nose on your face. How'd you make detective if you can't put two and two together? She was after him all along, said provocative things to him when she was in his mixology class and then threatened to register a complaint with the school authorities that he harassed her. Rejection, that's what made her do it."

Mrs. Davey lunged at Emily one more time, brandishing her shoe as a weapon. Enough of this broad, decided Emily. She countered the attack by ducking under the shoe and landed a punch on Mrs. Davey's right temple. *Damn. I was aiming for her nose.* She examined her fist and wondered if she should try the maneuver again. Perhaps retreat was the better option.

Lewis stepped between the two combatants, but he could see the altercation was over. Mrs. Davey was too busy yelling and holding her head to continue her attack, and Emily, a shocked look on her face, ducked behind the bar as if she intended to hide in the beer cooler.

Lewis knew things weren't likely to return to normal that easily. Mrs. Davey's wailing caught the attention of those passing the bar, which soon filled with interested spectators: men off the course early, Lenny Sharples and his student, the cook from the kitchen, and a few customers out of the pro shop.

Lewis had no choice. He'd have to do something police-like to calm down Mrs. Davey, get Emily alone so he could question her, and control the crowd of men who were yelling, "cat fight." He called for backup and took both women into custody.

When the police cruiser arrived, Lewis piled Mrs. Davey in the back. On Lewis' suggestion, Emily provided the widow with an improvised ice pack for the side of her face, although he couldn't see any bruise or redness there.

Lewis' actions did little to silence the widow. She yelled about suing the country club, Emily and the police department.

The detective loaded Emily into the back of his unmarked cruiser. She said not a word, but shot him murderous looks with her icy blue eyes from under long lashes, looks that Lewis found oddly attractive.

"Call Clara, Lenny," said Emily before they drive off, "or you'll have to close the bar. And Clara won't like that."

Lewis hit the button to close the window and caught another look of anger from Emily in the back seat.

"Air conditioning," he said. "It's more comfortable."

She turned her head and looked out the window. She made him feel as if he didn't exist.

When Clara closed at nine, she drove directly to the police station, sprung Emily for the second night in a row, and the two of them sat again in Emily's kitchen drinking coffee. This time Vicki joined them with a Key lime pie.

"It's so sour-sweet that it makes my teeth ache and gives me hot flashes," said Clara.

Vicki's mouth dropped open, and she looked upset. "Oh, my. Everyone tells me I make great pie."

"That's a compliment, dear. It is great," said Clara. She signaled for another slice, indicating the desired size by holding her thumb and pointer finger slightly closer together than the width of her first wedge.

Emily pushed her pie around the plate with no appetite.

"Eat," said Clara. "You look like an anorexic bird pecking at that food, and you eat like someone with lap band surgery."

"You're going to fire me, aren't you?" asked Emily. "I'm too much trouble for the business."

"Oh, you're trouble alright, but I'm thinking of taking you off as bartender and featuring you as the entertainment for the night. Think you can get your partner, Mrs. Davey to agree to show up too?"

"From what I've heard of the Davey family, she hardly needs the money," said Vicki.

"How do you know about them?" asked Emily.

"She belongs to the same quilting club I do. She likes to brag about the Davey family's thousands of acres of land and hundreds of head of cattle. And that they're fifth-generation Floridians."

"Of course, Marcus picked her up in an exotic dancer's club in West Palm," said Clara. "That was when he was tending bar in some dive down there, and his older brother was managing the ranch."

"He told the students in the bartending class he managed the ranch now, and he liked to keep his hand in mixology by teaching a course for his old alma mater, the Culinary Institute of the Palm Coast. So what happened to the brother?" asked Emily.

She watched the knuckles on Clara's hand turn white as she tightened the grip on her fork. For a moment Clara said nothing, then turned her face to Emily and gave her a tiny smile.

"Guess my eyes are bigger than my stomach," she said. She pushed away the plate with her second slice of pie half-eaten.

For a minute Emily thought Clara wouldn't answer her, but she did. Her tone was matter-of-fact, too matter-of-fact.

"He died in an accident with a crazed Brahman bull years ago. Freak thing. The bull went wild when the brother got into the pen with it. It happens sometimes."

Clara pulled the plate back to her, but, instead of taking a bite, she traced lines with her fork through the tart filling. "But I always wondered what got that bull so riled up just then."

"What do you mean?" asked Emily. Before Clara could explain, a car pulled into the drive.

"Company," said Vicki. She got up to peek out of the kitchen window. "Oh, yummy. It's that good-looking detective."

"Damn, Vicki. You know this guy? How do you know so much about everything around here?" Emily asked.

"He was in the diner down the street several weeks ago when I was in there with my bridge group having dinner. He took my breath away, so I asked the girls if they knew him. Peggy did. She waved him over and introduced us. He's such a hunk."

"You don't know the half of it," said Clara. Her tone was sarcastic, and something in Clara's voice spoke of tension between her and the detective.

"How well do you know him?" asked Emily.

Clara shook her head as if their past was of no consequence. "We went to school together, that's all."

The three women watched through the window as Lewis removed his hat and knocked on the door. "Do I have to let him in?" Emily asked Clara.

"No, unless he has a warrant, of course."

"You watch all those crime shows too?" asked Vicki.

"She was a lawyer once," said Emily.

"She's a lawyer, and you had to go out and hire that sleazy Palatier?"

"What do you know about him?" asked Emily. For a snowbird from Michigan, Vicki certainly had connections in the community.

"Not a lot," said Vicki. Lewis knocked on the door again. "But I did hear this rumor, and I'll bet it's true."

The three women leaned their heads closer together across the table. "Palatier had sticky fingers in the collection plate at church. He told everyone he was making change for a fifty. Of course there was no fifty in the plate, and I'd bet he had no intention of taking one out of his pocket," Vicki said.

As if the story revived her appetite, Clara shoveled a piece of pie in her mouth, almost choking on it when she tried to laugh at the same time she swallowed. Emily twitched her mouth from side to side in an attempt at a smile and reconsidered her choice of the man for her attorney.

"Don't look so distraught," said Clara. "He may be cheap and unethical, but he's a piranha in court if the money's right."

"Ladies." Lewis' voice came from beyond the front door. "I can hear you in there. Could you have this conversation later? I need to talk with Ms. Rhodes. Alone."

"Didn't you get enough alone time with her earlier this evening?" asked Clara.

CHAPTER 4

After shooing her friends out of the house and promising Clara she'd call if she needed help, Emily showed the detective into the kitchen.

"Coffee?" she asked. She'd be polite and throw him off balance with kindness.

"No."

Not even "no thanks," she noted. Her act wasn't working. He'd probably seen it many times before. She was expecting another round of questions about her relationship with Davey, but Lewis' next words surprised her.

"How well do you know Clara?"

Emily drew in a breath and did a slow exhale. Yoga. She needed to be careful here.

"You know her a lot better than I do. She's my boss. And we're friends, better friends now thanks to you and your propensity for carting me off to police headquarters the past two nights."

"Is she really your attorney?"

Emily didn't know how to answer that question. Would Clara suggest she tell the truth about the attorney thing or avoid telling a lie? Emily tossed this one around in her head for half a minute.

"I didn't think I needed a lawyer," she said. Lewis gave no reply, but picked up a spoon and began tapping it against the tabletop.

"Stop that," said Emily. She reached out and took the spoon away from him.

Lewis looked chagrined. "You sound like a teacher or a mother."

"I was."

"I know about the teacher thing, but my file on you says no kids."

"And my file on you says you snoop into areas that have nothing to do with police work."

"Okay. Look. Truce for now. I'm here to return your keys and your cell phone. We got..."

"...prints off both, and you checked my cell phone records. And they told you what? Or am I not supposed to know that?"

"The records told me that the call to the police station the night of Davey's murder was made from your cell."

Emily could feel laughter rising in her throat. Or was it fear that made her feel as if she was being strangled?

"That means the murderer was probably in the bar while I was taking out the trash. He was there? Within feet of me after he killed Davey?"

Lewis thought Emily looked as if she might pass out, and he knew he was no good with fainting women. His greatest fear was that she might swoon dead away into his arms, and he would have to resuscitate her. He began to sweat at the thought of Emily Rhodes with her Cupid 's bow lips close to his, her pale blonde hair lying across his arm, her long lashes shadowing deep, blue eyes. He needed air, distance, a stiff drink.

Good thing I'm not a fainter, thought Emily. Sharing close quarters with a killer was frightening, but she was still alive. Detective Lewis, however, was looking very gray, she noticed. No. That was green. *What if he passes out on me?*

⚬

No one passed out, and that was good, thought Emily. She was lying in bed with the early morning sun pouring through her windows, making the room too light and too hot for her to fall back asleep. Not that she'd done much of that anyway. She should have gotten up and turned on the air conditioning or opened all the windows, but she was too exhausted to move from the bed. She hoped she wasn't going to make a habit of spending most of each night in police custody.

She wanted to interpret what Lewis told her last night as evidence the police were looking in another direction for the murderer. Good news for her since she had Fred's ex-wife to fight in court soon, but bad news for Clara, if the investigation was going in that direction. And it appeared it was. Lewis told her the cell phone records indicated that, immediately before making the call to the police from Emily's cell the night of the murder, someone called Clara's home number.

Emily threw back the damp sheet and exchanged her hot pillow for Fred's cooler one. She pushed her nose into it and thought she could still smell his scent, impossible, she knew, after so many launderings.

How could Clara be involved in Davey's murder? Emily remembered Clara's look of pain when the death of Davey's older brother came up earlier that night. What was that about? If Emily had any gumption she should call Clara now and tell her what Lewis was up to and then ask her about Davey's brother. Instead she fell into a restless sleep for a few hours.

The words, "He's a man who needs killing," yanked her from her dreams, and she sat up in bed with a jolt. Who said that, she wondered, then remembered it was Clara, the night of the murder, when driving her to her car, who remarked on Davey's violent death. Emily had assumed Clara was simply trying to comfort her with the remark.

"No one deserves to be killed," Emily had said. Clara's response had been a dismissive laugh. But that was hardly hard evidence for murder. Was it?

⁂

She almost forgot her appointment with her lawyer in the afternoon. A water line in her condominium mobile home park had broken, and the water was shut off. That meant no shower for her, and after a night of tossing and turning preceded by being sweated out in the police station, she felt less than fresh. She wanted to make a good impression upon Palatier, both because she needed him and because she hadn't paid him the full amount of his retainer.

Emily was not one to use her feminine wiles on a man, but she did believe that cleanliness might help her case. She pulled her hair back into a ponytail and applied a bit of lip gloss. That'll have to do it, she thought when she looked in the mirror. The image there gave her reason to hope. She looked a youthful fifty plus, tan, fit, and petite—an appealing, nonthreatening client any lawyer should be happy to represent. She stopped at Mickey D's for a quick lunch and spoiled the effect by dribbling ketchup down the front of her white blouse.

❦

"Ms. Rhodes." Palatier stood as his assistant ushered her into his office. "Right on time."

He swept pudgy fingers through his coiffed white mane, then took her hand in his and shook it. To her surprise it was not at all like grabbing a dead fish as she expected, but more like holding warm, overcooked lasagna. And his palm felt a little sticky. Perhaps from the hairspray?

She took the chair in front of his desk and tried to look optimistic, but Palatier made her feel uncomfortable. His stare came to rest on her blouse. Emily wondered if he was looking at the condiment stain or her breasts. Either way, he couldn't seem to meet her gaze. She leaned forward so her chin was barely above the top of his desk, so he had nothing to focus on except her face.

"I'm afraid the news is not good," he said. "I spoke with Mrs. Costa's lawyer."

Emily corrected him. "The former Mrs. Costa."

"Right. The former Mrs. Costa's lawyer and I agree. The will is valid. You told me that to your knowledge Fred never made another will, although the two of you discussed it at times. Her lawyer says she is prepared to fight you for the house here and anything else in his estate." He began doodling on a legal pad.

Anger suffused her, making her cheeks burn and her heart pound. "Good God. Why would she do that? She's married an orthodontist who makes more money each year than Fred did in his lifetime. She certainly doesn't need the pittance his will would offer her."

"She maintains that it is for Fred's children—the two boys."

"She's lying. Fred gave his sons a substantial present of cash over the past ten years, ten thousand dollars a year to each one of them. And more. Loans, gifts. He was generous."

"Can you substantiate that?" he asked.

"I'll pull out Fred's bank accounts and his tax records." She slid back into her chair. Her shoulders slumped in defeat. This was going to be more difficult than she thought. "Do you think that'll make a difference?"

"It might," said Palatier. He stifled a yawn with his hand, a diamond pinky ring twinkling in the sunlight.

"Mr. Palatier, tell me something. Are you interested in this case?"

He dropped his pen and tilted his chair back.

"This is a small estate," he said, "and my percentage of recovery, should I make a case for your inheriting it, we've agreed is thirty percent. Of course, I'm interested in your getting your share of the estate, but it's difficult to argue your rights when the two of you never married."

Emily watched as he righted his chair and slid a document in front of him. He looked at it with intense concentration. Reading it with her usual upside-down skills, she determined it was merely an ad from the local western wear store.

"I thought perhaps the court might see me as a common-law wife."

"That's difficult to establish, especially here."

"Here?" Emily was confused. "Here, you mean as in this community?"

Palatier slid a notepad from under the document and began writing.

"Ah, yes, what was I saying? This community. We are dealing with a very conservative town where living together, no matter for how long, is not viewed as any kind of real commitment."

"And how do you think of it?" Emily asked. She was beginning to feel a fire working its way up her chest and into her head. And she was sure it was not a hot flash.

"My feelings are irrelevant," he said.

"No. They are not. I think they, along with your cut of the estate, pretty much dictate how hard you'll work on this case." She sat up straighter, hands gripping the arm rests of her chair.

He sprang out of his seat, his liver-like lips quivering, flapping. "See here, Ms. Rhodes, you've got no right...."

"Yeah, it seems in your book I've got no rights at all."

Palatier regathered his composure. He sat again and leaned into the leather back of the chair, his hands tented in front of his mouth. "I'm wondering whether we're a good match. I don't handle criminal matters, you see."

"But this is an estate, a will, not a criminal matter." Emily paused, then it hit her. "Oh, you mean because I'm a suspect in Davey's murder, is that it?"

"You're innocent until proven guilty in the eyes of the law, but people around here talk, and now they're talking about the relationship between you and Davey."

"What relationship?"

"His wife says you were coming on to him. That surely will make it difficult, if not impossible to prove your relationship with Fred was a committed one, won't it?"

Emily rose from her chair, and leaned across his desk. "I know I failed to pay the full retainer, but perhaps you can make up the difference by making change from the offering plate again this Sunday. What I've paid you should cover the time you spent on the phone with the former Mrs. Costa and her lawyer and for the long-distance call. I think we're even. I'm firing you. I don't need your services any longer." She turned her back on him and walked toward the door.

"You're making a mistake. This is a tightly knit legal community. I don't think you'll find anyone else to take your case. You're done for, and you'll be out of your little house in less than a month, I'd wager." He chuckled. "And don't think you can spread that lie about me and the offering plate around town. Client-lawyer privilege, you know."

"I didn't find that out from you, Mr. Palatier. That's common gossip now. I'll encourage my friends to do more of it. Watch your fingers in church. Everyone else will be."

Emily slammed the door behind her. It banged open. Emily turned and saw one of Mr. Palatier's diplomas fall off the wall in the outer office. Only the plush carpeting kept the impact from breaking the glass. Still, it gave Emily some satisfaction to see it plunge to the floor.

The hot air of the Florida afternoon hit her like a bread oven. She got into Stan the Sedan, turned up the A/C, and drove off toward Wal-Mart. Once there, she parked in the back, and, with her head on the wheel, wept. What did her newly found gumption get her? A job, accused of murder, arrested for assault, and out of a lawyer. One of four positives was hardly enough to keep the starch in her petticoat.

When someone banged on the car window, Emily was almost grateful for the interruption. With the engine off and no air conditioning, she felt as if she could grow water plants in the backseat. She rolled down the window to see Clara standing there with a bag of groceries and a worried look on her face.

"What's up?" she asked.

"I'll tell you, but not here. I don't want to confess my troubles in a Wally World parking lot."

"Coffee?" asked Clara.

Emily hesitated. "Do you own a gun?" she asked.

Clara's face remained expressionless. "Or I've got ice cream in here, melting unless we hurry to my place and eat it."

CHAPTER 5

Emily stirred her ice cream around in the bowl until it softened to the consistency of a milk shake. Clara watched, her own treat untouched. Not a word had passed between them since the two women entered the kitchen. "Want a straw for that?" asked Clara.

Emily shook her head and shoved the bowl away. Her eyes surveyed the kitchen and traveled to the living room beyond. Pictures of cattle drives, brandings and a large one of the sun setting over the lake hung on the walls. The hues of pink and fuchsia in the sky with the sun nestled behind a bank of clouds were like none Emily had ever experienced, yet she could tell it wasn't an artist's interpretation in oils. It was a photograph.

"Those colors happen rarely. I was lucky that evening. Had my camera with me. I usually don't."

"You took that?" Emily asked, impressed with her skill. "The others are yours too?"

Clara nodded, cleared the table of the bowls and began washing them.

Emily said, "Until I came to central Florida, I thought that large herds of cattle were found only in the west, Texas or Oklahoma, maybe. It's funny to see men on horseback driving cattle past palm trees."

"I grew up on a ranch west of town. Learned to ride and rope and..."

"Shoot?"

"Yes, but I didn't shoot Davey if that's where you're heading."

"You said he needed killing."

"I meant it. Lots of people around here felt the same way. There's not a whole lot of grieving going on. But still it was murder. I'd preferred he died by having a gator grab him, something that took more time than a shot to the chest."

The thought of one of those prehistoric-looking reptiles dragging a man into the water and rolling him under made Emily's nerve endings tremble.

"Speaking of large predators, Detective Lewis visited me early this morning and confiscated all my guns. He's looking for the weapon that killed Davey. As if I'd be dumb enough to keep it here." Clara pointed to an empty gun case in the hallway. "He forgot to look under my mattress though."

The shock on Emily's face said Clara had gone too far.

Emily watched her pinch back her smile and change the subject.

"So, wanna talk about what got you so down? I mean aside from the fact that I don't pay you a living wage as my bartender, and the tips are lousy." Clara winked and dried her hands, then sat again at the table across from Emily.

"Palatier and I met and had a disagreement. I fired him."

"Oops. That's trouble. How are you going to go to court without representation?"

Emily raised her eyes to Clara's, giving her boss a look of helplessness from beneath her lashes.

"Absolutely not," said Clara.

"What?" asked Emily.

"I'm out of the law business."

"You still have your license, right?"

"I said I'm out of the business. Look, I'll refer you to someone else."

"Who? You think I don't know that all of the attorneys around here are part of the same club? Who wants to take a case where their client is suspected of murdering a prominent local citizen, having an affair with the deceased and living in sin with her boyfriend? Who'd be crazy enough to do that?"

"Maybe my dad?"

"Who?"

"Most folks around here think he's nuts. He might do it, if he's bored enough."

"Where's his office? Let's go."

Clara pulled up in front of the Blue Heron Retirement Center with Emily in the passenger seat.

"Here we are. I can't promise you what kind of shape he's in today, but sometimes he can be pretty lucid. Other days I've found him running down the halls half-naked chasing one of the nurses. It depends."

Emily sat in total stillness. Not even her eyes blinked. She hadn't met Clara's father yet, and she was rethinking her decision to fire Palatier. At least he had an office and didn't work out of a home for the elderly. He might have been sleazy and unethical and a cad, but he was probably sane and usually clothed.

"Alzheimer's or Dementia?" Emily finally managed to ask as they walked into the place.

"Neither." Clara seemed to search for the right word. "He's odd. Always has been. I don't think age has changed that. C'mon. I think he'll like you."

Emily stopped walking.

"Oh, don't worry. I've never known him to get naked and chase any of my friends. Only the nurses. Well, once he chased my boyfriend when I was in high school. Dad had all his clothes on and a forty-five in his hand. My boyfriend was the one who was naked. Dad found us together in the barn getting friendly."

"He's on the sun porch," said the woman behind the desk when Clara and Emily entered the facility.

"Thanks, Maria. And how is he today?" asked Clara.

"Not bad. He challenged Monty Wallace to a duel this morning, but I think they decided to settle the argument over a chess board."

Emily grabbed Clara's arm as she started down the hall. "Maybe this isn't such a good idea. Your dad may not want to be bothered with my situation. I could represent myself in court, you know."

Clara stopped walking and turned to Emily with a look of incredulity on her face. "You confront one of our hanging judges alone? No way. They'll eat you alive. They'd like nothing better than to make the case all about cohabiting out of wedlock. You didn't read the interview with Judge Daniels last year?"

Emily shook her head no.

Clara continued her tale. "'If I had my way,' the judge said, 'I'd have the sheriff round up all those folks living together without benefit of clergy and throw them in jail.' I think his remarks were aimed mostly at winter visitors."

Before Emily could reply, a man with Albert Einstein hair poked his head around the corner ahead of them.

"That you, honey? I thought I heard your voice." He emerged from the room to their left and made his way down the hall toward them, the walker he used making his progress slow.

Emily had expected Clara's father to be as tall as she, but this man was short, perhaps only two or three inches taller than Emily.

"Dad," Clara said. She rushed up to him, throwing her arms around his small frame and hugging him.

"Careful or you'll break a bone or two. I'm not as young as I used to be, you know. Who's this?" He peered around Clara and gave Emily a look up and down.

"An employee of mine from the club. Emily Rhodes. My dad."

"You're real cute," he said.

"She needs help, Dad."

"She looks fine to me."

"Legal help."

"So help her," he said. "Don't be looking at your old dad."

"Not me. Not anymore. She needs rescuing," said Clara.

Emily came forward and thrust out her hand. "I need a lawyer."

The old man tipped his head to one side. She expected to see the eyes of an elderly man, vague, glassy, unfocused, but instead he surprised her with a look not unlike that of an eagle about to descend on his prey. She thought it would be a mistake to underestimate this man, and that made her glad.

"Let's talk in my room," he said. He grabbed the walker, but instead of using it to propel himself down the hall, he dragged it along behind him.

Clara grinned at Emily and followed him down the hall. As if in answer to the question that was forming in Emily's mind, he stopped and faced them.

"I just won it off Monty in a poker game."

"Maria said you were dueling over a chess board," Clara said.

"Hate chess. Too long and boring. Texas Hold 'Em's more my style."

"What'll you do with a walker you don't need?" asked Clara.

"I'm gonna give it to the Annual Hospice Yard Sale. They can sell it. It'd be dumb to keep it."

"That's what you said when you won the wheelchair in the monthly raffle here, and you kept that."

"When I walk, I walk. Otherwise, I ride. The wheelchair might be fun, but I can't see the point of shuffling along on a walker." He waved them on.

Each room in the facility had a bulletin board to the left of the door. As the three of them walked down the hallway, Emily looked at the decorations placed in each resident's space—message pads for visitors to leave a note, seasonal decorations and displays of crafts made by the residents. Clara's father stopped in front of the last door in the hall. His bulletin board contained only one item—a pair of steer's horns with a span of almost five feet.

Emily couldn't help staring at the display. They were beautiful, unusual and impressively huge.

"Those belonged to Jethro," said Clara's father.

"A friend?" asked Emily.

"No. A steer." He opened the door and ushered them into a room that would have been spacious were it not for furniture crammed into every corner and shoved up against all the walls. Paintings covered every inch of wall space, and three birdcages containing parakeets, cockatiels and canaries hung from a floor-to-ceiling metal pole. Navaho rugs were thrown across the floor and a totem pole sat in one corner. In another stood the wheelchair. The piece that dominated the room was an oak roll-top desk, the top open and papers and books piled several feet high on its surface.

"Have a seat, ladies. You can call me Hap if I can call you Emily." He pulled the wheelchair away from the wall and sat in it.

Clara took a seat on the bed, which also was covered with books and papers. The only other place to sit was the wooden swivel chair in front of the desk. It held several western-style shirts, a pair of chaps, a holster and...a pistol.

"Toss those things on the floor," Hap said to Emily. When she hesitated, Hap popped up from his seat and swept everything off the chair with one hand. "Don't worry. Gun's not loaded. They have rules in here, you know."

He threw himself back into the wheelchair, then rolled it across the room and positioned himself in front of Emily, their knees almost touching.

"I don't hear so well." He leaned forward so that his face was inches from hers.

"That's a lie, Dad. He's trying to see down the front of your blouse," Clara said.

"Can't blame me for trying." He winked and drew back a foot. "Now, what seems to be your problem?" he asked.

Emily explained about her and Fred, the lack of a will, and Fred's ex-wife's claim on his estate. Hap listened with his eyes closed and didn't speak when she had finished her tale. For a moment, Emily thought he had gone to sleep. She shot a glance of concern and irritation at Clara, but Clara was leafing through one of her father's ranching magazines and didn't notice Hap's napping or Emily's reaction to it.

"Let's go," said Emily. "He's not interested."

"I'm interested. Give a guy a chance to think about it, will ya? She's awful impatient, isn't she?"

"Sorry. I thought you might take the same stance as Mr. Palatier."

"Palatier? You've retained him?"

"I did for a moment, then I fired him today."

"Fired him, did you? I don't think anybody's had the nerve to fire Ignatius Palatier, although he could use some firing every now and then. The man's a weasel, a snake. No. He's not as good as that. He's dog doodoo on the bottom of a shoe. He's a fart from a wart hog, he's..."

"Dad. She gets the picture."

"Well, then that settles it. Anybody who has the sense to fire that toilet bowl ring is my kind of client. Of course, your involvement in Davey's murder complicates this case somewhat."

"I'm not involved in the murder," said Emily. "And if you think so, I'd better leave right now."

"Sit down, dearie. It's my job as your attorney to second guess what the court might think and what your husband's ex-wife might try to prove. Her lawyer will put your character on trial, don't think he won't, so you need to be up front with me about you and Davey." His sharp eyes met hers and held.

"There was no me and Davey," she said. Not really, she told herself.

"Then why did he hate you so much?" asked Clara.

Hap shifted his eyes from Emily's face to that of his daughter. "A good question," he said.

"I was the oldest student in the mixology class. The others were kids, and I asked a lot of questions. I even questioned his authority on occasion. He was a real ass, pompous, demanding and sometimes drunk in class."

Clara and Hap nodded their heads in agreement with Emily's assessment of the man, and Hap dropped the subject. Emily saw no reason why it should arise again.

And so it was decided. Emily had herself a new lawyer. When she inquired about his fee, he asked for twelve dollars' worth of Florida lottery tickets every week. He said he liked the excitement of not knowing whether he won better than he liked the certain money of a retainer.

Clara had left the room while he and Emily talked and planned strategy.

As Emily and Clara drove away from the retirement center, Emily felt more upbeat than she had in weeks.

"Your dad told me about your mother and him," Emily said.

"He did, huh? What did he say?"

"That he and your mom weren't married either, and he understood perfectly my situation. It's great to have a lawyer who's personally experienced the legal issue a person is confronting."

Clara threw her head back, guffawed and pounded the wheel.

"Watch it. You're all over the road." Emily grabbed the wheel to steer them out of the path of an oncoming truck hauling oranges from a nearby grove. Clara pulled over onto the shoulder, extracted a tissue from her jeans' pocket, wiped her eyes and blew her nose.

"What?"

Clara's reaction was ruining Emily's newly found mood of elation, and she told her so.

"I'm sorry, honey. That couldn't be further from the truth. My dad is nothing if not a marrying man. After Mom died, to whom he was married for 30 years, he wed three other women and outlived all of them. Dad's hard on women like a cowboy is hard on his boots. Dad likes the retirement facility for a lot of reasons, but mostly because he considers it a great place to hunt for his next wife."

"Why did he lie to me then?" asked Emily. Tears began to fill her eyes. She was getting to like her new attorney, and now she found he'd told her a lie, a big one. Could all lawyers have trouble with the truth? Emily hated to believe that.

"Because he likes you, and he wants you to feel comfortable with him. He thinks he's showing empathy for your case. And he wants you to like him too." Clara reached over and patted Emily on the shoulder.

"I think you really made an impression on him."

Not as much of an impression as he made on me, thought Emily, more confused about the future of her legal defense than ever, but not as bewildered as she was about Clara's arrest the next day.

CHAPTER 6

I don't suppose you'd like to go to the coast for some shopping?" asked Vicki. She and Emily sat on Vicki's back deck watching the calves butt heads and the foals race one another in the pasture across the canal.

Emily shook her head and reached for the binoculars sitting on the table. "I count three new ones, probably born yesterday or the day before. Time's getting away from me with this murder thing and my legal worries."

"I thought you had a new lawyer, and you were feeling better about your chances in court?"

"Oh. I am. I guess." Emily thought back to her meeting with Hap yesterday. He made everything sound so simple, but today her doubts returned. He admitted he hadn't been in court for over twenty years. Emily hoped he would wear clothes and keep them on during their court date.

"But, here's the thing, girl," he had said to her. "Being a suspect in a murder is bad for this case, but not as damaging as the rumors going around saying you came on to the victim. Gotta get to the bottom of those." Emily wondered how an issue of sexual morality could be more significant than murder.

Vicki's words broke into her thoughts. "Shopping might cheer you up, you know."

"Using what for money?" asked Emily.

"Sorry. That was insensitive of me. I could loan you..."

"And I'd pay it back working in the prison laundry, right?"

"Guess I did it again. Sorry."

"Oh, quit apologizing. I know you're trying to help. But to be honest, I never much liked shopping unless it was finding a bargain at a yard sale. *That* I find thrilling. Pre-used things so you don't have to guess whether they're tasteful. If you hit the good neighborhoods, you can rely on their judgment."

Vicki gave her a look of disbelief.

"Anyway," Emily continued, "I've got an errand to run today."

"Oh, good. What? I'll go with you."

"I'm going to have a chat with Lucinda Davey. You know. Marcus' wife. Still want to come?" Emily's eyes twinkled. She had told Vicki about her encounter with the victim's wife at the club.

"No thanks. I'd rather wrestle an alligator. The woman sounds dangerous. I don't think you should go either."

"Hap says I need to get to the bottom of her innuendo that I came on to her husband. I thought I'd confront her about her story in person."

"Take Hap along."

"Oh, believe me, I'm going to." Emily put the field glasses to her eyes again. "Oh, look," she said. She handed the glasses to Vicki. "Another foal, a black one."

They both agreed the foal's appearance was an omen for a good day ahead.

⁂

As with so many things in Emily's presently chaotic life, her sense that the day would go well was wrong. When she pulled up at the Blue Heron Retirement Center to pick up Hap, she found him in bed with a migraine and one of the female residents at the center.

"She's giving me a massage," Hap said, after he introduced the two women. "That's the only thing for a migraine. Massage and relaxation. Bed rest. Tomorrow we'll visit Mrs. What's-her-name. Now don't you go taking her on by yourself. I'll be out of bed by then. Or the day after." The white-haired lady in the red teddy smiled at Emily, shook her head in agreement and continued in her ministrations to Hap's scrawny neck and shoulders. That scene was more than Emily wanted to know about or see this morning.

Emily checked her watch as she left Hap's room. Vicki would have already left for the coast, but maybe she could get Clara to accompany her to visit the Widow Davey.

No one answered her knock at Clara's. Since it was Monday, the day the bar opened in the evening and the restaurant was closed at the course, Emily knew Clara couldn't be there. Maybe Clara had gone shopping, too.

Emily stopped at the Round-Up convenience store, bought a microwave burrito and asked for directions to the Davey ranch. She didn't want to call first. She thought it best to take Mrs. Davey by surprise so that she didn't have the advantage of loading her guns. Or getting the ranch hands to throw Emily off the property before she could talk with the woman.

<hr>

The convenience store clerk was right. You couldn't miss the turnoff to the property. On either side of the stone pillars marking the gate to the ranch stood life-sized bronze statues of horses, reared up with their forelegs off the ground.

The gate was closed. And locked. *Damn.* Emily considered climbing the fence and walking up the lane to the house. A herd of cattle grazing behind the fence deterred her. Several of them looked like bulls. She wasn't willing to risk her skills at making bovine friends today.

A brown sedan turned off the road and pulled up behind her car. Detective Lewis stuck his head out of the window. *Oh crap.* Emily wanted to go home and crawl under her covers. She never should have gotten out of bed today.

"Ms. Rhodes," he said. He tipped his hat to her. "Here to harass the Widow Davey?"

"That's not my style. In fact, I wanted a word with her about why she thought I was coming on to her husband. Given how he felt about me, it's an absurd tale. Why would he tell her that?"

"Let's ask her. Together." The detective used his cell to make a call. Thirty seconds later, the gate rolled back. "Well? Let's get moving before it closes on us." He swept his arm toward the driveway, a gentlemanly gesture for her to lead the way.

Emily jumped into Stan, then killed the engine trying to put it into gear, but she finally coaxed the recalcitrant vehicle down the road with Lewis close behind.

If Emily expected a ranch house, she was disappointed. The structure before her looked as if it walked off the pages of Margaret Mitchell's novel. Columns stood on each side of the wide double door. A veranda surrounded the house with floor-to-ceiling windows across the front.

Servants singing old spirituals and a woman with crinolines and a hoop skirt on the front steps would have completed the antebellum picture. Instead she got Lucinda in purple capris. Her blonde tresses hid most of her face with the exception of her carmine mouth set in a severe line across her teeth.

"You stretch my patience, detective, bothering me again with your questions. But now you bring that woman with you. I won't tolerate her on my property." She stood on the veranda steps, her hands on her hips, long crimson nails glistening in the sunlight.

"No choice, ma'am. She was waiting on the road, pulled in front of me, and got through the gate when it opened," he said.

Emily was about to deny his lie, but the detective cut her off. "I wanted to talk with both of you, so why don't we do it now? Here."

He brushed by Mrs. Davey and walked across the porch to a grouping of chairs and tables. He selected a rattan rocker and sank into it, throwing his hat on the glass-topped table alongside.

Emily followed him and positioned herself on the settee across from him. There was little hope of getting a lemonade out of Lucinda, but Emily was parched, and the burrito was working its way back up her esophagus.

"Mrs. Davey," she said, "could I trouble you for a drink of water?"

"You've troubled me and my family enough, haven't you? And now you want me to offer you southern hospitality? Marcus said you were a forward, Godless hussy."

"He said that about me? Well, I knew he didn't like me much, and the feeling was mutual."

"He said you hated him, that you were a poor student and he was going to deny you your mixology certificate. You tried to get it out of him by offering him favors, but he said no. So you killed him." She loomed over Emily, who inched back in her seat eyeing Lucinda's twitching blood-red fingertips.

"Did he say Ms. Rhodes threatened him?" asked Detective Lewis.

"Well, yes, of course. She grabbed him after class one night and suggested they get a hotel room. When he said no, she took a knife out of her purse."

Emily popped off the couch and stood nose to bosom with Lucinda. She wanted to grab her by her fake eyelashes and shake the truth out of her, but Detective Lewis held up his hand and gestured at the couch. "Sit," he said. And she obeyed.

"Were there any witnesses to this confrontation?" he asked.

"Witnesses?"

"Was anyone else there?"

"Are you saying dear Marcus was a liar?"

"In a criminal matter such as this, we need corroboration."

"No. He was alone. With just her there." She nodded her head at Emily, then slid into the chair beside Lewis'. She reached for a pack of cigarettes and a lighter on the table, lit one and took a deep drag off it.

"None of this makes any sense. I got my mixology certificate, so I had no reason to kill him," said Emily.

"You were a woman scorned twice over. Your man wouldn't marry you and then died, leaving you not a penny. When you tried to get my Marcus' attention, he blew you off."

Emily ignored the interruption. "And, as I was about to say, Marcus always drove to the class with Weston Quigley, and the two of them rode home together too. Ask Quigley about my coming on to him after class."

"I will," said Lewis. "Thanks for the information."

"Aren't you going to arrest her?" asked Lucinda. Each word she uttered produced a puff of smoke from her mouth.

"Corroboration, Mrs. Davey. That's what I'm after right now." He unfolded himself from the chair, removed his hat from the table and placed it on his head. With a tip of it to the widow, he started down the veranda steps to his car.

Emily followed, but stopped at the bottom of the steps. "I think you made up this whole story, Mrs. Davey. And I wonder why."

"Wait a damn minute," Lucinda said. "Now you're calling *me* a liar. Are you going to let her get away with that, detective?"

"She's not breaking any law, ma'am," Lewis said.

Lucinda jumped up, tossed her cigarette onto the porch floor and ground it out with her shoe. "I'm going to put in a call to your boss. You let her come here and insult me, then tell me you're checking on what my husband told me? She's a killer, a sex-starved killer, and everyone around here knows it. None of us are safe with her running free. I can't sleep at night unless I have a gun under my pillow."

"I don't recommend that, Mrs. Davey," Detective Lewis said. His voice held a cautionary note.

Emily wondered if he was suggesting Mrs. Davey choose something other than a gun to take to bed with her or she not call Lewis' boss. Before she could figure out the matter, a chair cushion thrown by the widow hit her on the back of the head.

Here we go again. She dashed for the safety of her car and spun out on the gravel as she hit the accelerator. In her rearview mirror, she saw Lewis close behind her, his cell phone at his ear.

Once they hit the highway, Lewis flashed his lights at her, but Emily decided whatever he wanted could wait. She headed for the safety of her tiny park model trailer. Lewis pulled up closer behind her and flashed his lights again. She ignored him and stepped on the accelerator, hoping she wouldn't have to break any traffic laws getting away. He continued the chase. She put on more speed. He turned on his flashers. *Oh, great.* Now she'd done it. She was going to get a ticket.

She pulled onto the shoulder and rolled down her window as he stopped his car, got out and walked toward her. "Why can't you leave me alone?" she asked.

"I want to talk to you. Could we go somewhere for a cup of coffee or tea? You said back there you were thirsty."

"Talk? About what?"

"Us."

What us? There was no us.

She hit the accelerator, throwing gravel, which he fended off by holding up his arm. When she looked in the rearview mirror, Lewis was standing at the side of the road, shoulders drooping, gazing at her car as she put distance between the two of them.

Her cell rang.

"What? I'm busy trying to evade the cops."

"It's me, honey. Hap. I'm feeling a whole lot better now. Let's take a drive to the coast and go shopping."

"I don't shop. And I certainly have no intention of shopping with my lawyer. Let's keep this professional, Hap."

"This is professional. I need a new suit for court, and I thought, since I can't locate Clara today, you'd be willing to advise me what's in."

She checked her mirror. *Good. No Lewis.*

"I'll buy you breakfast," he said.

"I already had breakfast."

"Okay. How about lunch?"

She burped the burrito not settling well on her stomach. "Okay. I'll pick you up in five minutes."

"You sound kind of funny. Something wrong?"

"No. But the day is not turning out to be what I was promised this morning."

"By whom?"

"By the horses."

"Girl, you're as wacky as me. How'd Fred tolerate you for all those years?"

"How does Clara put up with you?"

"You don't know my daughter real well, do you?"

Emily thought about that. Hap was the second person who mentioned her not knowing Clara well.

A bleep from her phone let her know someone else was trying to get through to her.

"Gotta go. See you in a jiff." She disconnected and clicked to get the caller on the line.

Lewis' voice came through the phone. "The station called. We arrested Clara for Davey's murder. I thought you'd like to know. And I want to explain about what I said back there. I think you misunderstood me."

Emily disconnected without responding and called Hap to say they needed to cancel their lunch.

CHAPTER 7

"I want you to stop by my house and get some things," Clara said. "My arraignment's tomorrow, and I don't have a toothbrush or a change of clothing."

Emily nodded, still numb with Clara's arrest.

She, Clara and Hap were talking in Lewis' office rather than in the jail. The location was the detective's doing, Emily knew, and it made her like him a bit more than she had earlier in the day.

"I'll be right by your side, honey," said Hap. Hap, dressed like a southern gentleman lawyer in a white linen suit, a bit yellowed with age, leaned forward in his chair with both hands on his mahogany cane. Emily had smelled moth balls when she picked him up in her car and surmised he had dragged the suit out of storage for the occasion.

"Leave it alone, Dad. I'm going to serve as my own lawyer."

"So I'll arrange for bail."

"I'll take care of that," Clara said. "If the charge is murder one, there won't be any bail, you know. Don't get your hopes up."

Hap kicked into lawyer mode. "Premeditated. Why? And you're no flight risk. You've got family here."

Clara cut her eyes to Emily, and Hap shut up. There was something the two of them did not want her to know.

"I could leave if you'd like to talk alone," Emily said.

"No, no. It's fine. This isn't your problem, and I hate involving you," Clara said.

"But it is my problem. Marcus Davey came into the bar and picked a fight with me, and you intervened. Now they think you killed him because of that altercation."

"No, they don't," said Hap. "Tell her. It'll come out at trial anyway."

Clara got up, ran her fingers through her hair and paced the length of the small space.

"The authorities think I killed Davey because I believe he murdered his brother. The problem is, I do think he was involved in his brother's death. I don't know how."

"A lot of people believe that, honey," said Hap. "If that's all they've got, well..."

"They've got more than that. They have the murder weapon—one of the guns they confiscated from my house."

"Your fingerprints on it?" asked Hap.

"Of course they are. It was my gun. The forty-five you gave me for my sixteenth birthday."

"That was supposed to be for target practice and an occasional critter like a rat or pesky snake in the hen house. Not for doing away with people, not even slime like Davey," Hap said.

Clara said nothing.

"Why do you think Davey was involved in his brother's death? I thought that was an accident," said Emily.

"A very convenient accident. Marcus was the younger brother, but by only one year. With Morton out of the way, Marcus took over the ranch," said Clara.

"But..."

"I went to school with the Davey brothers. Instead of looking up to his older brother, Marcus competed with him, tried to do everything he did better."

"Brothers often do that. It hardly makes him a killer."

"It's how he competed that bothered me. He got Morton thrown off the football team by telling the coach he was smoking. He moved in on one of Morton's girlfriends by leading her to believe Morton had gotten another girl pregnant. He was charming but scurvy in the way he manipulated people to make himself look better than his brother. Then before the big basketball game with our closest rival in senior year, he cut the brake lining on Morton's truck. That landed Morton in the hospital."

Clara slammed the palm of her hand on the desk, making Emily jump at the blast of sound and Clara's fury. "I was so mad at Morton for protecting his brother. He told the authorities that he must have clipped it by accident when he was working on the truck earlier that day."

Hap reached out and touched Clara's shoulder. "It could have been true, honey. You don't know for sure."

"I do know. Marcus was as bad as Morton was good. Everyone around here knew it too. They were too cowed by the Davey money and too scared of Marcus. And that included the police."

"If you keep up this single-minded focus on Morton's death, you'll make the D.A.'s case," said Hap.

"I told Emily I preferred he die a long painful death, not one taking seconds at most. Besides, as much as I hate practicing law, I still am a lawyer and an officer of the court. It's my duty to uphold the law, not carry out private vendettas."

"How do you think the killer got your gun? And how did he put it back in your house?" asked Emily.

"I don't know."

"And I think you do know," said Hap. "You're covering for him, as you always did."

Emily looked at Hap and then at Clara. The two of them were glaring at one another.

"Look here," said Emily, "if you don't want me to leave, then I'd better hear the whole story, not bits and pieces. What aren't you telling me?"

Hap pounded his cane on the floor, his face reddening with anger. "She's trying to protect that no good ex-husband of hers. Fat Eddie."

"Fat Eddie?" Emily asked.

"No way he's fast," said Hap. "He must weigh near three hundred pounds."

Clara smiled and shook her head. "Dad never liked my choice of husband. Ed's weight problem was years ago before he did time. He's a lot thinner now, but still not fast. He worked out while behind bars and slimmed down. He replaced the fat with muscle and a few tattoos. I couldn't care less about protecting him. If he did in Davey, I'd thank him for his service to humanity and then be happy to see his ass back in jail."

A knock at the door was followed by Detective Lewis' entrance. He couldn't seem to meet Emily's eyes.

"Captain's about due back, and he wouldn't like me letting you all use my office. Sorry, Clara. I've got to get you back in a cell."

Clara nodded, hugged her father and Emily and walked out of the room in the custody of a uniformed officer.

"This is a mistake, young man," said Hap.

"Probably, but the D.A. liked the evidence. It's not my call," said Lewis.

Hap picked up his cane and waggled it at him. "Who is the damn D.A. now anyway? I think I need to have a talk with him."

"Her. Charlene Miller."

"Married, is she?" asked Hap. He grinned and let out a small cackle of glee when Lewis shook his head. "See you, then." Hap patted Emily's cheek and walked off with a spring in his step, handling the cane as if he were a debonair river gambler.

Emily tried to follow him out of the office, but Lewis planted himself in front of the door.

"Look, we need to talk."

"I'm busy right now. I've got to get Clara a few things, then I've got to open the bar at the club and..."

"Us. I said 'us' and I think you misinterpreted what I meant."

"How could I? It's a simple enough word. It means you and me."

Emily tried to get around Lewis' body but whatever direction she moved, so did he.

"See, here's the thing. I think we got off on the wrong foot. I mean, we seem to clash with one another whenever we talk, and I wanted to say I..."

"Never mind. I know what you're going to say. You must think I'm stupid or something. I know you're doing your job." Emily feinted right, then ducked to the left and out the door.

"I'm apologizing for aggravating you, don't you understand?"

She continued to walk down the hall.

"I could arrest you," he said. "You like that better?"

Emily stopped and turned. "For what?"

"Speeding."

"I'll file sexual harassment charges against you then." She could see her remarks hit home as his mouth dropped open. His response gave her a moment of satisfaction, enough to encourage her to follow with another barb. "Don't think I can't figure out your game. Now you want to be my friend to try and pump me for information about Clara. It won't work. Stay away from me."

<hr>

In Clara's bedroom, Emily slid open several bureau drawers searching for underwear. She pulled out a lacy pink bra and several pairs of thong panties. *I wonder where she keeps her everyday undies, or does she wear this stuff all the time?* Emily thought of her utilitarian white cotton briefs, comfy, cheap and boring. But then, what difference did it make? She wasn't trying to impress any man now, was she? Her thoughts wandered to Detective Lewis' broad shoulders. *Forget it, Emily. You're a recent ersatz widow, and the world is watching you. Behave yourself. Besides, he's trying to use you.*

As insistent as she was that Clara and Hap tell her what was going on with Clara's arrest, Emily knew they were still keeping something from her. A no-good ex-husband wasn't the only thing Clara tried to hide. Hap said a number of people thought Marcus was involved in his brother's death, but what particular interest did Clara have in it? Clara was more entangled with the Davey family than either she or Hap admitted.

As she shut the drawer and turned to throw the items into the overnight bag she'd pulled from the closet, her sleeve caught the corner of a picture on the dresser top. It fell with a crash and broke apart, scattering the pieces across the carpet.

Clumsy me. Emily stooped to pick up the frame and the picture, a photo of Clara and a younger man. *A friend? Her son? She'd never mentioned him, but Hap said there was family, and she had been married to Eddie, fat or fast.*

She spotted another photo peeking out from the backing still lying on the carpet. She reached out for it. This one was of a man with dark hair and gray eyes. The photographer, probably Clara, had caught him grinning, the smile intimate, sexy and obviously meant only for the one snapping the picture. *That must be Eddie, and not fat at all.* He looked familiar to her, and she wondered where she might have encountered him. Perhaps it was the one night she worked as a bartender at the Burnt Biscuit. It was so crowded that she barely registered the faces of customers crowding around the bar.

Clara didn't seem keen to keep Eddie out on display. The boy with Clara certainly looked like Eddie, the same dark hair and strong chin. Emily inserted the photo back into the frame and tucked Eddie's face behind it. Thank goodness the glass didn't break.

—❦—

The arraignment outcome shocked both Hap and Emily. There would be no bail for Clara. The D.A. decided she was a flight risk, arguing that manager of a bar and restaurant wasn't a stable enough occupation to merit looking at her as an upstanding citizen. Hap's attempt to woo the D.A. hadn't helped, although he continued to wink at her throughout the proceedings.

What puzzled Emily was the equanimity with which Clara handled the outcome, as if she both expected and welcomed the arrest and her nine-by-twelve cell. Emily looked around the courtroom expecting she would see Clara's son and ex-husband there, but the room filled with reporters, a few police officers and a few other spectators Emily couldn't identify, except for Palatier, her ex-lawyer. He slipped past the guards and whispered something in Clara's ear as they led her away. Emily watched Clara toss her head back with a laugh, her bright curls bobbing in defiance. She waved off the ambulance chaser. His face reddening at the rebuff, Palatier looked around the courtroom. Emily caught his eye and smiled innocently. The red deepened. He wiped sweat off his upper lip and retreated out the courtroom door.

"What did he want?" asked Hap. The three of them, Hap, Emily and Clara sat in the visitation area after the arraignment.

"He thought I needed representation," said Clara.

"Honey, maybe he's right. How many murder cases did you take on when you were actively practicing?" asked Hap. "Maybe I should take over."

"You've got all you can handle with Emily."

"That's a breeze now that the focus is off her as the killer."

Emily's mouth dropped open at Hap's insensitivity.

"It's okay. Dad's right. This takes the pressure off you."

"How does putting it on you, also innocent, help anyone? The killer is still out there," Emily said. "You need your dad."

"I know what I'm doing. Now get out of here, both of you and accomplish something useful."

Emily's "useful" assignment was to find another bartender for the club. Clara had called the head of the country club's board and convinced him that Emily should take over as manager of the dining and bar areas. She had tried to tell Clara she knew nothing about handling the restaurant, but Clara insisted Emily would do fine.

"It's all in the computer," Clara had said, "ordering, billing, inventory and menus too. The cook knows the routine. You schedule and supervise the two waitresses and report to the board weekly. No problem." And then Clara played her last card. "I've got no one else. Please. Save my job for me." Clara's comments gave Emily hope she would work her way out of jail soon.

❧

Emily turned in to the Burnt Biscuit Bar and Restaurant around five, early enough that there wouldn't be a crowd in the dining room nor in the bar. She knew Randolph Whitney arrived in the early evening and she wanted to talk with him.

Randolph looked up from one of the back tables when she entered the dimly lit bar area. He waved her over. Randolph was small and slender, his facial features delicate, almost feminine in appearance. His apparent youthfulness, un-ironed white shirt and baggy black pants might have marked him as a waiter, or a poet, anything but the part- owner and manager of the Burnt Biscuit.

"I hear you're the bartender at the country club," he said. He shoved out a chair with his foot and signaled her to sit. "How do you like it?" He didn't wait for Emily to reply, but rushed on. "Sorry you didn't work out here, but my partner felt Davey's squeeze on her. We decided it was in everyone's best interest to let you go."

"You probably did me a favor. It's great working at the country club," said Emily. *Or was it?*

Now she had her hands full managing both the bar and the restaurant, positions for which she had no training or experience.

"Say, I don't mean to be crude, but since Davey's no longer in the picture, you could come back here if you wanted."

Emily thought back to the one night she had worked at the Burnt Biscuit when Marcus Davey entered, drunk, and insisted she serve him. At the time she had no inkling he would repeat this performance at the country club. The outcome was different, Emily admitted to herself. Clara defended her while Randolph and his partner, Sherry, had fired her. Both of them, but particularly Sherry, acted frightened of what Davey could do if they didn't get rid of her.

The waitress arrived at the table with a large steak on her tray. She set it down in front of Randolph and asked Emily if she'd like something.

"No thanks," said Emily. "And I appreciate the offer, Randolph, but I'm happy at the country club. In fact, I've taken on additional responsibilities, and I'm wondering if I could pick your brain for some information."

Randolph looked down at his steak. His nostrils contracted as he drew in the grilled aroma, and a satisfied look settled on his face. Then he did what Emily had seen him do the night she tended bar at the Biscuit. He reached into his pocket and extracted a switch blade, which he opened with a flick of his thumb.

CHAPTER 8

"**C**lara, you've got a visitor," said the guard.
Assuming it was Emily with some additional items Clara wanted from home, she followed the guard to the visitation area.

"Darren! What are you doing here?" asked Clara. "I told you to stay away from me, at least until I've sorted out everything."

Her twenty-year-old son took a seat across the table from her, folding his lanky frame onto the wooden chair.

"You need a haircut," she said.

He swept his dark hair off his forehead and shrugged. "How can you figure out anything from in here?" he asked. "Maybe I should tell the cops about that night."

"No! Stay away from the cops for now. You shouldn't have come here. Someone might see you. Where are you staying?"

"At my friend Todd's, but I don't feel safe there. The other night I saw the same black SUV driving past the house several times."

Clara knew that wasn't good. He had to get out of there, but go where? He couldn't stay with Dad in the retirement home, and she knew her house would be under surveillance by either the cops or the people responsible for Davey's murder. The killers had to know they weren't in the clear yet. Darren's other friends were unreliable, most of them druggies from his high-school days. On probation for smoking dope, the last thing he needed was to hang out with people who were dealing or still into weed.

"I've got an idea, but it'll take me some time to work it out. I'll get a message to you through Grandpa this afternoon. Now get out of here."

She got up from the table and signaled to the guard.

It wasn't that she didn't love Darren, but for now she wanted him as far from her as possible. The authorities were still building the case against her, and they must be wondering about that call on Emily's cell to Clara the night of the murder. Detective Lewis was like a blood hound when tracking down loose ends. He'd convince the D.A. that call was important and soon he'd find out who made it. Clara hated to bring Emily into this but it was a matter of family now. She'd have to manipulate her emerging friendship with Emily once again.

❧

Emily smiled as Randolph cut into his steak with the switchblade. "Maybe you should spring for new steak knives," said Emily.

Randolph looked up at her, shoved a large chunk of beef into his mouth and chewed. "The knives here are fine for the customers. I like the feeling of my knife cutting through a steak like a spoon through pudding. You should try it." He held out the switchblade to her and nodded toward his steak.

"No thanks. But you might give me a little help with a problem I have."

Randolph poked his fork at the baked potato, but returned to the meat. "Anything I can do. I have to admit I'm a little embarrassed Sherry and I caved so easily with Davey."

"Never mind," said Emily. "I don't think this setting would have been right for me anyway. But here's the thing. While Clara's in jail, I'm taking over her duties as manager so I need another part-time bartender at the club. Any suggestions?"

Randolph swallowed and propped his elbow on the table. His hand still held the knife, which he twirled around as a look of concentration crossed his face.

"Do you remember the old dude who came in here the night you were working? Had a long ponytail, drank Smirnoff's Silver."

Emily had a vague memory of someone dressed all in black at the end of the bar. *But old?* The guy was about her age. She shot Randolph a skeptical look. "Old, my ass. The guy was definitely cool looking and... "

"Okay, not so old. He fills in here sometimes when one of our bartenders gets sick. His name's Donald Green."

"Got a number for him?"

Randolph didn't reply to her question. Instead he posed one of his own. "What's the weather like? Is the wind blowing much?"

"Uh, no. It's sunny, a few clouds." Emily sighed, thinking about the perfect weather outside. Not too hot, not too humid, but the kind of day she wouldn't mind hitting drives into the pond on the first hole at the course, anything but sitting here in this dark cave of a bar and tracking down hired help. Emily straightened her shoulders and leaned forward.

"Then you can find Donald down at the river. He has the fastest bass boat on the lake. Ask whoever you see there, and they'll help you."

"Can't you give me his number? I'll leave a message for him. I don't really have the time to sort him out from the other guys fishing."

"The only way I've ever contacted him was to send someone to the river if I needed him. But you can try looking him up in the book if you like."

❦

There was no Donald Green listed in the white pages, and Emily had second thoughts about hiring him, but the other names Randolph gave her were employed elsewhere or weren't interested in the work at the club. She knew all her mixology classmates already had other jobs too, so it was Donald Green. Or no one, if she couldn't locate him.

❧

As she headed toward the local park where the river emptied into the lake, Emily tried to recall what she knew about Donald. She remembered him, and not for what he drank or his physical appearance, but for what he said to her after her run-in with Davey.

That Saturday night the customers were three deep at her station. Davey approached her drunk, and she refused to serve him. He grabbed her arm and almost pulled her onto the bar before Randolph rushed over with Sherry and pulled Davey away. "You'd better leave, Emily," Randolph had said.

"Pick up your check tomorrow afternoon," Sherry said.

Davey had humiliated her with his scene, and Sherry added to it by firing her in front of everyone. She grabbed her purse from under the bar and walked toward the door. Donald Green had stepped in front of her and uttered words all too similar to those Clara used. "There's a man I wouldn't mind killing."

At the boat launch area, Emily surveyed the large number of pickups with boat trailers. There had to be fifty or sixty trucks in the lot. The river and the mouth of the lake teemed with craft. If Green were out in his boat, how was Emily supposed to locate him, much less have a talk with him? She watched as a truck with trailer backed down the ramp. A man maneuvered a boat close and then drove it easily onto the half-submerged trailer. Neither the driver nor the one on the boat was Green, but she thought she might as well start asking for him. She began her search with the man exiting the pickup.

"Seen Donald Green around?" she asked.

"Yep. Over there." He pointed toward a boat anchored off-shore to the right of the launch. "The red one."

Emily followed his finger and recognized Green's long ponytail. Today he was dressed in a T-shirt and blue jeans and wore a cap with a bill. She began to walk down the river toward the boat. Maybe she could yell loud enough to make herself heard.

"Mr. Green," she said. Green sat on a high seat in the front of the craft. He didn't turn at her call.

"Mr. Green." She yelled louder. Still no response. I'll give it one more try, she thought. *If he's deaf, he's going to be a liability as my bartender anyway.*

"Mr. Green."

Not a muscle moved. Emily turned to walk back to the parking lot. "I heard you the first time you interrupted my fishing. C'mere, would ya?"

She retraced her steps. Green now stood in the back of his boat. "Catch."

Emily reached out and grabbed a ring of keys that flew through the air toward her.

"My truck's the black Ford with the fancy grill. Start it up and back the trailer on down here. Or is that too much for a little gal like you to handle?"

Why that arrogant S.O.B. Who does he think he is? Emily strode back to the parking lot and dumped the keys into the hands of the man who had given her directions to Green's boat.

"Green says for you to get his truck and pull him out of the water. He said he'd pay you twenty bucks for doing it."

Emily waited under the shade of a large palm tree at the river's edge. Once Green's boat was on the trailer, she smiled when she saw the man hold his hand out and say something to Green. The smile erupted into a chuckle as Green's face took on a deep shade of red and he turned to look her way. He got into his pickup and Emily was certain he was going to leave as he gunned the engine and headed for the entrance. Short of the turn onto the road, he stopped the truck, turned it around and parked a few feet from Emily's shady palm. She stood her ground as he slammed the door and moved toward her.

"I guess you thought that was pretty funny," he said.

As he advanced on her, she retreated along the river, backing up and not taking her eyes off him.

"Stop right there," he said.

Emily continued to retreat, but walking backward was far slower than the steps he took forward. Besides he had a good foot on her in height.

She was about to turn and run, when he grabbed for her and caught her forearm in a steel-like grip. She looked up into his icy blue eyes and rued having played her little joke on him. He seemed not to have much of a sense of humor.

"I'm sorry," she said. She tried to wiggle her arm out of his grasp, but he held on tight. "I wanted to talk to you, but you're so damn arrogant. You deserved what you got." *Wait a minute.* Was she apologizing or goading him into greater fury? "I mean, I'm sorry you lost that money."

"I didn't lose a nickel. I told him you were my ex-girlfriend and you were playing a joke on me. He wondered if he could ask you out, and I told him to go ahead. I was through with you. But I'm not done with you yet. We've got a score to settle here. No one drives my truck unless I give them permission. It's the same with my boat."

"You were going to let me drive your truck," said Emily.

"Nah. You wouldn't know how, and I knew it. I was playing with you." He smiled a bit, the anger lifting from his lined face. He also let up the pressure of his grasp, and Emily twisted away from him and ran along the river bank.

"Oh, hey. I forgot to tell you," Green yelled. "You're making straight for a gator on the bank there. About twenty feet in front of you."

Emily stumbled in her attempt to make her feet stop moving. Sure enough, a fifteen-foot gator sat in front of her, unmoving, eyes closed, but menacing all the same. Emily reversed direction, dashing back toward Green. She threw herself into his arms.

"Save me," she said.

"Tell me why I'd want to do that."

"There's a job in it for you. And twenty bucks," she said. She inserted her hand in her pocket, fumbled around with the change she carried there and withdrew a five.

"A down payment." She held the bill in front of his eyes.

He smiled. "Shoo," he said to the gator.

❦

The next morning Emily was having a little talk with herself in the shower. When Fred used to hear her in one of her "self" conversations, he kidded her that she was sharing the bath with another guy. Now Fred was gone, and she missed him. But she had to admit to herself that each day she was alone got a little easier. When she shared this with Hap, he cautioned her not to develop mental health too quickly after Fred's death.

"The court wants to see grief and suffering, not a merry widow," Hap reminded her.

She tried to squeeze out a tear of loneliness, but she had too much on her mind. Even if she could produce a tear, how would she know with the water running down her face?

She turned her attention back onto her new employee. The embarrassment of yesterday at the river flooded her thoughts. "Save me," she'd said, like she was a princess in a medieval castle. He had to think her an idiot. At least he'd let her know about that gator. Then he had the audacity to argue over the pay at the club. As if Emily had any say in what the hourly wage was. And he'd insisted on working nights so that he could get fishing in during the day. Emily was so desperate, she agreed. *When am I going to get a little golf in?*

The water in the shower cut off abruptly. Again this week, thought Emily. *And here I am with shampoo in my hair and a date to meet with my lawyer before I go to work.* Someone knocked on her door.

"Be there in a minute," she said. She grabbed a towel, dried off, and wrapped her terry robe around here. A young man stood on her steps. His eyes took in her sudsy hair.

"Oh, this," she said. She lifted her hand to her head. "Water shut off. Say, I know you. I saw a picture of you and your mother on her dresser."

"Maybe that will make this easier," he said. He handed her a note, which read:

Emily, I know this is unfair, but I have no choice. Dad wanted to contact you, but I told him it was better if I did it. My son, Darren, needs a place to stay where it's safe. He'll explain everything to you.

Clara

"So I guess we're roomies," Darren said.

As Emily gestured for him to come in, she spotted Mrs. Wattles and Mrs. Frey, the park's insatiable gossips, driving by in their golf cart. They slowed and took a long look at Darren as he walked into the house. They then proceeded straight up the road. Funny, thought Emily, they usually turned right at the corner to go to the pool for nine o'clock water aerobics.

CHAPTER 9

Darren left almost as soon as he arrived, saying he needed to pick up a few more of his things still at Todd's. Emily offered to drop him off when she went into town, but he said he'd take the bus outside the park's entrance.

"I'll be back here in a few hours. I've got to get some sleep before my night shift at the box factory in town."

"Be careful. Your mom wants you out of sight," said Emily. He'd promised his mother to fly beneath the radar by staying with Emily during the day and working at night. He agreed that hanging around with his old buddies wasn't smart.

Well, hiding out didn't last for long, thought Emily. But then, as she said to Vicki, twenty-year-olds needed some social life, the kind that couldn't be found in an over-fifty-five community.

A short time later she heard footsteps on her porch and saw the park manager through her front windows. *Oh, crap. This can't be good.*

"Could I have a few words with you?" asked Ralph Sturgis, a man as broad around the butt as he was tall.

Emily gestured him up the steps. He waddled into the living room and eyed the backpack Darren had dumped on the floor.

She didn't offer Sturgis a seat. The man always made her feel uncomfortable even when Fred was alive, eyeing her from head to foot.

"I hear you've got company," he said.

She didn't reply to his implied question. Let him ask a real one, and she'd give him an answer.

"Uh. I understand he's a young man. Under the age limit here. Relative of yours?"

"No. The son of a friend."

"How long will he be staying?" asked Sturgis.

"Not long. Just until some things are straightened out in his family."

"No one would mind if he was a relative, but since he's not, folks around here might think it odd you move in another man before Fred's, how do you say, cold in the ground."

Emily wanted to rush at him, fists flying, but she suppressed the urge. With difficulty. And she kept her distance from him.

"And you're suggesting I do what?" she asked. Her voice was as cool as a block of ice.

Ralph smiled one of his smarmy smiles, exposing two missing teeth. "Well, you might consider attending a little function with me tonight."

"What function?" Emily's eyes darted around the room, looking for something she could use to prod him out the door. Like a broom. Or a mop. Better yet, a sword.

"A small get-together in the Wildwood Hotel. Nothing formal or large. You and me. How about it?" He accompanied his obscene suggestion with an equally lewd grin.

The toilet flushed.

Ralph whirled on his feet in the direction of the bathroom. "Who's that?" he asked. The smile was gone from his face, replaced by worry lines on his fat, sweaty forehead.

"It's only me, Ralphie." Vicki emerged from the bathroom and stood in the hallway to the kitchen and living area.

"What did you...?"

"Oh, I heard all of it. Interesting. There have been rumors going around the park you were hitting on the single women here. I guess they're true. What must your wife think?" Vicki was almost dancing with glee as she jigged her way down the hall toward Ralph.

"You wouldn't tell my wife, would you?" he asked.

"No, of course not. I'd prefer to tell the Condo Board of Directors," Vicki said. She picked up a cookie off the plate she'd earlier carried over to Emily's and set on the counter.

"I'd lose my job," said Ralph.

Vicki was having way too much fun pushing his buttons. Emily wanted a piece of the man too. "You should've thought of that before you came in here and threatened me, but maybe we can work something out." She had no intention of cutting any kind of deal with Ralph, but the way his face lit up at the suggestion made it difficult for her to suppress a chuckle at the ignorant hope in his eyes. "Meantime, get out. You interrupted my morning tea with my next-door neighbor."

"Work what out?" asked Ralph. He rolled toward the door.

"I'll get back to you," said Emily. She slammed the door. It caught his backside and shot him down her steps.

"Now where were we?" asked Vicki.

A tiny smile tugged at Emily's mouth when she heard him muttering to himself as he pulled his golf cart out of her drive. Ralph remained a problem, but one she'd have to take care of another time. She turned her attention to a more immediate issue.

"Clara wants me to let Darren stay here for a while until she can think of some better place for him. How can I refuse her? She gave me a job when no one else would, and she's in jail partly because she chose to stand up for me. She seems to think her son's in danger, but she's not telling me about what's going on."

"You know very well what's going on," said Vicki. She bit into a cookie. "Don't you think Darren was the one who used your cell at the club to call his mom? Clara thinks he killed Davey, and she's hiding him from the authorities."

"But they arrested her for the murder," said Emily.

"Only because she's their best bet for now. Detective Lewis will follow up on that phone call."

"Clara and Darren also think he's in danger from someone other than the police. That doesn't make sense if he's the killer, and somehow I can't see him as a murderer."

"But you told me he's on probation for some crime."

"Smoking dope, and there's a long way from toking on a joint to shooting someone."

Darren couldn't be the killer. It didn't fit. He told her a car was following him, and he sounded more frightened of that than he did the authorities. She was about to assure Vicki she was in no danger when the phone rang.

Emily answered, listened for a moment, then said, "Yes, we should talk, but right now's not a good time. I'll get back to you." She jotted down a number, dropped the phone back into the cradle, and stood at the counter motionless.

"I sure didn't handle that well," she said.

"Emily, what's wrong? You're white as an albino rabbit."

Emily took a deep breath and let it out slowly. She somehow knew this day would come, but she was surprised at how unprepared she was for it. "I was about to say that Clara's son is no danger to me or you, but apparently my daughter is."

"I didn't know you had a daughter," said Vicki.

Emily suppressed a moan and drew in a shaky breath. "It was merely a matter of time before she looked for me. I've known where she was for many years, but..."

"Wait. Wait. Back up. Here. Sit down."

Emily shook her head as if gripping the counter would help her get back control of her life.

"I got pregnant with her in my thirties. I didn't want to marry the guy, didn't know him well, but I did tell him about the pregnancy, and we agreed it would be best if I put her up for adoption."

She doodled on the notepad with the number she'd written there, her eyes avoiding contact with Vicki's gaze.

"You didn't consider abortion?" asked Vicki.

Emily frowned, remembering the difficulty of making the decision. "I did, but I was so conflicted about the pregnancy. Should I keep the baby, give it up for adoption, get an abortion? I couldn't make up my mind, so time kind of did that for me. The adoption was a private arrangement, but at that time, we're talking over twenty years ago, adoptive and birth parents often didn't share in the child's life."

When she realized she had drawn hearts around her daughter's number on the pad, she threw down her pencil. She scrubbed away the tears that threatened to spill from her eyes and let out the breath she had held for over three decades.

"Timing's lousy," said Vicki.

"What do you mean?"

"The court better not hear about your daughter. A child born out of wedlock as they say. What would the judge think of that?"

Hap told her what the court would say. "Woman lives with a guy for over ten years without getting hitched. Seems to be a pattern with her. She had a baby without being married."

Emily groaned. "Well, the good news is that no one knows about this except for Vicki. She can keep a secret."

Emily sat with Hap at the local ice cream parlor, watching him spoon a hot fudge sundae into his mouth. His current squeeze, Elvira Bonnet, was there too, indulging in a low-fat, low-sugar yogurt cone. Emily sipped a cup of coffee and thought about the phone call from her daughter. She wondered if the young woman would really come visit her as she'd said on the phone. Her feelings about the daughter she'd given to others to parent were confused: anxious delight at being able to see her, mixed with fear about what the young woman would say to the mother she'd never known. And then, there was the other thing. Vicki was right. The timing was lousy.

"And I can't say I was happy about Clara having Darren move in with you."

Emily brought her attention back to what Hap was saying. "Hmmm? Oh, he'll be no trouble." She hoped. While she was divulging information about her personal life, she thought she would also tell Hap about the park manager's visit.

"How'd he find out about Darren?" asked Hap.

"I think the rumor patrol saw Darren arrive." She explained about Mrs. Wattles and Mrs. Frey and their drive-by in the golf cart.

"Cripes," Hap said. He scraped his spoon around the bottom of the sundae dish. "You have less privacy in that place than I have in the retirement facility, and we live under one roof! Right, Elvira?" He put his arm around his companion and squeezed so hard that she giggled and burped. "Sorry, honey."

"Listen, I've got to go. I have to open the bar, and set up for lunch and dinner at the club. And I've got a new bartender to break in." She wondered if Donald Green could be broken in any easier than a wild mustang to a saddle. Not likely.

"Here's some good and bad news together. We've been assigned a court date for challenging the will. I've got all the records from you about the years you and Fred lived together and shared expenses, but I need you to generate a list of people who will serve as character witnesses. As long as Clara is in jail, we can't use her, so dredge up some of those folks out at your condo park."

Emily grabbed her purse off the chair and waved goodbye at the door, then stuck her head back in. "I could have Mrs. Wattles and Mrs. Frey testify to my generosity in sharing my house with a twenty-year-old hunk." She chuckled at the look of horror that crossed Hap's face. "Just kidding."

❧

Emily piloted Stan the Sedan along the highway, careful to keep her speed under the limit, but chafing at the slowness of the drivers ahead of her. She hoped to be able to get things in order at the club and also play nine holes of golf this afternoon. Vicki arranged a replacement on the golf league earlier in the week, so she'd missed her usual play time. The waitresses, the cook and kitchen staff would do their jobs as usual, but Donald Green as the bartender gave her concern. She had the uneasy feeling it was a mistake to hire the man. He was too cantankerous and single-minded, a man who probably didn't take directions from a woman well.

She'd find out, and soon. He stood with his hands on his hips waiting for her outside the side entrance to the club as she turned into the parking lot.

"You said eleven. It's five past." He looked at his watch, then shook his head at Emily. "I thought you'd be here before me to handle opening. You said bartender. I didn't think I'd have to do setup too."

Emily wondered if anyone could see the thin plume of steam rising out of the top of her head. Lately it seemed as if she was learning the fine art of how to hold your temper around difficult men. And to make things even harder for her, Detective

Lewis stood at the door of the bar as she and Donald came around the corner. The two men eyed each other. Emily should have made introductions, but she didn't feel like it. Let them figure out who the other was.

"Donald," said Lewis.

"Detective," said Green.

Of course. How could she be so stupid? The two of them knew each other. They probably played together in the sandbox at preschool.

She unlocked the door, gestured for Donald to go ahead, then turned to Detective Lewis. "You'll have to excuse us, but Mr. Green is one of my new employees, and I'm training him today."

Lewis barked out a laugh. "You're training him? To do what?"

"Bartend. Here. What's so funny about that?" she asked.

With his hands in his pockets, Green lounged against the wall next to the open doorway to the bar and said nothing.

"Well, that'll have to wait for a while. You go on ahead and do what you need to do. Mr. Green and I have business."

"What business?" she asked.

Green finally stepped forward and placed himself between her and the detective.

"You find it yet?" Green asked.

"No, but we're working on it. Anyplace we can talk around here?"

"Let me ask my boss." Green turned to Emily.

"Oh, go ahead in. I don't expect anyone will be itching for a beer until the league that's playing the back nine finishes. I'll get things going here, and I'll catch you up when you're finished."

Whatever the "business" was between these two men, Emily was curious. Not that it was any of her concern, but having their discussion in her barroom gave her access to whatever was going on.

The snatches of the conversation she caught as she moved in and out of the bar gave her all the scoop she needed. Someone had stolen Green's bass boat. Maybe that was why he was so testy over her being five minutes late today, but more likely it was simply his unpleasant personality.

He'd called the theft in early this morning when he decided to take the boat out for speck fishing. The truck was still in the drive, he told Lewis, but the boat and trailer, parked down near his barn, were gone. When he reported it to the police, he informed the station he would be at the club the remainder of the day.

Lewis asked Green if he had any enemies and then laughed. "Okay. I'll rephrase that. Got any friends that might want to play a joke on you?"

Green lowered his voice in reply. Both men looked up at Emily, then laughed.

"What's so funny?" she asked.

"Nothing. Donald was just telling me about how the two of you met. He figures you might be upset you missed a golden opportunity to run off with his boat and came back to pick it up."

"Ha," Emily said. She walked into the kitchen. When she reemerged, Lewis was on his cell and giving her one of those police looks.

He finished, stood up, and walked over to her. "You've got some explaining to do."

"Me? What?" she asked.

"We found Green's boat parked in your driveway."

CHAPTER 10

Vicki flitted around Emily's kitchen, setting up the coffee, placing cookies on a plate and taking out mugs from the cupboard. Emily was exhausted and sunk down onto the couch, content to let her friend take over playing hostess.

"I don't know anything about that boat, except someone backed it into your carport, and then left with their truck. I saw them as I was returning from the pool. By the time I got to your house, they were pulling out," said Vicki. Her eyes danced up and down. Emily could tell she was thrilled to be part of the investigation.

"And you didn't get a good look at the person driving the truck?" asked Detective Lewis.

"The windows were tinted too dark."

"Describe the truck."

"It was huge. And dark," said Vicki. She gave him an embarrassed smile. "I'm not good with trucks. They all look the same to me."

It was after ten that night. The boat and trailer still sat in Emily's carport. Donald's truck was pulled in behind them, while Emily's car, and Detective Lewis' police-issued cruiser were parked in Vicki's drive. It looked like the beginnings of a block party with neighbors walking or driving by or standing around on the street, craning their necks to see what was happening. The gathering was inside, and the atmosphere was anything but festive.

"I should set up a satellite police station here," said Emily. She wanted everyone to go away.

"Coffee's a whole lot better in this place though," said Lewis.

Green had entered her living room only moments earlier, after he'd gone over his boat inch by inch looking for any damage the thieves might have done. His examination of the craft rivaled the meticulousness of the police investigators who had collected evidence from it earlier.

"I don't think the fingerprint analysis is going to get us much. They wore gloves. But we did find something we're following up on," Lewis said. He took another cookie offered him by Vicki.

Emily arched her eyebrows at Vicki in a look of disgust. "I'm not running a tea room here, you know," she said.

"What's that?" asked Green. He slid into the leather lounger.

"A tea room," said Vicki. She stood in front of the chair, the plate of cookies n her hand.

Green flapped his hand at Vicki as if chasing off an annoying gnat. "What did you find in my boat?" he asked Lewis. He grabbed the recliner's handle, maneuvered it backward, and relaxed into the leather comfort.

"That's Fred's...," said Emily. She was about to say the chair was Fred's favorite. Green shot her a look that said she was beginning to annoy him too. *Such a sensitive man.*

"Blood on one of the seats. Looked like transfer from something or someone," said Lewis.

"Likely mine or belonged to one of those speck I pulled from the lake yesterday," Green said.

Lewis nodded. "Well, we'll check it out anyway." His eyes shifted to Emily. "What I don't get is why someone dumped the boat at your place. You seem to be the center of a lot of criminal activity in this town lately."

"You explain it. You're supposed to be the detective," Emily said. *Go away.* She was exhausted and sleeping was the only activity she yearned for right now.

"Cookie?" asked Vicki. She offered the plate to Green.

He again performed his dismissive wave. "So can I have my boat back?" he asked. He was looking at Emily.

"Don't ask me. I'm going to bed. You all lock up when you're done with your café klatch." She headed toward the bedroom, hoping everyone would take the hint and hit the road. And that included Vicki, whose hostess acts were beginning to irritate her. Before she closed her bedroom door, she called down the hall to Green. "I didn't steal your boat. And that's that. Don't forget. Tomorrow you open at ten. Set up. And if you're late or don't show, you're fired." She slammed the door, but continued to listen from her bedroom.

"We're releasing your boat," Detective Lewis said.

She lay down on her bed and let her thoughts drift to the call from her daughter.

Green nodded to Lewis, tipped his hat to Vicki, and left. Lewis followed, and Vicki could hear the two of them talking in the carport. She moved closer to the door to eavesdrop, but the voices faded off into the night as the two men retreated farther down the driveway to get their vehicles. She soon heard the roar of Green's truck engine as he hooked up the trailer and drove off with the boat.

Vicki turned back toward the kitchen and decided to wash the cups. She knew Emily was bone weary from everything happening in her life. The least Vicki could do was get rid of the cookie crumbs and prevent the ever-present ants from setting up housekeeping on Emily's kitchen counter. As much as she enjoyed Florida, heading north for Michigan in April felt like returning to civilization, or at least a place where fire ants couldn't devour your foot in five seconds.

"Vicki? You still here?" She heard Emily's voice drift down the hallway.

"Yeah. In the kitchen."

"C'mere. But be quiet."

Vicki entered the darkened bedroom and could make out Emily's silhouette backlit by illumination coming in the window from the streetlight.

"I think I fell asleep for a few minutes, but I woke up when I heard a phone. Listen," Emily said.

Both women could hear Detective Lewis talking on his cell phone as he leaned against his cruiser.

"That blood on the boat? I want you to check it. I think it's human. If it is, compare it against Marcus Davey's blood. If they're a match, we may have found out where he was killed before someone moved his body into the dumpster." The detective flipped the phone closed and turned to look in the direction of the house.

Emily ducked down below the window and pulled Vicki onto the floor with her, not that he had much chance of seeing them in the darkened bedroom, but Emily didn't want him to know they'd been spying. Of the two difficult men in her life, Lewis was on the right side of the law, but she still didn't trust him. As for Green, Emily now had another reason to suspect him of being a murderer.

As if reading her mind, Vicki whispered, "And you hired the man. You'll be working with him every day."

How better to get at the truth about Green's role in the murder and help get Clara out of jail? Emily was delighted, a feeling she knew better than to share with Vicki.

Instead, she and Vicki finished a pint of Haagen Dazs and the remainder of the cookies. Vicki argued that playing detective at work with Green was too dangerous, and Emily listened, but she knew it was an opportunity to get to the bottom of the murder. She wasn't passing it up.

When she reentered her bedroom and gazed lovingly at the bed she had spent far too few hours in of late, it was after two in the morning. In a few hours, Darren would be coming home from his night shift at work, and he deserved a hearty breakfast.

Someone hammered on her front door. Emily turned her head to look through the windows onto the front porch, but it was still dark outside, and all she could see was a figure silhouetted by the streetlight. Her bedside clock read 3 a.m., too early for Darren to be returning from work. Besides, she'd given him a key. *It better not be an impromptu visit from the park manager, or the hell with trying to protect his wife. I'll march over to his place, dragging the letch by his feet, and wake up the entire park.*

She shrugged into her robe and grabbed the broom as she walked by the washing machine. *She'd give him such a whack. She'd give a whack to anyone standing out there interfering with her sleep.*

Anyone except the person standing on her steps. Emily recognized her at once. How could she not? It was like looking into the mirror thirty years ago. Long, sun-washed hair, blue eyes, a few inches taller than Emily. And she seemed to have the same habit of biting her full lower lip. *Her daughter.* She wasn't shocked, yet surprised was too mild a description for the feeling that jolted through her body. She knew someday this would happen. Why hadn't she prepared herself? But what was the right thing to say or do when confronted with a daughter she'd never laid on eyes except for the thirty seconds after her birth?

The young woman broke the silence. "You never got back to me, so I thought I'd drop by. I figured if I was here, you couldn't very well ignore me." The hands on her hips and the pugnacious look on her face said what the matter-of-fact nature of her words did not: she was here and not leaving despite the early hour.

All Emily needed was a clone of herself sitting waif-like on her front steps for all of the park to ride by and see.

She tried to match her daughter's blasé tone, but her voice broke and her heart raced wildly. "You might as well come in. Ah, hmmm. I suppose you'll want coffee. You know it's 3 a. m."

"The bus had a flat."

Her daughter had a lousy sense of timing. Emily remembered her own sense of entitlement with her parents when she was in college, often appearing on their doorstep with a wayward friend who needed food and a place to crash for the night or leaving them with a stray cat she found along the road. That's what parents did. They went out of their way for their children. I suppose that feeling I can't quite label has to be something like maternal love, thought Emily. It both frightened and pleased her, and she hoped she wouldn't break down and cry in front of her offspring.

"I stopped by the all-night coffee shop in town. I'm caffeined out."

Emily nodded and gestured toward the couch while she sat on the edge of Fred's recliner.

"Oh, by the way. My name's Naomi."

"I know."

"You do? Oh, of course, Mom and Dad must have told you. And my call to you? Didn't you want to know what I wanted? Weren't you even a little curious after all these years why I was contacting you?"

This was what Emily had expected. The accusing tone and, soon to come, the questions about why she abandoned her child. She knew this was coming, and yet she still wasn't ready for it, nor had she gotten together any explanation that would be acceptable to a rejected child. Anything she might say would sound defensive, but she had to try.

"Yes. I am curious, but you contacted me, and I thought it was your move whether to pursue it further. All this time I thought I had provided you with the best home possible. Was I wrong?"

"Oh, no. Mom and Dad were great. Are great." Naomi's attitude had shifted from that of accuser to one of explorer. "I wanted to find my roots. That's all."

"You sound like a hippie from the seventies," Emily said. *This is so weird. Her voice is mine. And for some reason, she's lying to me.*

"My favorite part of history. And you lived it. Right?"

"I remember it. It wasn't glamorous, I can tell you. People were dying in Viet Nam, and the war split the country."

Naomi nodded. "Uh, I guess you're not too happy to see me."

"That's not it at all. I suspected you might show up in my life one day. I didn't think it would be now."

"Timing's not good, right?"

Emily nodded, but smiled. "But you're here, and I can't deny how happy I am to finally meet you."

Naomi hesitated. "Did you know I was married?"

Ah, thought Emily, now we get to the real reason she's here.

"No. When did this happen?" Emily asked.

"Several months ago. Mom and Dad warned me he would be a problem, but I was in love. He's a cop, but that's not the issue." Naomi extracted a tissue from her pocket, blew her nose, then began to tear it to shreds as she continued talking.

"He was possessive and jealous when we were dating. Mom said it would lead to trouble, and it did."

Emily got out of her chair and picked the shreds of tissue off the floor, threw them in the kitchen wastebasket and returned to the living room with a box of Kleenex in her hand.

"Here," she said. She kept one for herself. "I'm thinking this story is going to be as ugly as that jagged cut on your chin. So I might need a tissue too."

Naomi touched her finger to the angry red mark and produced a smile that barely lifted the corners of her lips.

"He's been, uh, he's been beating me. At first a slap here and there, but in the past two weeks, he's accused me of coming on to his pals at the station. He hit me hard enough that I had to go to the emergency room for stitches when I fell into the cupboard."

Emily's eyes filled with rage, and she opened her mouth to speak.

"And don't tell me to go to the cops or to a shelter. He is a cop, and he knows where all the shelters in the area are located. And I can't go home to Mom and Dad. He'll come there and make trouble."

"I wasn't going to say any of those things. I'll bet he doesn't know about me, does he? I was going to suggest you could move in here." The words fell out of her mouth, surprising even her.

"He knows I was adopted, but that's all he knows. I didn't come here to have you rescue me." Naomi's mouth formed a determined line across her face.

"No, of course not. But then, I'm not the kind of person to give you away twice in your lifetime. Maybe once when I couldn't take care of you, but not now when you need help."

"Thanks, uh. What do I call you?"

"The name's Emily."

"Right."

"You need to be prepared for close quarters here. I've got another roommate, and he's using the only spare bedroom, so it's bunk with me in the king-sized bed or sleep on the couch. Oh, and, cops seem to wander in and out of here, something I'll explain to you later. And sometimes stolen merchandise appears in my drive. I'm one of several suspects in a recent murder, I tend bar for a living, and one of my close friends is in jail." Emily paused to catch a breath. "So there. I guess you're all caught up on my life. If you still think moving in here constitutes some kind of refuge, you're welcome. The pool and spa are across the street. Try to ignore any gossip about me you hear there. I've got to get some sleep. How about you?"

Emily arose at six, in time to make pancakes for Darren. She eyed his torn sleeve and several scratches on his face. All the young people in this place were arriving damaged this morning.

"What do you do at the factory?" she asked.

He noticed her scrutiny of his face and shirt and laughed, a laugh she couldn't quite believe. "Oh, this? I work the press that makes the depressions for folding the flaps on the boxes. I got my sleeve caught in the mechanism and scraped my face when I tried to pull it free. It's nothing."

Maybe, but Hap should know about this. And about her newest live- in.

—❖—

"Can you keep her at the park?" asked Hap. Emily had called him on her way to work.

"A lot of good that will do. Information in the park drifts out the gates like smoke from a sugar cane burn. Plus she looks like my twin sister. Well, she's a lot younger, but you know what I mean."

"And you can't send her back to her parents?"

"It's not safe, Hap. He'll find her. She could use legal advice from you."

"She might be safer getting protection from a big, brawny cowboy or a cop like Lewis."

"Lewis?"

"He might want to do you a favor," Hap said. "Ask him."

"Is that a friend talking or are you giving me your legal expertise?"

CHAPTER 11

After her call to Hap, Emily increased her speed, hoping she wouldn't run into traffic in town. She had spent too much time with Naomi and Darren at breakfast. After an initial shyness when they were introduced, the two began chattering over their pancakes about their favorite musicians and what movies they'd seen recently. Despite the age difference, they seemed comfortable with one another, like an older sister with her brother.

Without revealing the details of her situation, Naomi asked Darren if there were any openings at the box factory. "I need a job, but I don't have much experience."

"I'll ask around this afternoon when I get back to the factory," said Darren. "Most of the work there is pretty physical."

Naomi chuckled. "I know I'm small, but I'm stronger than I look. I work out." She lifted her arm and made a muscle, a small, but obvious bicep. "I'll arm wrestle you for the last pancake."

Emily had tried to convince Naomi that Darren could sleep on the couch, so she could have the spare room. Darren also insisted he'd take the couch, but Naomi said she was fine where she was, sharing Emily's bed. It seemed to Emily that Naomi liked being close to her.

Until now Emily hadn't realized what she had missed all these years—the feeling of family—and she wondered if Naomi, raised an only child, felt some of that too. Emily had been reluctant to leave the casual camaraderie, laughter and joking the two had established so easily. And now she was running late.

When she turned into the parking area at the golf course, she spied Green's truck with the boat and trailer attached. She figured he was reluctant to let his baby out of his sight.

The bar was set up, and a few golfers sat on the stools shooting the breeze with Donald. He didn't look like a golfer in Emily's estimation, and she hadn't asked how familiar he was with the sport because she'd been desperate to get some-one to work the bar. He was swapping tales with the two men about the fifth hole and telling them how his drive hit the water and bounced onto the green. A possible, but unlikely hit, but she was thankful Green could entertain in several sports languages.

"You did a nice job setting up," Emily said.

"It was that or be fired," he replied. He grabbed a knife and began slicing lemons and li-mes.

She decided to play the friendly boss, but not lose time getting information out of Donald. "Do you think the blood on your boat was human?" asked Emily.

"Oh, probably. That happens a lot when you're hauling around dead bodies." Green held the knife in his hand and tested the blade on his thumb. "A little dull. Want me to sharpen it. I'm good with a sharpening stone."

Emily gulped. "Sure. Go right ahead." She scurried out of the bar and into the kitchen, turning her head back toward him in time to see a tight smile on his face. Was that amusement at her awkward attempt to cross-examine him or pleasure at scaring her off?

After conferring with the chef about the specials for lunch, Emily was about to reenter the bar when she heard a familiar voice. She peeked through the window from the kitchen to see Lucinda Davey perched on a bar stool gabbing with Donald. *Now what could they be talking about?* Since she had no interest in encountering her again, she decided to stay hidden in the kitchen and listen in on their conversation. She cracked the door open a bit to hear better.

"Would you make me a pucker sour apple martini, sweetie?" asked Lucinda. She swung her right leg over her left and wiggled her pink and green Capri-clad butt around on the stool. "Oh, I hope I don't fall off this thing and hit the floor. Would you catch me if I did?"

Green gave her one of his usual grim, unsmiling looks. "I'm the bartender here, Lucinda, not the bouncer."

"Oh, aren't you the funny one," she said.

He placed the green concoction in front of her, and she took a sip. "Just sour enough," she said.

Emily wondered if she meant Green's manner or the martini. "So I heard someone stole your boat," Lucinda said between sips.

"You didn't come in here to ask about my boat. What do you want?"

Emily thought their conversation had a note of a past connection to it. Were they ever involved? Could she find out?

"No dearie, I didn't come to talk about your damn boat. As if I cared about anything of yours. I have a golf lesson with Lenny." That surprised Emily. Lucinda didn't seem like the golf playing kind of gal. Her foundation and mascara would run by the second hole, and the smell of her hairspray and perfume could attract every fly and mosquito on the course.

"Good thing I went light on the vodka," Donald said. He turned, Emily's gaze caught his. Her eavesdropping was over, yet she was reluctant to face Lucinda. Every time she was in the presence of that woman, she risked bodily harm.

Donald busied himself around the bar, sending out cues that he wasn't interested in further discussion with Lucinda. He jerked his head to one side signaling Emily he could use her help, but she did a thumbs down signal and hung back near the kitchen door, yet close enough that she could spy on Lucinda.

Lucinda turned around on her bar stool, sipping her martini and gazing out on the driving range. Lenny was giving another lesson to the young woman Emily had seen him instructing at least three times every week. The woman hit a drive that went over one hundred and fifty yards. Lenny, in his usual over-friendly way, grabbed her around the waist, and kissed her. The woman drew back, as if she wasn't enjoying this kind of attention from her instructor, but she continued to smile.

"That's enough of that," said Lucinda. She slammed her half-finished martini on the bar, slopping green sticky liquid on the shiny wooden surface. For a gal carrying more than her share of necessary weight around the hip area, Lucinda was fast. By the time Emily pushed open the kitchen door to get a better look at what was happening, the Widow Davey was on the driving range standing over a surprised Lenny Sharples. His student grabbed her club and jumped into the golf cart, hitting the accelerator hard enough that the cart did a wheelie as she sped for the safety of the clubhouse.

"What happened?" asked Emily. She and Donald stood at the windows of the bar, watching Lenny and Lucinda.

"She decked him," said Donald. He turned back to the bar, grabbed her martini glass, and began to wash it.

"She may want the rest of that," Emily said.

"She may, but she shouldn't," said Green.

"You seem to know Lucinda. Tell me about her and Marcus," said Emily. She watched as Lucinda threw her arms over her head and gestured wildly. She looked like a human windmill. Lenny backed up to his golf cart while Lucinda advanced on him. Emily couldn't hear what she was saying, but her mouth worked like a chute in a grain elevator, words flowing without stop, burying Lenny under their assault.

Donald turned at Emily's question and joined her at the window. "Like that," Donald said. "She yelled some, cajoled some, managed him, and Marcus retreated."

"What I knew of Marcus Davey wasn't someone who could be put off by a woman," said Emily.

"Maybe not by you," he said, "but you're not a southern woman. You're a little bitty northern babe. No danger at all. But Lucinda? Lucinda's another story. Rumor has it Marcus was dedicating himself to booze, and Lucinda was managing the ranch."

"That had to have been difficult for him. Or didn't he mind?"

Donald thought for a minute before he answered. "As long as she let him believe he was the boss, no problem. And, like I said, Lucinda is a southern woman who knows how to manage her man. His problem was with his older brother."

"I heard about how he died. What was the problem?" She thought she could guess from what Clara had said, but she wanted to hear Donald's view of the brothers.

"Don't know for sure, but folks around here suspect Marcus had a hand in the so-called accident. No one could prove it, of course." Again Donald paused and considered his words. If they got any slower in coming out, cobwebs would grow on his tongue.

"Marcus wasn't half the cowman his brother was," he said.

"Ah," said Emily, "that explains a lot. He carried himself as if he was waiting for someone to insult him, to question his competence or status. Look how he reacted when I told him no to another drink. A drunk with a chip on his shoulder. But he'd have been as prickly without the booze. It made him less certain of himself, meaner maybe."

Donald turned to her with a look that she found unsettling, a look that said he almost had found respect for her.

"Well, I'll be damned," he said. "That's quite an assessment. Aren't you smarter than Johnny Reb dressed in blue in a Yankee camp? Now you know why Detective Lewis has more suspects in the murder than this county has cattle."

She guessed Donald's comments about her were meant as a compliment, and one she wasn't sure she welcomed. She hadn't yet made up her mind about what kind of man Donald Green was.

The next day her phone rang at six in the morning. *Too early*. She and Naomi had talked until two, catching each other up on their lives. Emily felt nauseous from lack of sleep.

"If you can be ready in fifteen minutes, we can get ourselves a mess of specks. They're biting fast and furious in the river near the state park."

"What the hell? Who is this?" Emily asked.

"Donald. I thought you might like to see what folks here live like."

"I know what they live like. They kill each other on occasion, arrest their womenfolk and steal one another's boats. Besides, I have company here." *The nerve of this guy*.

"Invite them along."

From the other side of the king-sized bed, Naomi yawned and her eyes opened. "What's happening?" she asked.

Emily turned her head and watched her daughter awaken. What an odd feeling, to be sharing a bed with a child she hadn't seen since her birth. This would take some getting used to. *Or perhaps Naomi wouldn't stick around that long*. Emily was shocked at how saddened she was to think her daughter might leave soon.

"Want to go fishing?" asked Emily.

"Fine with me. You got a boat?"

"I got a... Well, I know someone who does," Emily said.

"I won't get eaten by alligators, will I?"

Emily covered the receiver. "No chance of that. This guy can scare off the biggest reptile by simply waving his arms. On the other hand, he may kill people." Once the words were out of her mouth, she wanted to take them back. She shouldn't frighten Naomi with suspicions that she herself didn't quite believe.

Naomi looked closely at Emily's face. The weak morning light hid Emily's facial expression from her daughter. *Could Naomi see she wasn't being serious about Donald? She wasn't serious, was she? Naomi had to believe she was rational enough not to hang out with murderers. She hoped.*

"Great. I can be ready in five minutes, if we can stop at the convenience store and get coffee, real coffee not that decaf stuff you live on."

"I heard that," said Green.

What did he hear? The part about killing people or Naomi's need for caffeine?

"Naomi needs coffee first. Where do we meet?" Emily asked.

"No, I mean I heard the part about killing people. Haven't done that in a while," he said.

Emily assumed he had to be kidding, but just in case... "I'll let Vicki know we're going," she said. "I mean, there might be an emergency at the course." *Or if the authorities want a lead on the killer should our bodies be found floating in the lake.*

Green laughed. "Meet me at the boat launch on the river in ten minutes. I already got coffee. We'll be back in time to open the bar."

"You didn't really mean that about his killing people, did you?" asked Naomi from the bathroom.

Emily didn't know how to answer her daughter's question.

❦

Emily drove Stan the Sedan along the river road leading to the state park. The sleep was barely out of her eyes, and she wondered why she was doing this. She was going fishing with a possible murderer, she reminded herself, to help get her boss and friend out of jail. The next time she visited Clara she should ask her about Donald Green. Clara knew everyone in town, so she must have the scoop on him. And, Emily reminded herself, she had to tell Clara about Green's boat being found in her drive.

"So is this a boyfriend or what?" asked Naomi.

Emily's mouth dropped open at Naomi's question. "Boyfriend? Oh, good God no. He's an employee, someone I need to talk with. And I hear he's pretty good at fishing. That's dinner for tonight," Emily said.

She steered the car into the parking area and saw Green's boat positioned on the ramp ready to be launched.

He beckoned her over after she parked the car.

"A friend. Naomi," she said introducing her daughter to Green. Naomi was not only a friend, but he didn't need to know that. She watched Naomi's face and thought she caught a hint of irritation there at the form of introduction. *What was she to Emily after all these years, but most important, what did she want to be?*

"Donald Green, my employee," said Emily. She watched his eyes snap at the designation.

Emily had managed to annoy both her companions.

He held out his hand. "Also a friend," he said. He paused, looking from one of the women to the other, comparing the two. "You gals look..."

"What?" asked Emily.

"You look kinda small, both of you. Think one of you can handle backing this trailer down the ramp while I maneuver the boat off it?"

"I'll do it," said Emily. After their first meeting, she was eager to show him she could handle the huge dually truck. Short didn't mean she was dumb or inept. It did mean she'd have a hard time reaching the pedals, however. She crammed her backpack behind her on the seat, shifted into reverse and hit the accelerator with her toe. The truck shot backward.

"Slowly!" yelled Green.

She stuck her head out the window and looked back at him. "I thought you were in a hurry to get out on the river." This time she applied less pressure.

"Stop," said Green. "I only want the boat in the water, not the truck."

Emily toed the brake.

"That's good," he said. He backed the boat into the water. "She's in. Park the truck and trailer, and I'll come around to the dock."

Emily eased her toe onto the accelerator and drove the giant truck vehicle up the ramp and chose a parking place. Naomi was already at the dock accepting a cup of coffee from Donald. He offered one to Emily, but she shook her head when she inquired about a bathroom and Donald told her she'd have to use the tin can on board like everyone else.

Donald pulled away from the shore and signaled the two of them to settle back into their seats. He throttled forward, and they shot into the channel.

The mouth of the river provided a panoramic view of the lake ahead. The sun was low on the horizon, and the sky spread blue color from one side of the tea-colored water to the other. Emily tried to tie her hair back into a ponytail, but the wind whipped it free. She gave up struggling with the strands and welcomed the feel of the cooling breeze blowing through it. She'd cautioned Naomi to wear long sleeves and trousers against the bugs, but now, with the sun climbing into the cloudless sky, she wished the two of them had on shorts and light shirts. Emily rolled up her sleeves and let the wind evaporate the perspiration from her bare arms. When she turned her head to see how Naomi was faring, she saw that her daughter had removed her shirt and had a sleeveless tee underneath.

Donald said something to her, but she couldn't make out his words above the sound of the motor. He throttled back a bit.

"Ahead, around this bend and toward that sand bar, we'll drop our lines."

Emily saw other boats in the main channel of the river, their lines out, and men pulling in fish. "Why not around here?" she asked. "It seems everyone is catching something in the open water." She wasn't comfortable with the idea they should tuck themselves away from the other boats, where no one could see them.

"This is my secret spot. Only I know about it. It's a honey of a fishing hole," he said. Pride shone through his usual emotionless tone.

He piloted the craft around the bend, throttled down more and steered sharp right so that the trees, reeds and cattail along the bank obscured them from the other boats in the channel.

Donald tossed out the anchor and helped Emily and Naomi set up the lines. "Now all we have to do is wait," he said and settled back in his seat.

Not a breeze caught them in their hideaway. Sweat began to track its way down Emily's face and onto her chin. Naomi appeared to be sleeping with her head resting in her hand. Donald remained motionless. A half-hour passed and nothing moved on the bank or in the water.

"If there are fish here," Emily said, "they're all asleep."

Donald shook his head and signaled her with a "shush." Another fifteen minutes went by. Naomi took heavy breaths, almost snores, and Donald's head dipped. Emily wiped the perspiration from her upper lip and wondered why she was sitting in the middle of a body of water that seemed devoid of life unless one counted the gators, which were keeping a low profile this morning.

"Something on your right-hand line," said Donald. "Play it in easy like."

Emily did what he suggested but the line didn't move.

"How big is this damn fish?" she asked. "I can hardly pull him toward the boat." Emily tugged harder and kept the line taut. To her delight, she saw a shadow under water and then it broke the surface alongside the boat.

"Must be a big bass," said Donald. He got out of his seat and worked his way back to where Emily was sitting.

"What ya got there?" he asked. He leaned toward the water and squinted his eyes to get a better look at her catch. "Well, you wouldn't know the kind of fish, would you? Pull 'er over here, so I can see."

"You're wrong. I know what I've got here," she said, looking down into the water at the line next to the boat. "It's a hand."

CHAPTER 12

"I hate to do this, Donald, but you'll have to come with me to my office. There are some questions you'll need to answer," Lewis said.

Green, Emily, Naomi and the detective stood at the boat ramp several yards from a crowd of fishermen now more curious about Emily's catch than their own. Several police vehicles encircled the ramp, keeping the nosy spectators at a distance. Emily could see the lights of an ambulance and additional police cars surrounding the bank of Donald's secret fishing hole down river.

"Me. Why me?" asked Green. "She found the damn thing." He gestured toward Emily. "And she's already involved in one murder."

And just when I was beginning to think kindly of him. Emily guzzled water from a thermos some kind spectator handed her when she couldn't get her hiccups under control. She took a tentative breath.

"No one said this was murder," Lewis said. "But there is the issue of that blood found in your boat. The lab says it's human. Let's go."

Green eyed him with suspicion, then his glance swept through the crowd of fellow fishermen, many of whom he knew. Emily suspected Green would want this conversation private. He nodded at Lewis, and the two men headed toward the police car.

This time, thought Emily with some pleasure, she wasn't the one under suspicion. She looked at her watch and noticed she had only minutes to get to the course.

"So can I go now?" she called to Lewis' retreating back.

He stopped and walked over to her. "You don't seem very curious about the identity of our victim," said Lewis.

Emily turned her back on the ambulance, then shifted around to look across the river, anything to avoid seeing the body being transported from the rescue boat. "It's too grisly. I'd prefer not thinking about it. Besides, I don't mean to sound callous, but everyone I know and care about is accounted for," said Emily. "So, how about it? Can we go?"

"I need a statement from you and your, uh, friend." Lewis' gaze traveled to Naomi who was leaning against the bumper of Donald's truck.

Emily's shoulders slumped. She was spending more time being questioned by the police than she was working. "I've got a job I have to get to. You might as well question me there. By now everyone at the course is familiar with police interrogations in the clubhouse."

Lewis nodded his agreement. "How about...?" He gestured with his head toward Naomi.

"My daughter. It's a long story, and one you don't need to know about. I'm going to have her drive me there and take the car back home. She's exhausted. This was her first fishing trip, and no one liked the catch."

Emily turned on her heel, slipped her arm around Naomi's waist and directed her toward the car. Her daughter felt as limp as a Raggedy Ann doll missing most of its stuffing.

On the way out of the parking area, Emily changed her mind and turned toward home instead of the course. She berated herself for letting her curiosity about Donald Green overwhelm her better judgment. It was foolish to be out on the water with him alone. What was he doing, taking them to that spot and letting Emily latch onto his most recent victim? Showing off? Although he *had* used his cell to put in a call to the police right away. Maybe it was a coincidence that the body floated where he usually fished. The man confused the hell out of her.

Emily looked across at her daughter. Naomi leaned against the passenger window and said not a word the entire ride. As they pulled through the security gate, she sat up in the seat. "I thought we were going to the course."

"This has been a shock, especially after what your husband did to you. You need rest. I'll be home..." Emily paused. When would she be home? How long would they question Donald? And what if they arrested him? She'd be working the bar alone until closing tonight. "I'll be home when I can. I'll go in with you."

"I'll be fine."

Emily knew she needed a little time to recover from the morning's unpleasant surprise, but she grabbed her daughter's hand to lead her into the house. To her surprise, Naomi laid her head on her mother's shoulder and leaned into her.

"I hope that's not how fishing is usually done around here," she said.

The sight of Darren on the couch watching television seemed to perk her up.

"I thought you'd be asleep by now," Emily said.

"Nah. I've got too much on my mind. Wow. You two look like someone ran over you. What's up?"

Emily explained how their fishing expedition went wrong. "So who was it?" he asked.

"I don't think the body was in any shape to be identified then," Emily said. A shiver ran down her back as she remembered the sight of the bluish white hand on the end of her line.

"Oh, yeah," said Darren. "I'll bet the gators got to it."

Naomi's jaw dropped, and her face turned white. "I'm going to bed."

"Sorry, Naomi. I wasn't thinking. It must have been awful for you," Darren said. He got off the couch and came over to pat her arm.

"It's okay. I need some rest." Naomi gave them a tiny smile and headed down the hall toward the bedroom.

"I've got to run to work. Could you keep an eye on her while you're here?" Emily asked Darren.

⚬

She scurried around the bar, wiping spots from the glassware, checking the tap lines and slicing up lemons and limes. She noted with satisfaction that Donald had sharpened the bar knife, and it cut the fruit easily.

Lenny stuck his head through the doorway. "Open yet? I need a quick shot of Crown Royal."

"Sure. This is the first time I've seen you in here in the morning."

Lenny approached the bar and removed his sunglasses. He was sporting quite a shiner.

He caught her staring at his eye. "Lucinda. Yesterday. She's very possessive about her golf instructors."

Emily set a generous shot of whiskey on the bar in front of him. "Instructors? She's had more than one?"

"Several months ago before you came here, she took a few lessons from our assistant pro, but she likes to be the center of attention. He had other students, and she wasn't happy about that. Now she's doing the same thing with me. She doesn't seem to understand that I have to give everyone the same consideration I give her." He grabbed the glass and threw the contents down his throat. "Hit me again."

Emily poured him another shot, and he tossed that one away with equal dispatch, then waved goodbye. Through the bar windows, she could see him as he wheeled his golf cart out toward the driving range. The young woman who had fled from Lucinda's wrath the day before was on the range hitting balls. She looked up at Lenny's approach, and glanced at her cart. Lenny ran up to her and put out his arms as if to embrace her. Emily watched as the woman backed away from him, and Lenny pursued her to her cart. She shook her head at him, and sped off toward the clubhouse.

Less than ten minutes later, Lenny reappeared in the bar and asked for another shot.

"Do you think that's wise?" asked the assistant pro, Mike Graham, who had followed Lenny into the bar. "You're booked with lessons for the remainder of the morning and into early afternoon."

"You take 'em," said Lenny. He planted himself on the barstool in front of Emily.

"Fine, but you'll have to mind the pro shop then," said Mike.

"Righto. I'll be here on this stool in case I'm needed."

By noon, after helping himself to the bar wares, Lenny could no longer hold himself upright on the stool, and Emily had to call his wife to pick him up.

"This is wonderful," Emily said to Mike. "You and I are the only ones working here aside from kitchen staff and two waitresses."

"I'll see if I can rearrange lessons, but if I can't, you'll have to take over the counter at the shop when I'm on the range."

"I can't do that. I'm the only one on the bar," Emily said.

But there was no choice. Emily ran between the bar and the pro shop, and Mike shuttled back and forth from the range to the shop. Emily managed a quick call home to check on Naomi after the lunch crowd.

"That you, Darren? Your voice sounds funny."

"Do you know anyone with a brown Mercedes sedan?" he asked.

"No. Why?"

"It's been driving by here all morning. It must have passed more than five or six times. I thought maybe a friend of yours looking for you, but didn't stop when they noticed your car was gone."

"Well, don't worry about it. Whoever's in it would have to have a gate card to get into the community." The line for the pro shop rang. "Wait a second," said Emily. "Mike. Would you get that? I'm on the other line." But the phone kept ringing. "Darren, honey, I've got to go. I'll call you again when I get a chance. But Naomi's fine, right?"

"Right," said Darren. There was no conviction in his voice.

"Darren?"

"No, she's sleeping. She's okay. I'm... Never mind. See you later." Darren hung up, and Emily hit the button for the bar line.

By three o'clock there was a lull in golfers needing carts, food or drinks, and Emily leaned against the counter at the pro shop. Both she and Mike were exhausted.

"Does Lenny drink like this often?" she asked Mike.

"I've never seen him do it before, but I can attest to how unnerving Mrs. Davey can be when she demands attention. I considered quitting my job here when she hit on me earlier this season," said Mike.

"Hit on you?"

"She was interested in more than smoothing out her swing," said Mike. "And Lenny seemed to encourage her. But then Lenny has a habit of encouraging all the women."

"I guess her performance yesterday put him over the edge."

"That and Lenny's gambling issues." Mike straightened up a round of golf clothing.

"He gambles?"

"He's always over at the casino on his days off, and lately he's been taking calls here that sound as if he owes money to someone. But you never heard it from me," said Mike.

The phone rang. Emily saw the bar line light up. "Now what?"

"It's me," said a masculine voice. It was one Emily had forgotten about during the rush of the work at the course.

"Mr. Green. I hope this call isn't to invite me and my daughter on another fishing adventure. We had all we could handle this morning. In fact, she's home in bed in a state of shock."

"You're testy today, now aren't you? Why blame me if someone saw fit to pollute my fishing hole with a floater?"

"Donald, get your sorry butt in here. I've been running around all morning and afternoon trying to keep up with the bar and the pro shop while you've been exchanging fishing stories with the local gendarmes."

There was silence on the other end of the line, and Emily thought for a minute he'd hung up on her. She really didn't believe he'd been responsible for the corpse she'd snagged, but she was enraged that whatever the police thought he was involved in, he had left her short-handed today of all days.

"And then you have the nerve to suggest Lewis question me instead of you because you believe I had a hand in Davey's death. If you want this job, you'd better get out here. Now."

"I took that job to help you out. I don't need it, and I might give it up if you take this attitude every time a little something goes wrong in your life."

Emily hung up on him.

"Donald coming in?" asked Mike.

"I doubt it."

A brrrring of the phone and the bar line lit up once more. Emily grabbed it off the cradle and pressed it to her ear. "I don't want to talk to you," she said. She assumed it was Donald calling back.

"It's me, Emily. Clara."

※

Donald appeared fifteen minutes after she received the call from Clara. Much as she wanted to fire him on the spot, she didn't. He took up his position behind the bar, and she told him she'd be back when she got back.

"And if you don't get back here tonight?" he asked.

"Close up." She tossed the keys to him. "Be careful taking out the trash."

"Oh, right. Never can tell what I'll find of interest to the local police." He chuckled in his sardonic way.

"There's an old gator likes to sit behind the dumpster looking for someone to get close. But then, that shouldn't be a problem for you. You're a real gator wrestler, aren't you?"

"All you'd have to do was glance his way, and the look on your face would scare him into the next county," Donald said.

She turned on him, and he held up his hands as if to fend off her attack. "Leave me alone. It's been a bad day," she said.

"You think I like sitting in an eight-by-ten room sharing crummy coffee with a detective who has one murder and another suspicious death on his hands, and who's trying to tie them together, maybe with me as the suspect?"

"I've been there. Remember? Leave the keys on the counter, set the alarm and put the automatic lock on the door when you leave. Lenny will open up tomorrow. That is, if he's not too hung over."

❦

When she pulled into the jail parking lot, Clara stood at the door to the building waiting for her. Emily got out of the car, and the two women hugged, an embrace that neither of them wanted to end. She stepped back and looked into Clara's face. Her eyes lacked their usual sparkle, and her rumpled clothing looked dirty and hung loosely on her body. Emily vowed to pamper her, to do anything she could to put the zing back in Clara's step.

"They finally got smart and dropped the charges, did they? Not enough evidence? Motive a little weak?" asked Emily.

Clara threw a small paper bag with her possessions in it into the back seat of Emily's car. "We'll talk law later. Let's get out of here. I want to go home and take a hot shower. And I especially want to shave my legs," said Clara. "How's Darren?"

"He's fine, I guess. He's babysitting my daughter today until he leaves for work, so I'll drop you by your house and head right home." She explained the discovery of the body in the river to Clara.

"That poor child," said Clara. "An abusive husband and a corpse all in the space of a week. Watch it." Lewis' police cruiser pulled into the lot blocking their way out.

Emily stuck her head out of the car window. "Detective Lewis," she said, "we'd appreciate your moving out of our way. Clara's got an important meeting with a bubble bath now that the police have come to their senses and released her."

He got out of his car and approached their vehicle. "I'd like to talk to Clara alone."

"You can say what you need to in front of Emily."

Emily thought the expression on his face puzzling, a combination of the look of police business coupled with something like compassion. "Well?" said Clara.

"The body in the river? It was in bad enough shape that we had some trouble identifying it, but the wallet in his pocket contained a driver's license—your husband's."

CHAPTER 13

Emily ran hot water into the tub for Clara and searched through her bathroom cabinets for something to scent it.

She found a bottle of bubble bath and emptied half into the tub. *There. That should remove any lingering odor of imprisonment.*

She stuck her head around the bathroom door and called down the hall to Clara. "Madam, your bath awaits. It'll be good for removing jailhouse grime and for relaxing. I poured you a glass of chardonnay. It's on the edge of the tub."

"I'll make it a short soak. I have a lot of things to arrange. I've got to call some of Eddie's friends and relatives, what few he has...had, I mean. Did you call Hap?" asked Clara. She stood in the hallway clad only in her bra and panties. "I probably should burn these. I'll never get the stink of jail out of them. Oh God, I forgot. I've got to get a hold of Darren and tell him about...."

Emily had never seen her friend so disoriented and confused, but then the death of a husband was a shock. Emily could relate to that. She took Clara by the hand and led her into the bathroom. "Your address book is in the desk in the hallway, right? I'll make the necessary calls. You get yourself together."

Emily shut the door behind her, hoping that the scent of lavender bubbles and a sip of cold wine would put things right. *It might help me too*. She poured wine into another glass, extracted the address book from the drawer and slid onto the couch in the living room.

Clara's head peeked out from the bathroom doorway. "Your daughter..."

"I'm calling her right now, then Hap, and then Darren. Don't worry. I won't say anything. I'll call the factory and tell them to have Darren call you as soon as he gets the message. Go soak."

There was no answer at her house. It was after five in the afternoon. She guessed Naomi was napping and not answering the phone, or she'd gone to the hot tub and pool for a swim. When she called Darren's employer, he informed her that Darren had not shown up for work. *Both children not available?* Emily began to worry. She got Hap on the phone and told him about Eddie.

"I'll be right over," he said. "I'll get a ride from one of my lady friends here."

"Could you swing by my place on your way and see if you can rouse Naomi? She may be napping or at the pool. I couldn't get her on the phone. And it seems Darren never showed at the box factory today. I don't want to say anything to Clara right now, but Darren looked as if he'd been in a fight. He said it was an injury from work, but... He called me earlier today saying that a strange car kept going by the house."

"What don't you want to tell me right now?" asked Clara. She wore a towel wrapped around her and held the wine glass, now nearly empty, in her hand.

"Talk to you soon," Emily said. She hung up the phone. "That was Hap."

"Uh, huh. What are the two of you keeping from me? I walk out of jail to a dead ex and whispering between you and Dad. What's up?"

Emily looked up at her friend and saw that the old in-charge Clara seemed to be back. "Guess lavender and wine are some kind of miracle cure."

"No, I think it was having a bathroom to myself and looking down and seeing smooth legs." She poured herself another glass of wine, refilled Emily's and joined her on the couch.

"Okay. I can't get in touch with my daughter, and Darren didn't go to work today. He also was worried about a car that drove by my house several times. I'm concerned it could be Naomi's husband. Maybe the batterer found her."

"Then I think you need to go home and take care of her. I'm fine. Hap can help me out here."

"No, no. I want to stay. Hap's checking my house now."

"My dear Emily, you've been more than an employee. You're a true friend. But you've done enough. Now skedaddle on home and check on your daughter. Dad and I will worry about Darren."

Hap, driven by yet another of the blue-haired ladies from the center, pulled up to the curb as Emily exited Clara's. After introducing his chauffer as Sadie, he said, "I found your daughter poolside chattering with some young ladies down from Michigan visiting their grandparents. I told her about Clara and Eddie and said you'd be home soon."

"Thank God she's safe. And thanks for looking in on her."

"You're like Clara. You worry too much about your grown kids. Must be an occupational hazard of motherhood." Hap waved goodbye to Sadie who laid rubber as she pulled out in front of another car. "She's a little reckless in the driver's seat. And in other ways, too." Hap chuckled and waggled his bushy white eyebrows. "How's my little girl doing?"

Emily knew he wasn't asking after her. *Look who's worrying now.* "Clara worked through the shock of dead Eddie in the bathroom."

"I never knew her to be one for throwing up," Hap said.

"Not that. She took a bath and drank a glass of wine in record time. She's fine, I think. She tossed me out, so I'm on my way home. Or do you think I should stay for a while?"

Clara opened the front door, took her father's arm and drew him inside. "Go home and see how your own little chickadee is doing."

"Hap says she's at the pool."

"She may need sunscreen. Emily, I'm fine. Go. Go." Clara made shooing motions at her.

"If you need anything...."

Clara closed the door. Emily felt so useless. *Shouldn't she be doing something for Clara? The woman had just gotten out of jail and now had to deal with the death of her ex.* Emily thought of chicken soup, but in the ninety-degree heat, that seemed silly. Clara stuck her head back out the front door.

"There is one thing, however," she said.

Emily turned back toward the house with lightness in her step and eagerness to help written on her face. "Yes?"

"Who's taking care of the bar?"

"Donald's there now. I told him to close up tonight."

"You'll go back and check on him, right?"

"Sure." That wasn't her intention, but, of course she could do that, if Clara thought it was necessary.

"I'll see you there later, then," Clara said.

"You don't need to come in," Emily assured her.

"Oh, yes I do. For my sanity, yes I do."

❦

Naomi returned from the pool, sunburned, hair hanging in tangles and a look on her face that said she'd had an afternoon of fun and had recovered from her morning's fishing event.

"Did you make some friends?" asked Emily. She stood at the sink washing up breakfast dishes. It sure looked as if her daughter could overlook messes someone Emily's age would not.

Naomi halted inside the door. "Oh, I should have done those before I went out. I'm sorry."

So let's revise that assessment. She's slow to see the mess.

"How's your friend Clara? Hap told me about her husband." Naomi threw her beach towel toward the couch. It fell short and landed on the floor. As Emily was about to ask her to pick it up, Naomi said, "Sorry about that," and grabbed the towel. She glanced around the room with a questioning look.

"Oh, hang it out back over one of the chairs." Emily gestured with her head toward the backyard.

"Right."

Several minutes passed and, when Naomi didn't return, Emily dried her hands and followed her daughter out the door. Emily stood motionless on the patio facing the water. A mare and her foal, their coats burnished bronze by the sun nearing the horizon, turned their heads toward the house and examined Naomi from the safety of their pasture across the canal. When

Emily appeared by her daughter's side, the foal nudged his head between the mare's legs and began nursing. With a flick of her ears, the mare dropped her head and fed again on the stubby grass.

"They know you," said Naomi.

"I usually have my coffee out here on those mornings when I have the time. And they have their breakfast across from me. So, yep, I guess you could say we're acquainted."

"It's beautiful here. So quiet and peaceful. I can understand why you want to stay even though Fred is gone."

Naomi's comments jerked Emily away from the pastoral scene before her and back to her predicament. Her case would come before the judge soon, and she had been so distracted by recent events that she had forgotten how tenuous her hold on this property was.

"Did I say something wrong?" asked Naomi. "Your expression changed from contentment to depression in a second."

"Oh, no, honey. I was reminding myself I have to get to the club and worrying you'll be bored here by yourself. I could drop you at the mall to shop and then you could walk to the cinema if you'd like." Emily thought there was no point in telling Naomi her troubles, not with an abusive husband breathing down her daughter's back. And that reminded her. "So that I can keep an eye out for that no-good husband of yours, not that it's likely he'd find you here, what kind of car does he drive?"

"A blue Ford Explorer. Is there something wrong?" Fear crept across Naomi's features.

"No, honey. I wanted to keep my eyes open for his car, that's all. So how about it? Want me to drop you at the mall?"

"Thanks, but I've got an invitation to go to the coast with my new friends this evening. There's a Thai restaurant there they want to try. Unless you'd prefer I stay here."

Emily wouldn't admit it, but she wanted Naomi near her and considered taking her along to the club. But Naomi wasn't a child.

"You go ahead and have fun." She stopped herself short of giving Naomi a curfew for when she was to be home.

❧

Clara stood looking out the windows of the bar. Emily wondered what she could see out there. The lights in the bar remained on, but it was pitch black outside. There were no lights on the driving range. Mike had closed the clubhouse an hour ago, leaving the grounds dark with the exception of the sensor light, which lit when Donald left by the back door several minutes before.

Emily sat with her elbows propped on the bar watching Clara at the window.

"This certainly has been some day for the club. And for you," said Clara. Before Mike closed the course, he and Emily had let Clara know about Lenny's drunkenness.

"Do you think it had something to do with Lucinda's visit yesterday?" asked Emily. If Clara wanted to talk shop, and it took her mind off her husband and son, Emily didn't mind.

Clara continued to stare out the window, as if sheer concentration would be enough to light up the subtropical night. "You've had your run-ins with Lucinda."

"The woman is crazy," said Emily.

Clara faced Emily, her mouth set in a grim line. "No, she's not. Don't be taken in by her woman-trapped-in-the-sixties appearance. She uses the tacky look and a cheaply made up face to detract from what's under her teased hair—a sharp mind. Don't underestimate her. She's dangerous."

"You know something about her you're not telling me. What is it?"

"Nothing you need to know about, but be wary of her. Lucinda is not a silly woman."

"Do you think she's involved in her husband's death?" asked Emily. Clara faced the window and began scanning the darkness once more.

"I wouldn't go that far, but I'm sure she'll be able to make it work for her somehow. If she knew what I have planned for her, she'd...."

A chill ran down Emily's spine. She didn't want her friend in any more trouble, and Clara's tone of voice said "revenge" although she couldn't imagine for what. "What are you planning?" asked Emily.

"You can't keep secrets forever."

"Me? I'm not. I never tried to keep Naomi a secret." Emily's voice sounded defensive to her own ears and no wonder. Why was Clara accusing her of keeping secrets?

"Not you. I meant me. It's time to give up what I haven't admitted all these years." Clara turned from the window to face Emily across the dim bar. As she opened her mouth to speak, the window behind her exploded. Shards of glass flew across the room showering Clara and Emily like sleet. The noise of the window blowing inward was accompanied by another, a loud pop or bark.

"Get down," said Clara. "Someone's firing a rifle at us."

Both she and Emily dove for the floor. They lay there for a minute in silence. Then Clara shimmied on her belly across the room and quickly jumped up to hit the light switch. The room was bathed in comforting blackness.

"That's why you kept looking out the window," said Emily.

"I thought I saw car lights coming up the club road. Then nothing. Someone had to have turned them off. And I wondered why."

"I guess we know why now," said Emily. She began to prop herself up on her elbows. "Ouch. Damn. There's glass all over the floor. I jabbed some into my arm." Aside from the unreality of being shot at and the glee at being alive that followed, Emily took comfort in there being no follow-up shot. She shakily began to get up.

"No. Stay down. They could still be out there," said Clara. She reached out and placed a restraining arm on Emily's shoulder. The two women continued to lie on the floor for several moments, but the first shot was an orphan.

"You okay?" asked Clara.

"You were closer to the windows. How about you?"

"Scratches from the glass shattering. I think I'm going to need another bath though."

"That much blood?" asked Emily.

"It's a bar floor, for God's sake. It smells like beer, booze and the fifth green."

Clara was making jokes, so Emily figured they had to be okay, and she wasn't hiccupping, a very good sign.

Lights from a car hit the broken window. Okay, so she was wrong. They weren't okay.

"I'm calling the cops," Emily said. She flipped open her cell and made the call.

"Too late," said Clara. The rumble of a heavy engine drew closer, and the vehicle stopped within inches of the window. The two women watched as boots appeared when their wearer opened the driver side door and approached the building. A big man stepped over the sill, crunched through the broken glass, and walked to the other side of the bar. He flipped on the wall switch.

Clara stood up and faced him. "Donald. What the hell are you doing here?"

CHAPTER 14

Rifle in hand, Donald stood among the shat-tered pieces of the plate glass window. "You ladies sure have a real mess here, now don't you?"

His eyes swept the barroom and came to rest on Clara and Emily who had risen off the floor and were shoulder to shoulder. Drops of blood from flying glass dotted their faces and arms, and they stood amid larger shards covering the bar-room floor. Closer to the window when the shot hit, blood poured from Clara's shoulder.

"The cops will be coming down the club road in a few minutes." Emily hoped that letting Don-ald know the authorities would be on him any minute would encourage him to put aside his weapon and not shoot the two of them.

"I don't think the club road is the fastest way out of here. Any four-wheel drive truck can cut across the field and come out north of here on Swamp Road."

"Is that what you have in mind, Donald?" asked Clara.

"What? No way. If you take a wrong turn past the field there you'd end up in some real swampy country, bad enough that even a four-wheel drive wouldn't help. I'll stay here."

Clara looked puzzled for a moment, then reached out her hand. "Let me see your rifle." Donald handed it to her. She sniffed the barrel. "It hasn't even been fired," she said, and gave it back to him.

Green produced a bark that passed for his version of a laugh. "You thought I was responsible for this? Hell no. I had turned onto the highway when I met a truck coming toward me. After he went by, I watched him in my rearview mirror, and he turned onto Club Road. I thought that was peculiar since no one was here except for you two, so I turned around first chance I got and followed him back here." Donald ran his hand across the back of his neck. "Then I lost him. I figured he must have turned off his lights so you wouldn't see him coming."

The sound of sirens and lights from police vehicles turned his attention away from Emily and Clara. Clara let out a low moan. "I've got to sit down a minute."

Emily turned toward her friend and got a good look at her in the light. Glass shards in her hair glistened like stars, but what might have been the romantic effect of diamonds nestled among red curls ended with blood spatters dotting her face and arms and a larger stain seeping through the sleeve of her blouse. She helped Clara onto a bar stool. "This can't all be from the glass. I think the shot grazed your shoulder."

Detective Lewis stepped through what was left of the windows. "Why am I not surprised to see the three of you at this scene?"

Emily gritted her teeth, but couldn't keep herself from letting go at Lewis. "Before you say another snarky word about us, could you call an ambulance? Clara's been hit."

Detective Lewis crossed the room in two long strides and stood in front of Clara. "Where?" he asked.

"Right here," said Emily. She pointed to Clara's blood-stained blouse. Clara turned her head to look at her shoulder, blanched white and fainted into Lewis' arms.

❧

An ambulance prepared to transport a protesting Clara off to the hospital. "I'm fine, fine. It was that damn jailhouse food that got to me. A delayed reaction, that's all. A bit of food poisoning, gratis of the county."

Emily waved to her as the E.M.T.s loaded her into the vehicle. "You fainted from shock. You need medical attention. I'll meet you at the hospital. Try to be good, will you?"

"You two could have been killed," said Lewis. "I think the perp would have finished what he started if it hadn't been for Green driving up and ruining his plans. I've got my men checking the land between here and the road."

"If your fugitive knows this terrain, you won't find him. He'll hole up somewhere in that swamp or work his way around it to the west. That's a lot of territory to cover with a few men," said Green.

Except for catching Clara when she fainted, Detective Lewis hadn't taken his eyes off Green since he arrived. "I like your story, Donald, unless you were trying to put a scare into these two," Lewis said.

Emily wondered about that, too. Donald always seemed to be in on whatever criminal activity happened recently. The stolen boat, the discovery of blood on it, fishing Fat Eddie's body out of the river and scaring or saving Emily and Clara. What was his game? Or was there one? Clara said his rifle hadn't been fired. The man was an enigma.

Green shook his head as if Lewis' words were more disappointing than a bare hook in a bass tournament. As Green opened his mouth to make a comment, Lewis' cell phone rang. He held up his finger to signal Green to hold what he was going to say, listened for a minute, then walked off to take the call.

"Well, where the hell is he?" Lewis spoke loudly enough that both Green and Emily heard him. "He's supposed to be on for Detective Stiles who's taking maternity leave. I need him here. Now." Lewis flipped the phone shut.

"Damn Toby." He muttered the words under his breath, but had moved back toward Emily so she heard his comment.

"He was impersonating you the night of Davey's death," she said.

"He wasn't impersonating anyone." Lewis' voice had a snappish quality to it.

"Sorry," said Emily.

"Can I go now or are we going to do that down-to-the-station thing you do so well?" asked Green. "I've got to get up early tomorrow. The annual bass tournament begins at six."

"Get out of here," said Lewis. "But don't..."

"Don't leave the county. I know. And me with a brand new passport." Green started his truck and backed onto the road.

Emily watched as he rolled down his window before he shifted into drive.

"Oh, that reminds me. I won't be in for a couple of days what with the tournament and all." He waved to her and sped off.

"Oh, damn," said Emily.

"Problems?" asked Lewis.

"The same as you have. Lack of personnel. With Clara injured and Donald off to catch fish, I'm missing a bartender or a manager, take your pick. Regardless, it means I'm the only one working the bar for the next few days."

Emily's cell called out with its salsa ring.

"Hi. It's me. Naomi. I got back from the coast and you weren't here. Is everything okay?"

"Fine, honey." Emily paused and thought for a second. *Oh, why the hell not.* "Would you like a job?"

⸺⸺

Emily picked up a still annoyed and uncooperative Clara from the emergency room several hours later. "I don't need all these pain meds, and I can walk out of here. Get away from me with that wheelchair."

Hap walked through the trauma center doors with Sadie in tow. "Now you listen to me, little girl," he said. "You do what these folks say and save the sass for later."

Emily stifled a laugh. *Little girl, indeed. Why, she's five inches taller, outweighs him by twenty pounds and hasn't even begun the diatribe I know she's fostering inside.*

But to Emily's surprise, Clara grabbed his hand and looked down at her father with the same blue eyes as his.

"Daddy," she said. Tears rolled down her cheeks, their path interrupted by the stitches and butterfly dressings placed over her cuts.

"It's okay, baby. You've had a rough couple of weeks. Now Emily's going to take you to her place. You know I can't take care of you, and you need some help with your arm in a sling, so I'm sure Emily won't mind, will you?" He looked at Emily who moved her head up and down.

Oh, what the hell, she thought. *I might as well be running a boarding house.*

Once in the passenger's seat of the car, Clara wiped away her tears with her good hand and stared straight ahead.

"We'll stop at your place, and I'll run in and grab some clothes and a toothbrush and comb for you," said Emily. She took her eyes off the road for a moment and looked at her friend. Clara said nothing and continued to stare straight ahead.

"You want me to get anything else while I'm there? Cosmetics, books to read, bath beads, shampoo, your tongue?" Emily asked.

Still Clara said nothing. Emily slowed the car as they passed under a street light to get a better look at her friend.

"Clara?"

"Pull over a minute, would you?"

Emily steered the car to the curb, put it in park and scanned the dark for police cruisers who might find two women parked on the street at four in the morning odd.

"Okay," said Clara, "about that crying thing back there with Dad. It must have been the shot they gave me when they stitched me up. It's not what Dad said. I handle these things very well, unless they pump me full of drugs."

"It was a little Novocain, a local."

Clara looked at her friend, exasperated. "Could you let me have this one fantasy? It was embarrassing. I never cry."

"Oh, I know what you mean. They must have given you an overdose of the local or they mixed it up with another drug, one that makes you cry."

Clara checked Emily's expression to make certain she wasn't being sarcastic. Emily's look was guileless, but then, Emily was the master of innocence when she wanted.

"Do you want to register a complaint with the hospital, sue them or something?" asked Emily.

"Don't push it, girl."

The two of them continued to sit in the darkness. Emily rolled down her window and let in the night air. "I sometimes forget how wonderful it is to be here. When the night is dark with no moon like now, I feel as if I'm being wrapped in velvet, warm, soft velvet. There's nothing like this in the north."

"Hmmm," said Clara as if in agreement. "There is something else you can get me while we're at my house."

Emily started the engine and looked at her friend with curiosity. "Yes?"

"I might find a use for several of my guns."

"Not in my place," said Emily.

"I'm not going to use them in the house. Unless it's necessary. Besides with this bum arm, I'm going to have to teach you to shoot. Maybe Naomi too."

Oh good, thought Emily, now I'm rooming with Annie Oakley.

-❧-

"No, I'll take the pull-out," said Clara. "You and Naomi can stay put in your room, Darren in the guest room and me here." She pointed to the couch.

Naomi, Emily and Clara stood in the living room of Emily's park model and discussed the sleeping arrangements. The conversation had gone on for several minutes. Someone rapped on the front door.

"Hi. It's me. Vicki. I heard you pull in and then saw your lights on. What's up?" Her glance ran up and down Clara first, then turned to Emily. "The two of you look like you tangled with barbed wire, but you, Clara, you must have been bundled in it and thrown in the back of a truck."

"Naw. It wasn't as bad as that. Someone shot at us, that's all," Clara said.

Since Clara's comment necessitated their telling Vicki all about the incident at the club, Emily decided to make coffee. Vicki scuttled back home for some rolls she had bought at the store. Soon the four women were sitting around Emily's table and discussing the evening.

"What are you going to do?" asked Vicki. Her facial expression changed from horror to excitement and back again.

"Sleep," said Emily. She stretched her arms and yawned. "If we can figure out where."

"Someone can stay at my place," said Vicki. "My husband is usually out on the course by eight every morning. He'll never even notice if there's anyone else in the house."

"Thanks, Vicki, but there's plenty of room here. People will need to be flexible and move around a bit," Emily said.

After Vicki left, Clara remained immovable when it came to the couch. When she insisted that she wouldn't stay unless she got the couch, Emily relented, opened it for her, and she and Naomi headed for the back bedroom.

As tired as she was, Emily remained awake, waiting for Darren's return. By six in the morning, he hadn't shown up. Emily tiptoed out to the living room to check on Clara.

"I'm still awake, waiting for Darren, like you." Clara swept her hand through her tangled curls. "He's a resourceful young man, but he's also one for finding trouble, like Eddie."

"Like father, like son?" said Emily, then regretted saying it. "I didn't mean to imply he'd end up in prison like his dad."

"Never mind. I wonder what he's gotten himself into this time. I hate to admit it, but the kid's not very reliable. He's lost more jobs than I've applied for. I'm sorry to cause you all this worry." Clara rolled over, but Emily didn't believe she was sleeping. Emily dragged herself back to the king-sized bed and Naomi's soft snoring.

At eight in the morning, Emily awoke to the smell of coffee brewing.

Naomi slept curled in a tight ball beside her. *Who made the coffee?*

"I'm in the other bedroom," said Clara.

Emily peeked in on her. "How did you manage the coffee pot?" she asked.

Clara had Darren's backpack out on the bed and was searching through it with her good hand, pulling items out of the zippered pockets and dumping them onto the bed.

"Vicki came over and did the coffee. Also offered to make breakfast, but I said we'd manage with toast." Clara looked up at Emily. "Did I do wrong? Were you wanting pancakes, sausage and grits?"

Emily shook her head and sat down in the desk chair next to the bed.

"I know I'm being nosy, but I thought maybe I could get some sense of what Darren's up to. I haven't kept a close eye on his movements and don't know much about his friends."

"I don't know much about Naomi's life either," said Emily.

"You haven't been her mother all these years. You've got an excuse. As for me, I damn well gave up on him. Not a very parental thing to do. I was a lousy mother."

"Well, I don't mean to sound judgmental about your recently departed ex, but he certainly wasn't much of a father to Darren, was he?"

"Of course not. Why would he be?" asked Clara. She pulled a stack of papers from one of the pockets and began to go through them.

"Why wouldn't he be?" asked Emily. She was confused at her friend's attitude toward Darren's father.

"Oh, well, I mean, how could he be any kind of a role model for the kid when he was off in prison most of the time, and, when he came home, he planned most of the escapades that would land him right back in jail." Clara continued to rifle through the papers. "What's this?"

"What?"

Clara held up a sheet with a seal impressed onto it. "An official copy of his birth certificate. Now why would he want that? Did he talk to you about what he was doing? Or when he got this?" Clara asked.

She threw the paper onto the bed and then began to dump items out of the backpack onto the floor, scratching through the pile with her good hand like a one-armed squirrel frantic to dig up an acorn in deep snow.

Emily shook her head while she watched Clara search through the meager collection of Darren's possessions: a razor, shaving cream, a lighter, some store receipts and a half-pint of cheap gin.

"I know he left early for work some days. He usually took the bus, but I think several days he got a ride into town with one of his friends. Maybe they dropped him at the courthouse." Emily was puzzled about why Darren would need a copy of the birth certificate too, but not as concerned as Clara seemed to be.

"Do you know what friend?" she asked.

Emily shook her head no. "Maybe he was applying for a passport."

Clara looked up at Emily, seemed to take measure of her and for a moment Emily thought Clara had something she was going to share with Emily, something important. Then her expression became shadowed.

"It's better you not know. I hope the fool didn't let anybody else in on this." Clara replaced the document, tossed the backpack onto the bed and got up. "There's coffee, and I can sure use a cup."

CHAPTER 15

Detective Lewis sat at his desk, his eyes heavy with weariness from the long night he had put in searching roads that intersected with the Club Road, scouring the fields adjacent to the course, and directing his men to set up a road-block on the main highway. They had found nothing. He knew they wouldn't. Every four-wheel-drive vehicle in the county must have driven that area in the last few days, either hunting coyote or using the clubhouse road to access the isolated swamps to the west. His men rousted drivers and passengers from their trucks and sent high school couples and good old boys with hooch in paper bags home to their beds.

They examined plenty of rifles, but none that had been fired recently. Nobody they interviewed had spotted a truck traveling through the area at a high rate of speed. But then, how observant can a bunch of tipsy cowboys and teenage lovers be at that hour, Lewis asked himself.

He heard footsteps outside his office. They didn't slow in front of his office, but continued on. A door closed. *Toby*. Lewis jumped up and ran down the hall, throwing open the door at the end.

"Where the hell were you tonight?" he yelled at Toby Walker as he bent over and took a shot at his spit can on the floor next to the desk. Toby dug into his pocket for a handkerchief and wiped his mouth, then glanced up at Lewis, a look of surprise on his fat, sweaty face.

"I was working." He slipped the brown-stained handkerchief back into his pocket.

Lewis tried to hide his disgust at Toby's tobacco habit. He knew everyone in the station had complained to the police captain, Aaron Worley, about the chewing and spitting. Captain Worley and Toby went way back to grade school days so the only concession he would make to the near mutiny of his officers was to move Toby to the smallest office in the building and insist he keep the spit can there. No one ever went to Toby's office, not even Worley. Only rage at Toby's absence at the crime scene propelled Lewis into Toby's den tonight.

"Working where?" asked Lewis. "I needed you out at the course, helping me at the scene, or at least taking part in the search."

"I figured you would handle the scene so I searched the east range. When I got to the course most of the men had headed for the swamps. I knew you'd want me to take up the slack so I followed Bobby Aldrich, who headed toward the rodeo grounds." Toby tilted his chair backward and propped one polyester clad leg on his desk.

"Bobby never told me you were at the rodeo grounds with him," said Lewis.

"Well, I wasn't. I saw a car pull out of the grounds and head into town, so I followed it."

"And?"

"Nothing. Kids where they shouldn't be." Toby turned his head to one side and spat. It hit the outside of the can, and the dark juice ran down onto the floor.

"And you didn't think you should check with me about what needed to be done before you took off, and you didn't let me know what you found?"

"I'm a detective here too. I may be your partner until Detective Stiles pops that kid, but I have as much say in what happens on a case as you do."

"What you don't get, Toby, is that partner implies cooperation, sharing. But you probably don't understand that."

Toby slid his chair back onto its front legs with a bang. "Maybe we should take our disagreement to the captain when he comes in to work."

"Go right ahead. I'm beat. I'm going home for a few hours of sleep. You can tell Captain Worley how you're on the job." Lewis walked out, slamming the door behind him. He gulped a lungful of air once in the hallway, aware he had been taking shallow breaths while in Toby's office. The place stank. He smiled to himself, pleased that he had maneuvered Toby front and center on the case while he went home to rest. He wondered how long it would take Toby to figure out what he'd done.

He did need some shut-eye, no question about that. The hours he'd been putting in since Davey's murder had given him little time to eat, much less get some sleep. He blinked as the sunlight hit his face at the station door. Must be after eight in the morning, he thought. He checked his watch. Nine fifteen. His cell rang.

"Lewis here. Yep. Fine. Yep." He flipped the cell closed. Now he had two murders on his hands. The medical examiner found a bullet hole in the back of Fat Eddie's head. The wound wasn't obvious when they pulled him out of the river because of the damage done to the corpse by the water and the gators. The weapon was a rifle, a twenty-two, the same kind of weapon that had been used to take out the window last night at the golf course.

Lewis now felt confident the target was Clara, not Emily. He was also certain the two murders were connected. He didn't get the connection now, but something tickled his brain cells. Some link between Clara, her husband and the Davey family, something that went way back. He'd have to take a look at his old high-school yearbooks when he got home. Correction. He'd look at them after he got some sleep.

Two days later, Clara paced up and down Emily's living room, gesturing angrily with her good arm while she flopped the arm in the sling up and down like a duck's wing.

"Now I'm mad, furious really. Where is that boy? Hasn't been at work for the past two days and no word from him. And this afternoon is Eddie's funeral. He's always been irresponsible, but not this bad."

Clara was demonstrating her usual bravado, because Emily thought Clara was more worried, scared even, than she was mad. Emily was concerned about Darren's absence too. With the murder, the death of Fat Eddie and the shooting at the club, Emily felt as if the bad guys, whoever they were, were closing in on her and Clara.

Hap and Sadie, her hair freshly coiffed and sparkling blue in the sunlight streaming into the park model's windows, were seated on the couch. They had come early to have a bite of lunch before the ceremony. Hap sat quietly with a look of deep concern on his face as he watched his daughter pace. He wore his white linen suit and each time he shifted position on the couch, a scent of mothballs wafted across the room and out the windows. Naomi helped Emily make iced tea and tuna sandwiches.

"Something wrong, honey? You're awfully quiet today," Emily said.

Naomi kept her head down and continued to slice lemons for the tea. "No."

Emily didn't know her daughter well, but something in her tone of voice and her unwillingness to make eye contact with anyone today said she was upset. *She looks guilty, but about what?*

Clara, perhaps because she was the queen of denial when it came to her own feelings, possessed radar for cover-up when it came to others hiding theirs. Emily had seen her do it before, home in on what someone was trying to hide, like the day she figured out how angry Emily was at Fred's death and how much she pitied herself because of it.

Clara stopped mid-stride and focused on Naomi, narrowing her eyes as if to see through Naomi's lowered lids and into her head. "Naomi, you're hiding something. Tell me." Clara crossed the room in two steps and stood over Naomi. Her mouth was set in a tight line, her eyes dark with threat.

"Nothing. I'm sad, that's all," said Naomi.

Emily stepped between Clara and Naomi. "Leave her alone, Clara. She's got enough on her mind right now. She doesn't need to have you browbeating her for no reason except that you're upset and looking for a target for your anger."

Naomi threw the lemons down on the counter and slipped around Clara. "I've got to get dressed now. Excuse me."

She retreated down the hall and slammed the bedroom door closed. "She knows something about Darren," said Clara. She prepared to follow Naomi down the hall.

Hap rapped his cane on the floor. "Stop it, both of you. This isn't helping anybody. If Naomi has something to say that you should hear, she'll tell you in her own time. Now, I'm starving. I thought we came here to eat."

Emily gave a sideways glance at her friend, ducked her head and tore open a bag of chips.

"I'm sorry, Emily. I'm frantic. Darren's not the best kid, but he's better than this."

"I know. I'm worried about him too. Let's eat now. I'll see if Naomi wants a sandwich, then I'll talk to her after lunch."

Emily never got a chance to confront her daughter about what she was hiding—and she was certain she was hiding something—because of the phone call that interrupted their meal.

"It's Detective Lewis," Emily said. She held out the receiver. "He wants to talk with you, Clara."

Clara took the phone, listened for several minutes and finally said, "Okay. Thanks for letting me know." She turned away from the table, her shoulders slumping. Then she took a deep breath as if fortifying herself for a difficult task and turned back to everyone.

"The medical examiner reported a bullet wound as cause of death for Eddie. He didn't drown as we first thought. It was the same kind of weapon that was used to shoot out the clubhouse window the other night. And Lewis thinks there's a connection between the two murders. I think so too."

"You think Darren's involved," said Emily.

"He is involved. He called me from the bar on your cell the night Davey was murdered, so he was there. I haven't told Lewis it was Darren, but I think he suspects."

Hap looked up from his sandwich. "As your attorney I advise you to keep your mouth shut, my dear. There's no need to involve these other folks."

Emily grabbed the edge of the table and leaned forward, a pugnacious look on her face. "We're not 'other folks.' We're friends, almost family," she said.

Naomi hadn't said a word since she rejoined them at the table. She seemed mesmerized by her sandwich, picking at the crumbs of bread and not looking up from her plate.

"I don't know who killed Davey and my ex, but I'm trying to protect my family and my friends. The fewer people who know what I do, the better," said Clara.

"Maybe you should talk to Lewis, tell him about Darren's call to you. And you were upset about his birth certificate. Tell him about that too," Emily said.

Both Naomi and Hap looked at Emily in surprise. "He knows?" asked Hap.

Clara nodded. "I found it in his backpack."

"That's not good," said Hap.

Naomi threw her fork down on the plate. "You went through his things?" Her tone was one of indignation. "You palm him off on my mother while you're in jail and then you get so interested in his life that you snoop in his backpack? Mothers." Naomi pushed away from the table and sat with her arms crossed over her chest, her lips drawn tight in a grimace of disgust.

Emily held her head in her hands. Everyone seemed to know more about what was going on than she did. Even her daughter appeared to hold a piece of the puzzle while Emily's hands were empty.

"Let's leave this until after the funeral," said Clara.

Hap looked relieved, while Naomi remained silent and brooding.

Emily wondered if Naomi's allusion to mothers included her.

⁂

Few people were gathered in the Partridge Funeral Parlor when Emily and Clara walked in followed by Naomi, Hap and Sadie. Clara scanned the mourners seated in rows in front of the casket and nodded to a few, as did Hap, who then went over to talk with another older man seated at the very back of the room.

"That's Eddie's uncle, Archibald Clapp. He's all the family Eddie had. Except for Darren and me. I'll be back in a minute," said Clara. She followed Hap over to the man and embraced him.

He sure didn't look anything like the Eddie Emily had seen in the photo in Clara's bedroom. This man reminded her of the detective she first met in the police station, Toby-the-Spitter. Both men were short, square of build and had thinning hair. But maybe Eddie didn't look anything like his uncle. She found a seat in the front and pulled Naomi and Sadie into chairs beside her.

"I'm surprised," said Naomi. "The coffin's open. I thought the body was, well, you know, not in great shape."

Sadie leaned over and, in a stage whisper, said, "Oh, you'd be surprised what they can do nowadays. My cousin's next-door neighbor was found in her house days after she died, and they made her look like a fairy queen. Cousin Betty said she looked better lying in that coffin than when she dressed up for church on Sunday. C'mon. Let's have a peek. I mean, we ought to pay our respects."

Sadie grabbed Emily's arm and pulled her out of her chair. Emily didn't want to view the body, but Sadie wouldn't let go of her, and she found herself in front of the casket. She glanced at Eddie's face. Not bad, if you didn't focus on his features too long. No evidence of what several days in the water did to him. *But, oh, my God. This is awful.* She turned away from the casket and rushed to the back of the room. "I've got to talk to you," she said to Clara. "The body in the coffin. It's not Eddie's."

Clara whirled around and practically ran down the aisle and peered into the casket. Emily followed her. "Well?"

"How would you know what my ex looked like? You've never met him, have you?" asked Clara.

By now Naomi, Hap and Sadie had joined Clara and Emily in front of the coffin. They were drawing curious stares from others in the room.

Uncle Archibald approached. "What seems to be the trouble?"

"No, I've never met him, but I saw his picture in your bedroom when I picked up clothes the day you were arraigned."

"What picture?" asked Clara. She had grabbed Emily's arm and was holding on so tight that Emily thought it would go numb.

"I dropped the one of you and Darren on the floor and another photo behind it fell out. It was a picture of Darren's father, Eddie. I could tell because he and Darren have the same hair and gray eyes."

Clara's eyes shifted away from Emily's face and to Hap's. He shook his head and turned away.

"That's not the man in the picture." Emily gestured toward the body lying among the satin folds of the casket. "That's not Darren's father." Once the words were out of her mouth, she realized she'd made a mistake.

"Eddie's not Darren's father?" asked Archibald. "Is that what you're saying? What's going on here?"

"I'd kind of like to know that too," said Detective Lewis. He had entered the room without attracting attention and now joined the group at Eddie's coffin.

Clara turned on him, her eyes snapping with irritation. "What business is this of yours, Detective? This is a funeral. People are mourning the dead here. Shouldn't you be ticketing speeders or better yet, solving two murders?"

Emily recognized her response as penultimate Clara—attack when you're feeling cornered. Lewis merely smiled and rolled his eyes revealing he too knew Clara's penchant for offense when she felt trapped.

She put out her hand to her friend. "Clara, we need to talk, but not now. After the service."

Emily then turned to Lewis and confronted him, the top of her head barely at his chin level. But her voice was firm. "She's right. We're mourning the death of a husband and father. Anything else can wait until later. There's a seat in the back." Emily gestured toward the row where Uncle Archibald had been seated. Now another man sat there also. Donald Green. "Next to Donald, Detective."

She led Clara back to the first row. They took their seats as the minister entered. Archibald still stood in the center of the aisle, confusion and anger making a play for expression on his face. He started forward toward Clara, but then turned and walked back to his seat.

"You were spying on me," said Clara. Her voice was low enough that only Emily could hear her.

"I accidentally knocked the picture over and the frame loosened, that's all. I was not spying on you. I had no reason to spy on you. Maybe now I do."

The funeral director closed the coffin lid, obscuring the features of Clara's ex, and the mourners quieted as the minister began his remarks. "We are gathered here to celebrate the life of our friend, husband," he nodded in Clara's direction, "and father." He looked around the room, as did everyone else, but Darren was absent.

From the back of the room, Emily heard Archibald clear his throat. Clara looked uncomfortable and wiggled in her seat as if she was impatient to get the service over. The clergyman droned on for several more minutes, but since Eddie hadn't had much of a life beyond that in prison, he found little to say about how it could be "celebrated" aside from his remarks about Eddie's dedication to his son, Darren.

Clara muttered something about, "Oh, right. Visitation days were a load of fun for the little guy."

He quickly moved on to mentioning Clara as the ex-wife, "now a good friend, who feels his loss deeply."

At this point, Clara leaned forward and looked accusingly at her father. "Did you tell him to say that, Dad?"

He leaned back at her. "I had to give him something to say or this would have ended in five minutes."

"That would have been better than lying."

Emily pulled Clara back into her seat and told her to "hush up." She turned her head to look at Uncle Archibald, Lewis and Green and found them with their heads together, deep in conversation. *That can't be good.*

"Would anyone like to come forward and say a few words about Edward?" asked the minister.

In the silence following the minister's invitation, people shifted restlessly in their seats. When no one stepped forward, the gathering gave a collective sigh of relief, relief that this ordeal was over and relief that no one was willing to say anything, bad or good, about the man. "Well, then, let us bow our heads in prayer for..." the minister began.

"I have something to say." The voice came from the back of the room.

All heads turned in that direction. "Darren," said Hap.

"Thank God," said Emily.

"Oh, damn that boy is dumb," said Clara.

CHAPTER 16

Ignatius Palatier wiped his full lips with the linen napkin and gazed approvingly over the marina next to the restaurant in which he and his brother-in-law, Thomas Brookfield, were having lunch. Motorboats were tied up at the docks, and farther out, he could see sailboats bobbing at their moorings. He loved being on the coast, soaking up the cosmopolitan atmosphere of fine restaurants with their pandering waiters and costly menu offerings. He chose to ignore the curious glances of those who thought his boots and cowboy hat too gauche for West Palm.

Towering clouds rolled by and cast their shadows on the deck. The temporary shade offered a welcome reprieve for diners braving the gathering heat of the afternoon.

"This is a far piece from cows and gators," said Thomas. His gaze followed that of Ignatius. He took another sip of his martini and sat back in his chair with a sigh of pleasure. "I can't imagine why you want to stay there when you could move down to West Palm with me."

Ignatius knew his brother-in-law wasn't serious. Why would Thomas want to bring a cowboy from the rangeland of central Florida into his up-scale east coast practice? And Ignatius had no il-lusions about himself. He was a boot-wearing, string-tie kind of guy. If he moved into a fancy law firm like Thomas' he'd have to account for his time as well as change his mode of dress. Ignatius liked his freedom, and the last thing he wanted was to have Thomas riding herd on how he prac-ticed law. No, making contact over an occasional lunch was fine with him as long as Thomas picked up the tab.

"Are you still representing that little lady from up north, the one whose partner left her with nothing?" asked Thomas. He chewed the last bite of his lemon sole with a look of ecstasy on his face. Ignatius had finished his burger several minutes before and was working on his third Crown Royal on the rocks.

Ignatius searched his mind. What had he said about Emily Rhodes to his brother-in-law over one of their three-martini lunches? Was it some-thing he should have kept to himself? The two of them had no compunctions about crossing ethi-cal lines, so he wasn't worried Thomas could call him on breach of conduct for talking about Ms. Rhodes. But Thomas might use something Igna-tius let slip about her to manipulate him in some manner. He knew better than to answer too quickly without getting more information. Yes, Thomas was up to something. Ignatius crunched his ice and signaled the waiter for another drink.

"You know the ex-wife came to me, and I thought if you were still representing the partner, we could work out some kind of a deal that benefited both of us." Brookfield cleared his throat and took another sip of his martini. "I mean, something of benefit to both our clients."

Ignatius considered his words. Thomas sometimes threw bits and pieces his way. If some pistol-toting, spur-wearing cattle rancher wandered over to the coast for representation, Thomas might toss him back onto the range and give him to Ignatius to represent. Thomas certainly didn't want that kind of client sitting in his waiting room scaring away all the diamond-ringed, gold-adorned wealthy female clientele who made up the bulk of his practice.

Ignatius decided to be circumspect. "Maybe. If I am, we can't talk about it, and, if I'm not, then I've got nothing you want, brother."

"Between us chickens, I could use any information you have about her. I think she's gonna make a pitch to the court based upon her many years of devotion to him, and I don't want any pretty blonde preschool teacher messing up the case for my client."

"How could she? Your client has a will in her favor." Thomas nodded and signaled the server for the check.

Ignatius was puzzled about Thomas' interest in the case. "And aren't we talking about a piddling estate here? So what if this Rhodes woman gets some of it? It won't hurt your client. I hear she's loaded."

"Oh, she is loaded. That's the problem. It might look bad for her in one of those friendly working folks' courts you've got over there. Big, bad, rich lady divorces the guy, then years later takes all of his money leaving little suffering partner nothing. You know your rural judges and the ranchers, wealthy as they might be, wouldn't take well to screwing the underdog."

The waiter stood over the table with the check, lingering for a signal to place it down in front of one of them. Thomas waited for a reply from Ignatius, who ignored the waiter, as did Thomas.

"Well, if Ms. Rhodes were my client, that's the way I'd play it."

"She's not then."

Ignatius would never tell the truth, that Emily Rhodes had fired him. So he pressed Thomas. "Why should you care how this case goes, money-wise?"

The waiter still stood at the table, eyes staring out the window, awaiting his cue.

"If I win this one, I win all the business for the ex-Mrs. Costa. Get it, Iggie?"

Ignatius hated being called Iggie, and Thomas knew it. "Oh, I get it, Tommie. I just wanted you to say it."

Thomas nodded to the waiter, who placed the aging check in front of him.

"You're making me say it like you're wearing a wire. You're not working for some state legal ethics commission, are you?" Thomas slapped a credit card on the tray.

Ignatius snorted the question away. "How can I help you, Tommie? I wouldn't want your income to dip below seven figures." Ignatius swabbed at his forehead with the linen napkin. The problem with these places on the coast was that they thought dining al fresco was chic even when the weather was in the nineties. He longed for a tall one in the sixty-five-degree air of the Burnt Biscuit.

※

Detective Toby sat at the bar of the Burnt Biscuit waiting for his contact. It was three in the afternoon, late for lunch, and, in fact, the Biscuit had stopped serving an hour before. Toby drank vodka and tonic with a twist, confident the smell of booze could be hidden by a mouthful of Tic Tacs when he returned to work. He loved the Biscuit, especially liked the aromas of cigarettes mingling with food odors from the kitchen and the ever-present fragrance of beer and booze that leached off the carpets. The place was dark and cool, unlike the office he occupied with its ineffective air conditioner. He loved taking his coffee breaks here.

There was only one thing wrong with the Biscuit. Although they allowed cigarette smoking after eleven at night when they stopped food service, the bar would not countenance chewing and spitting. At any hour. Toby knew he was a man born too late. If he'd been in rural Florida half a century before, he could have run this town and had his own private brass spittoon in every bar in the county. Toby smiled at this thought.

"Something you want to share with me?" asked the lawyer.

He took a seat on the stool next to Toby's and looked around the bar. No one was left in the place except for a couple who sat at a table in the corner. Damn tourists, thought Palatier, noting the man's Bermuda shorts and sandals with black socks. The woman wore a sleeveless, backless dress, and it was clear she'd had too much sun by the reddened skin on her arms. They were finishing up a real Florida lunch of blackened gator and sweet potato fries. The waitress brought their check, then hovered over the table signaling them she wanted to be paid so she could get the hell out of here.

"Nothin' special," Palatier heard the man say as he punched the toothpick dispenser and stuck the wooden picker in the side of his mouth. "Tastes like chicken. Not worth the money." A whoosh of warm air blew through the bar as they opened the door and left.

Toby raised his hand to get the attention of the bartender who was caught up in a late-afternoon television game show.

"Watcha having?" asked the bartender.

Ignatius had worked up a ferocious thirst driving up from West Palm. They must have put too much salt on my burger, he thought. He almost ordered another Crown Royal, but he remembered he had several late appointments, so he reconsidered.

"A sweet tea," he said.

The bartender turned away to get the drink and rolled his eyes knowing that he wasn't going to make any money off this guy.

"You paying?" asked Palatier.

Toby nodded. A buck for a sweet tea. That shouldn't break Toby's bank.

"You rousted me out of my office and got me over here. I hope this is worth my time. I'm working on a big case you know," Toby said.

Big case, my ass, thought Ignatius. He knew that even though Toby and the captain were boyhood friends, the captain rarely let Toby work anything more important than caballeros off the dairy farms doing weekend shoplifting from the local Mexican flea market.

"That shooting out at the country club, the other night? That's my case. I wouldn't be surprised if the captain turned both the murders over to me also. Lewis isn't making any headway on those."

"Good. Glad you're doing so well. And what I'd like from you is somewhat related. I need to have someone do some snooping for me." Ignatius wanted to conduct his business and be on his way.

"As long as it's not a conflict of interest. Or illegal," Toby said.

Palatier reached in his pocket and pulled out his wallet from which he extracted a twenty-dollar bill. He shoved it over to Toby, saying, "Let me buy the drinks. You can keep the change."

Toby's sausage-like fingers grabbed the money, and it disappeared below the bar. "I'll take care of your drink. What can I do for you? Not that a small amount like that will buy you much other than another tea."

"I need any smut on the Rhodes woman you can dig up for me."

"Smut? What kind of smut?"

"Shady associates, but especially any lover interests she might have. Men she's seeing. Like that."

"Men? The only man she's been seeing is Detective Lewis. Oh yeah, she hired Donald Green at the club and went fishing with him. They caught a dead body."

Ignatius' eyes narrowed when he heard about Lewis. Every time the man testified against one of his clients, Ignatius lost the case. Wouldn't that be fine, now, if Lewis could be made to look derelict in his duties by hobnobbing with a murder suspect? Even if there was nothing going on, Ignatius could help Thomas make it look bad for Emily and Lewis. That would be pay back for that

Yankee gal firing him and for Lewis' constant in-
terference in his cases. And Thomas would be in
his debt.

"Lewis? She's been seeing Lewis?" he asked.

"Well, maybe not seeing him per se, but...,"
Toby paused. "Yeah, I guess you could say he's
overstepped his official role."

"This could work out fine for you, Toby. Help
me out and you get money to do a little spy work
and perhaps enough dirt on Lewis to get him
bumped back to patrol. I know you dislike the
guy as much as I do."

"Yeah, he got all uppity on me the other night.
Chewed me out. He said I wasn't doing my job,
and then he goes and dumps all the paperwork in
my lap."

"Yeah, yeah." The last thing Palatier needed
was to sit here and listen to Toby complain about
imagined slights. He didn't mind hiring the man
for any number of jobs where the work was ever
so slightly illegal, but he'd be damned if he'd listen to him moan about his life. "So you can add
this piece of action to your other off-payroll work.
Make yourself some money. Maybe retire early."

"Anything I can get you gentlemen?"

Toby and Ignatius jumped when they heard
the voice coming from behind them. Randolph,
owner of the Biscuit, stood there with a smile on
his face.

"Eavesdropping on your patrons' conversation?" asked Toby. His voice sounded both defensive and frightened.

"Certainly not," said Randolph. His smile never wavered. "I wanted to make certain you were being well taken care of by Justin here." At the sound of his name the bartender turned his attention from the television and hustled over to the three men.

"Justin's been very attentive," said Palatier. He wanted both men to go away so that he could finalize arrangements with Toby. He was relieved to see Toby looking eager to get to the bottom line also. The mention of money usually speeded negotiations up with him. Toby liked to see the green stuff sooner rather than later.

"Then we'll leave you to your conversation," said Randolph. He hesitated a moment, still standing behind the two men.

"And, ah, two more of the same," said Palatier. It was better not to offend Randolph in case he ever got curious about meetings between Toby and Palatier and decided to chat too freely with local authorities about the relationship.

Justin got the drinks, slapped them onto the bar's lacquered surface, and waited for his money. Palatier pulled a ten out of his wallet. The bartender returned three dollars and fifty cents in change and returned to his television. Randolph dipped his head goodbye and left, the smile broadening.

"That guy's creepy," said Toby. "I'll bet you anything he's queer."

If police training included sensitivity seminars, Palatier figured Toby must have called in sick that week. "Nevertheless," he said, "we have business to finish up here. Say a thousand dollars, five hundred now, the rest when you get me something substantial on the lady. Or the man."

Toby grinned his acceptance, and Palatier slipped five one-hundred-dollar bills into Toby's hand.

Both men chugged the remainder of their drinks. As they got down from their stools to leave, Palatier grabbed the three ones in change on the bar and left the fifty cents.

What a cheapskate, thought Toby.

◈

Once on the road, Toby regretted not having used the men's room at the Biscuit. Toby had experienced this problem many times before so he did what he was used to doing. He pulled off the road and relieved himself next to his vehicle.

Mrs. Wattles and Mrs. Frey, residents of Emily's condo park saw Toby engaging in his bathroom break at the side of the road and noted the lettering of the city police on the car. They were offended at his ungentlemanly act and felt it their civic duty to report his lewd behavior to his superior.

Mrs. Frey punched the number of the station into her cell phone, and she got lucky. Any other time of the day and the officer on the switchboard would have answered and jotted down the particulars. Then she would have placed the complaint in Captain Worley's in- box where the note would be lost among the other notes he'd avoided reading for the past month.

This afternoon the officer was taking her coffee break. The call rang into Worley's office. He listened to the offended Mrs. Frey, heard the angry Mrs. Wattles' voice in the background and assured them he would personally take action.

As Worley put down the receiver, Toby pulled up outside the captain's office window. Worley watched him get out of the four-wheel- drive vehicle and walk with a stagger across the parking lot. He tripped on the bottom step leading into the station. Worley's eyes narrowed. *It's bad enough the man is utterly incompetent and a slob to boot. But now he's coming to work drunk. This is too much. Too much.*

By the time Toby tried to pull himself together and started down the hall, the captain was waiting for him. Toby barely had time to shove three more Tic Tacs into his mouth before the captain beckoned toward his office. All the officers in the main station room saw Captain Worley's face; his huge mustache quivered, his teeth ground together and his jaw worked back and forth and up and down.

The men and women under his command would have preferred standing on the levee in a

Category Four hurricane rather than face the captain when he got himself into this state. He'd make certain watering roadside palmetto wasn't something Toby would soon repeat.

⁕

At the funeral home, Darren walked to the front of the room and swallowed the lump in his throat. He never thought he'd be addressing a group of people about his family, but it was something he had to do.

Clara held her breath, afraid he would reveal family secrets she'd kept for all of Darren's life. She crossed her fingers and hoped he'd be discrete.

Darren worried his quaking legs wouldn't hold him upright, so he gripped the podium in front of him for support. He began speaking about the man he'd always known as his father, of the times, however few, they'd had together.

"I remember once he took me to the carnival and we rode the Ferris wheel. I was little, probably not more than five. I got sick and threw up all over myself and my dad's lap. He didn't get mad, just took me to the restroom and cleaned me up. He was an even-tempered guy when he was around, and I liked watching television with him. He never hit me. I remember he smiled a lot. We were going to go hunting when he got the time." Darren paused. "He did the best he could." Darren shrugged. "I guess that's all."

Clara lifted her chin. No fancy words, no dishonest praise, but bless the kid. He stood up there and paid tribute to Eddie in a way the man would have respected. It struck her that she didn't know her son well, and she wondered what he would have said about her if she had been the one lying in the coffin.

Darren walked from behind the podium and sat down in the seat in front of Clara. She leaned forward and clasped his shoulder. He hesitated only a moment, then reached back and took her hand in his.

After a final prayer, the minister announced refreshments at the Blue Heron Retirement Center's dining room. There would be no internment. Eddie was to be cremated.

On the steps outside, Clara held Darren's arm while people stopped to express their condolences. Darren whispered in his mother's ear loud enough that Emily heard him, "We need to talk about my real father. I'll skip the cookies and see you later at home." By his tone of voice, Emily could tell he was sitting on a tinderbox of anger at his mother.

"I don't mean to be snoopy, but, as one of your closest friends and someone who cares for you and Darren, and the person who cared for both of you in my home, I…"

"Okay. You've got the right to know, but can this wait until we have some privacy? There's a long story behind Darren's birth."

Someone took Clara's arm and drew her away to a group of people surrounding the minister. Emily stood alone until Hap walked up to her.

"I guess you'll finally get the story on Clara's youthful indiscretion. Like mother, like son, although Clara doesn't like to admit her son is a chip off the old block."

"And who is the 'old block' if not Eddie?" asked Emily.

"That's Clara's story to tell, not mine." Hap sucked on his teeth and chuckled.

CHAPTER 17

Darren, Naomi, Clara, Emily and Hap sat in Clara's living room following the get-together at the Retirement Center. The sun was falling toward the horizon, dusty mists riding its slanted rays as it shone through the window. The room felt hot and stuffy to Clara. She had opened the front door when they entered and now she walked toward the kitchen door and opened that also. The cross-ventilation produced a gentle breeze, making the sunny particles move about like tiny dancers.

Darren stood at the window, his back turned toward the others in the room. Everyone's eyes were on him, and he cleared his throat several times before he found his voice. It shook when he spoke. "Once I got my birth certificate and found out who my father was, I needed some time alone. So I hid out at that old shack at the edge of Rendezvous Swamp."

"There are huge gators and all kinds of snakes out there. You might have been attacked or bitten. And besides, what the hell did you need with your birth certificate?" asked Clara.

"The truth about myself, something you've kept from me all these years. The floor is yours, Mom. Let's hear what you have to say." Darren's voice continued to quaver, and this time Clara heard anger in it, not nervousness.

She stopped picking at the couch's nubby upholstery and looked up at her son. Resistance to telling a secret kept for so long made her throat close up for a moment. Then relief swept over her. She only hoped her son could hear beyond her words.

"Let me get my story out before you jump on me, Darren. Don't go off half-cocked because you're mad I didn't tell you about this sooner. Okay?"

"Have at it, Mom. I can't wait till you explain this one." Darren dropped into a kitchen chair and glared at his mother.

Clara took a deep breath and began. "My senior year of high school I had the opportunity to study abroad for a half-year. I jumped at the chance. I wanted to be out of this cow town and away from my parents." She looked at Hap. "Well, away from Mom who was strict with hours and dating.

"One of the teachers on the trip, Neville Landry, and I got to be friends and, then before long, it was more than a friendship. We slept together on and off through the rest of my senior year." She paused, and when she continued her tale, she quickened the pace. "After I got out of law school and was in practice on the coast, we ran into each other again and took up where we'd left off. But this time, I got pregnant. By now, Neville had married and had children of his own. There was no chance we could marry." She finished the story with a dismissive flip of her hand.

Darren seemed about to interrupt, but Clara shot him a look, and he backed down. His fists clenched and unclenched and a red flush spread from his neck to his jaw.

She looked at her son with love in her eyes and her voice took on a pleading note. "I know what you're thinking, sweetie. You think it was some old letch teacher taking advantage of one of his students, but it wasn't that way at all. I might have been the one who seduced him."

"That wasn't what I was going to say."

Clara held up her hand to silence her son. "Let me finish this, and then you'll understand. Neville was a nice man. I took advantage of his attraction to me. I was pretty wild in the days after law school. I liked to bend the rules, a lot. I knew exactly what I was doing.

"Eddie and I were good friends in high school so when I got back here, he helped me out of my predicament. He married me and tried to be a father to you, Darren. But as you said at the funeral, there were few times you were together. While I balanced motherhood and my law career, he settled into a life of petty thievery. We were too busy doing our own things to be good parents.

I'm sorry you had to find out the way you did. What I don't understand is why you went to the courthouse for a copy of your birth certificate. Or did someone goad you into doing it?"

Clara watched as her son's once angry face grew calm. She sensed he had made some kind of decision.

"I guess my story won't be as interesting as yours, but some of the guys at the factory talked about spending spring break in Mexico. I needed my birth certificate to get a passport. That's all. You do believe me, don't you?"

"No one suggested you get the birth certificate?"

"No. It was my idea. Why?"

"Nothing. I wondered if any of your friends were curious about your dad. You didn't tell anyone did you?" Clara's voice was tinged with suspicion.

"No one knows about the birth certificate except for all of us in this room. Why so suspicious?"

"Nothing." Clara relaxed back into the couch, freeing her injured arm from the sling. "I think I can get rid of this thing in another few days." Clara fiddled with her sling, then looked up, her eyes moving from one person to the other in the room, daring them to continue with the topic she had decided was ended.

No one spoke for a moment until Hap arose from his chair. "Well, then, I think we need to mosey along, dear Emily. If you would be so good as to give me a lift to my door."

Of all the people in the room, Emily thought she understood Clara's dilemma best. Unmarried and pregnant. What to do? Emily had considered abortion, yet Clara made no mention of that possibility. Who was this Landry guy? He seemed to have faded from Clara's life as if he never existed. And why hadn't Darren expressed an interest in his father's whereabouts? Perhaps Neville Landry was the one love of Clara's life, the one man she couldn't talk about. Somehow Emily doubted that.

But Emily had other matters on her mind. "There's something else we need to talk about before we leave. I think we all know that Darren used my cell phone to call Clara from the bar the night of Davey's murder. And more recently Darren had marks on his face that he said he got at work. I know better. From years of dealing with preschoolers, I think I know the signs of a scuffle between two people as well as anyone."

Her gaze traveled around the room and settled on Darren. "You were at the bar that night. You saw something you shouldn't, and now someone is threatening you physically to keep quiet."

Darren looked back at her with defiance. She wasn't going to get anything out of him. Clara and Hap gave her similar looks. The family was hanging together. Naomi dropped her eyes and stared at the pattern on her skirt. Emily wasn't about to give up.

"Okay, let's try this. You haven't told the police about Darren's using the phone. They don't know he was there. And, Clara, you and Hap have been eager to keep Darren out of sight if you can. Darren, did you see who killed Davey?"

"No," said Darren.

"But you're scared the killer doesn't know that. Right?" asked Emily. All four heads nodded yes.

"Someone threatened him over the phone the other night," said Naomi. Darren shook his head no at her.

"Then that someone shot at us. Actually, they shot at Clara at the clubhouse," said Emily. "Am I right?"

Heads wagged up and down.

"You know what I think?" asked Emily.

Four sets of eyes filled with curiosity looked at her. "I think someone had better go to the police."

"But we have no information," said Clara. "Besides, they'll be as likely to arrest Darren as protect him."

"Do you have any idea who beat you up and threatened you?" asked Emily.

Darren shook his head, but she wasn't convinced he was being truthful. She felt everyone in the room knew more than she did. Did any of the others think Clara was lying about Darren's father? She did. Did Darren? When they talked about the birth certificate, what they didn't say to one another seemed more significant than what they did say. But only the two of them seemed to comprehend that unspoken language.

"I can understand after the incident at the clubhouse the other night you'd want some protection," said Clara.

Emily thought of the tall, muscular, competent Detective Lewis and nodded affirmatively.

"Then we're off to the shooting range tomorrow for some practice," said Clara.

"I don't have a gun," said Emily. If she thought the lack of a weapon would end her shooting lesson, she was mistaken.

"I've got plenty of guns. So does Darren. And Dad has a few too," said Clara.

The image of Lewis faded, replaced by one in which she held a large gun, which went off accidentally hitting her big toe. That was not what she had in mind at all.

❖

Emily drove Clara's pickup west down the highway, past the turnoff to the river where it emptied into the lake. Today she sailed past the trucks and trailers parked in the lot next to the boat ramp and continued toward the road leading to the casino.

"Take a right here," said Clara. Emily glanced at her passenger. Clara had her arm out of the sling and was massaging her hand.

"You sure you can handle a gun with that arm?" asked Darren. He and Naomi sat in the back seat of Clara's crew cab pickup. Clara had insisted all of them go to the range: Emily to learn how to handle a weapon; Darren, who had been shooting since he was around five, to update his skills; and Naomi, because no one wanted her home alone.

Clara turned around in her seat to talk to Naomi. "Did your husband teach you to shoot?"

"Yes. And I hate guns." Naomi sat with her arms crossed over her chest, her lower lip trembling with defiance and fear.

"But you do know how to shoot, right?"

Instead of answering, Naomi looked out the window. "Why did I think it would be safer for me in cowboy land? It's like the wild west here."

"Yes, it is," said Clara. "But here you have some protection."

"Guns?" Naomi gave a snort.

"No. People who care about you and can make good on the promise to keep you safe," said Clara.

Emily privately still thought telling the authorities about Darren's presence at the bar the night of the murder made more sense than forming this vigilante group for protection. Sure, they might arrest him, but he'd be safe in custody.

Clara must have read her mind. "And where would that leave us?" she asked. "We're also in danger because whoever's after him doesn't know how much he's told us about that night. And

Naomi's husband will figure out where she is soon enough."

Emily cranked the wheel left to avoid hitting a turtle sitting in the middle of the road, then as quickly pulled it the opposite direction as the left front wheel caught in the soft sand on the shoulder.

"Hap thought I should tell Lewis about Naomi's situation," Emily said.

"Oh, like he'd take her under his wing," said Clara. "Ha."

Emily ignored Clara's interruption. "And as for Darren, he hasn't told me anything. The rest of you seem to know more than I do."

"Let's keep it that way. It's safer for you," Clara said.

Safer, maybe, but disconcerting to have so many questions unanswered. That picture hidden in the back of that frame in Clara's bedroom still nagged at Emily's conscience. Something about the man felt so familiar. His eyes? Or his hair? Or the way he looked into the camera at Clara? She'd never laid eyes on Neville Landry, but she felt she had seen this man many times.

She turned her attention back to driving as a pot hole jarred the front of the truck and the wheel threatened to twist out of her hands. She wouldn't call this a road. It was more of a washout, maybe, but not a road. The truck thudded on down the track which soon led into a grove of palm and cypress trees. They passed through a fenced-in area and by a weathered sign that read "Bi Water Ever porting Clu." Filling in the missing letters, Emily thought it meant "Big Water Everglades Sporting Club." She asked Clara if that was correct.

Clara nodded and said, "With the arrival of fancier indoor ranges on the coast, our membership's dropped, and we don't have the money we used to."

Emily pulled up alongside several other trucks and parked. Shooting stations, bare patches of dirt with poles alongside, lined one side of the lot, but nobody stood at them. It was so quiet that Emily heard mocking birds calling in the nearby bushes. Darren grabbed the guns, and the three women followed him over to a shed open on three sides. Clara introduced the man sitting in the shed to Naomi and Emily.

"Friends of mine, tender-footed Yankees, who need some lessons, just to scare off a few skunks and gators. Earl, this is Emily and Naomi. Earl Pucket, who takes care of the range here."

Mr. Pucket reminded Emily of an aging walrus with his crop of white hair and a mustache that covered an area of his face where his mouth must have been. He was large and his skin was very pink. Emily might have taken him for an albino were it not for his inky black eyes. He wore a short-sleeved shirt with a pattern of faded coral and yellow hibiscus flowers on it and patched denim shorts. Emily's eyes traveled down his legs expecting to find sandal-clad feet, but instead he sported a pair of highly polished alligator cowboy boots.

He watched Emily take in his footwear. Were it not for the size of his mustache, Emily thought she might have caught the makings of a smile on his hidden lips.

"Shot 'im right over there," said Pucket. He pointed downrange of the shooting stations. "A big one. Got a vest out of 'im too. I wear that to church on Sundays."

Before she spent winters in rural Florida, Emily might have thought his choice of Sunday apparel odd. Now she merely nodded her head in acceptance.

Pucket took Clara's money, stuffed it into a cigar box, and handed over ear protectors and shooting goggles. "It's slow today."

"I noticed a couple of other trucks," Clara said.

"Some fellows dropped them off here to hook up with a buddy to go to the casino. I'm keeping an eye on them."

"They didn't want to leave them at home?" she asked.

"Didn't want their wives to know they weren't going to work."

"Ah," said Clara.

"You want to give these ladies the lowdown on how we do things or should I?" asked Pucket.

"I think it would mean more coming from you, Earl."

He walked out of the shed and beckoned them to follow him down the line of shooting stations. Emily noticed at each station an electric drive trolley and a wooden post with some kind of a button on it. Mounds of dirt were piled down-range and a paper target hung off the trolley. It didn't make much sense to her, but Earl seemed ready, although not too eager, to explain how the system worked. He looked at Emily as if he wanted to wish or pray her away. She wanted to fulfill his wishes, go home, make herself a strong drink and spend the rest of the day watching mindless television. Clara pushed her along.

Earl bypassed the first station. "Trolley's broken," he explained and walked to the next.

"Now I'm only gonna tell you once, so listen up. Send your target out to the desired distance." He depressed the button and the target swung along the chain toward the mounded dirt. "Use one weapon at a time. I'll throw you out of here if I see you change weapons back and forth."

He leered at Emily as if she seemed likely to violate this rule. "Only load when you're ready to fire. The barrel of your gun must be pointed downrange at the targets at all times whether loaded or not. I don't want my shed accidentally shot up like it was last year by Billy Myers, that dumb kid. And you must wear ear protection and shooting goggles. And don't be forgetting to put them on and try to do it after you load." He yelled his last admonition at them making Emily and

Naomi jump. Darren and Clara smiled as if they were expecting it.

Pucket gave Emily and Naomi a final look, shook his head as if he considered the situation hopeless and trudged back to his shed, kicking up small clouds of dirt with his beloved boots.

"Why don't you go first, Darren?" said Clara. "You can demonstrate how it's done."

Darren nodded, punched the trolley button sending the target out fifty feet, then donned the shooting glasses and hung the protective ear covers around his neck. From the weapons they'd brought, he extracted what Emily deemed to be the largest pistol she'd ever seen.

"This is a forty-five Remington six shooter, single action. I won junior champion with one just about like this, a twenty-two, huh, Mom?"

Clara stood with her hands on her hips, head cocked to one side. "That was years ago. Let's see what you can do with it now."

He flipped out the cylinder and loaded six bullets into it, and with a flick of his wrist, returned it to the ready position. Emily noted he did all this with the barrel pointed at his target.

"Everybody behind me and put on your glasses and ear protection. This is going to get loud." He took his stance facing the target, both hands on the gun. "Now, with this gun, you need to cock it," he pulled back the pin, "before each shot."

He fired off six shots in quick succession. Even with the protective ear coverings, Emily and

Naomi jumped with the sound of the shots. Emily watched the target flick back with each one. A push of the button and the trolley rushed the target back to them.

"Not bad. Five in the bull's eye, one just outside," said Clara.

"Are you up to trying it, Mom?" he asked.

Clara nodded and repeated Darren's steps for setting up the target, loading and firing. Clara made certain Emily and Naomi were behind her, then popped off three shots in succession. She brought the pistol down, paused for a moment, then shot three more times.

"My arm's weaker than I thought," she said.

She punched the button on the pole and the target came racing back to them. All six shots missed the bull's eye, but were within several inches of it.

"You would have stopped the guy, right?" asked Emily.

"Do you see a spot on that target saying 'aim here, not in the bull's eye'?" asked Clara. "Your turn, Emily."

"I'm not sure about this," said Emily as Clara and Darren set her up to shoot. This time they sent the target out half the distance. Emily settled into her stance, took aim, then brought the pistol down. "How do you aim this damn thing?"

"Just point it at the target," said Darren.

She aimed at the target, watching her arms waver slightly, disturbed at the weight of the gun in her hand and the cold feel of the metal.

"Here I go," she said. She cocked the gun, aimed and pulled the trigger. The revolver jerked skyward and made her take a half-step back to keep balanced. "How's that?"

"Fine, but this time, open your eyes," said Clara.

CHAPTER 18

Keeping her eyes open while she aimed at the target was the hard part for Emily. She managed to get off her last two shots with her lids at half-mast only because she imagined she was shooting at Ignatius Palatier, her former sleazy lawyer.

Emily slipped the protectors off her ears. The air was still. Even the birds had ceased their songs.

"How'd I do?" she asked.

The target raced back to them. In it were the twelve shots fired by Darren and Clara, but not another one.

"I missed it entirely." She knew she'd hate this.

"Takes practice," said Clara. "Like golf."

"Yeah, but with golf, no one ends up dead or bleeding all over the green," said Emily.

With great reluctance, Naomi took her turn. Her aim was far better than Emily's, the target offering up four shots left of the bull's eye.

"Not bad," said Darren.

"Okay. Time to switch guns. Maybe this one will tickle your fancy," said Clara. She extracted a smaller weapon from its case. "This will be simpler for you, Emily, and you may like the feel of it better. The balance is great." She placed it in Emily's hand.

Simple. She needed simple. "What is it?" asked Emily.

"A .380 Walther PPK-S."

The name sounded familiar to Emily, and she did like the way it nestled into her hand. *Balance? Is that what Clara called it?*

"You know, James Bond's weapon."

"Oh," said Emily. Her mouth opened slightly and her lips formed a round "O." "A spy's gun. How exciting."

She loaded the clip as Clara instructed.

"It's an automatic. Pull back the slide, aim and shoot."

"I know. I know. I've seen the movies."

Emily struggled with the slide, but finally got it back into position. When she pulled the trigger, she found the kick was not as powerful as the revolver, or if it was, she was prepared for it. Perhaps the gun did have better balance for her. She got off eight shots and recalled the target. As she counted the holes in it, she realized she'd hit it three times.

"Now it's Naomi's turn." Clara held her hand out for the nine millimeter.

"I want to go again," said Emily. She moved the weapon out of Clara's reach. Hitting the target with the Walther PPK stirred up her competitive spirit. "If I can put three shots in someone that ought to stop him."

"I don't know why you'd have reason to shoot anyone, but even eight shots from a .380 may not put a man down," said Detective Lewis. No one had noticed his arrival. "You might do better with a shotgun."

Emily froze in position. She would have turned to face the detective, but she remembered Earl's caution to keep the barrel of the gun pointed at the target or downrange. She wasn't intending to shoot the detective, at least not right now.

"What are you doing here?" asked Clara.

"Trying to get in a little target practice so that I can be sure to pass my annual exam, that's all."

Clara's shoulders, which Emily noticed tightening up when Lewis arrived, slumped in relaxation.

"But while I'm here, and since Darren has been difficult to find of late, I'd like to ask him a few questions about the night of Davey's murder."

Clara stepped between Darren and Lewis. "Such as?" she asked.

"Where were you that night, Darren?"

"I told you. He was with me. At home," Clara said.

"I'd like to hear it from him."

"Would you take your conversation someplace else," said Emily. "You're ruining my concentration."

She had put on her ear protection, sent the target out again, reloaded the clip and punched it back into the .380. She pulled the slide back, took her position, and fired all eight shots. When the target came back, she found she'd planted six of them within several inches of the bull's eye.

"I'd still recommend you try a shotgun," said Lewis.

Emily handed the gun to Darren and stomped away from the shooting station. *The nerve of the guy. A shotgun? When she was doing so well with James Bond's weapon.* The theme from *You Only Live Twice* ran through her head. She turned and stuck out her tongue at Lewis. Earl saw the gesture and cackled.

Two days after her love affair with James Bond's weaponry at the range, and the day after she was finally able to get in eighteen holes of golf at the club, Emily could almost not bend her right arm. And she was on tonight at the bar. She decided a soak in the hot tub might ease the discomfort. Since she wasn't due at work until late afternoon, an hour or so in the sun might make her feel better also.

Naomi had borrowed Stan the Sedan to get to the course. She was still subbing for Donald, who hadn't yet returned from the bass tournament. Emily didn't understand how a grown man could spend so much of his time sitting in a boat with a line dangling in the water, especially when the prize was another rod and reel that would only allow him to dangle yet another line in the water.

He was due back at the bar this afternoon, and she supposed she'd have to listen to his fish stories the entire night. Clara had put both Emily and Donald on duty because of the annual hospital golf tournament. She expected a busy night. Maybe she wouldn't have time to listen to Donald yammer on about fishing.

When she got to the hot tub, there was a notice posted saying it was closed for repair for three days.

"Damn, just when I need it most," she said to herself. She flipped her towel over her shoulder and walked the block back to her place. There was a message on her answering machine from Hap.

"We've got a court date in two days. We need to meet and go over our case. How about you and me meet for lunch tomorrow? Pick me up at noon. Call me."

With all the excitement over the shooting at the club and her practice at the range, she'd almost forgotten about her case. She'd gathered together all the necessary paperwork—cancelled checks, credit card receipts, mortgage and car payment information—demonstrating that she and Fred had shared, not only their bed, but their finances, for the past ten years. Now she and Hap had to decide what witnesses could testify to her devotion and fidelity to him during that period.

They were life partners, Hap had said, like husband and wife, but with no license.

But Hap also mentioned that no marriage certificate was one thing, understandable in terms of tax and dependency issues. Lots of older people did that, but, Hap wondered, why hadn't Fred made out a will favoring her? Why let the old one stand? Emily didn't understand that either, and every time she thought about it, she felt the anger at Fred rise up from her toes and travel throughout her body. *If he weren't already dead*, she thought, *I'd like to kill him.*

She knew all the questions nagging at her were ones the judge would want addressed also. Could she answer them to her own satisfaction and the judge's?

She dialed Hap's number. "I'll pick you up around noon tomorrow. We can get a booth in the back of the Burnt Biscuit and have some privacy there."

She put down the phone and considered the time she had left to her this afternoon. Vicki had volunteered to take her to the club when she returned from her bridge game later, but Emily had two hours to kill before she was due at work. Knowing Vicki's fondness for hot fudge sundaes, she wrote her a note saying she had errands to run and she would meet her at the ice cream parlor several minutes before three. Meantime, Emily slipped into work clothes and met the bus outside the gate. She had some research to do at the town library.

—✥—

With one elbow propped on the table holding up her chin and refrigerated air blowing across her shoulders, Emily turned pages with her free hand. She had skimmed three of the yearbooks from the time Clara was in high school and now turned her attention to senior year when Clara had gone abroad for study. *Here it is, the picture taken of the students who participated.* Neville Landry stood in the back row behind the eight students. *Well, he certainly could be Darren's father. No doubt about that. Same long, lean body type.* But it was difficult to tell about eye and hair color. Maybe gray like Darren's. But Landry was not the man hidden in the picture frame in Clara's bedroom.

She scanned the faces of the students: five girls, including Clara and only three boys. Given Landry's youth and good looks along with the excitement of exotic gay Paree, Emily imagined the girls would find studying abroad socially as well as intellectually interesting. And the boys? Well, like all males, these youths might have found the idea of French girls tempting, as was the chance to be with their female classmates unsupervised by parents.

Emily read the names below the picture. The end of the line read, "Absent, Morton Davey." That must have been Marcus' brother. She flipped to the index in the back, looking for a page where he might have been photographed in a club or perhaps his senior picture. Nothing. The guy certainly wasn't a joiner, or if he was, he was camera shy.

She found several pages listed for Marcus Davey and turned to them. Youth Rodeo. Marcus sat on a pinto pony, hat pulled down over his eyes. He looked exactly like any other teen in the club. He was younger than his brother, so Emily turned to the junior class photos and found Marcus. Same shifty eyes she remembered from mixology class, only a lot younger. The nose, however. The nose reminded her of the hidden picture. Maybe Clara had the hots for Marcus back then. That couldn't be. Clara hated Marcus. Or at least she said she did.

She turned to Clara's senior picture. The woman had aged very little in the years since it had been taken. The face that looked back at her from the photo revealed the same sense of self-confidence Clara exhibited now. The lines time had written on her forehead and around her mouth gave her face more character than the youthful Clara, but the eyes were the same—mischievous, almost dancing their way out of the yearbook.

She flipped back a few pages and stared at the picture of Detective Stanford Lewis. His hairline had receded a bit and a deep furrow had grown on his forehead, but, as with Clara, these signs of aging simply added distinction and interest to his face. She drew her finger across the lips. Full, but not too large.

"See something that interests you?" The voice came from behind her. Emily's head snapped up, and she shifted her body around so she could see who was speaking. Not that she needed to see the face. It was the same as the one before her. Besides, she recognized the voice. She slammed the book shut.

"Detective Lewis. What are you doing sneaking around the library?"

"Not sneaking. I'm doing what it says." He pointed to the sign asking patrons to turn off cell phones and observe quiet in the building.

Emily looked at her watch. "Oh, my. Look at the time. I've got to meet Vicki."

"I'll return these to the shelves if you like," said Lewis. He reached for the yearbooks, but Emily beat him to it.

"Never mind. I know where they go." She grabbed all four of the books, fled into the stack nearest her, tossed them on the shelves without searching for the proper place and ran out of the library.

Once out in the bright sunshine and humid air, Emily paused to catch her breath. That man had a way of turning up at inconvenient times. *I hope he didn't see me touching his photo like some lovesick teenager. And why were you touching it?* asked a tiny voice from inside her skull. She shook her blonde head to free herself from the voice, looked again at her watch and realized she had another hour before she was to meet Vicki. She stood under the acacia tree in front of the library looking up and down the street, trying to think of what she now could do. A hand touched her arm and she jumped.

"Your sweater," said Detective Lewis. "You left it on the chair."

"Thanks." She grabbed it and threw it across her shoulders.

"I'm glad I caught you. You were late meeting someone?"

She looked up into his brown eyes. Heat permeated her body, and she wondered if it was a hot flash or simply due to the temperature change from the library's coolness. *Or was it because of him? He was so close.*

She glanced around in desperation. She knew she should look as if she were on her way. "Ah, well, I must have misread my watch."

"Good, then. We can have coffee." Hand on her back, he guided her to his police cruiser, opened the door for her, and in a daze, Emily got into the passenger seat.

Neither of them saw the man pointing a camera phone in their direction.

CHAPTER 19

Naomi stepped out of the bar's doors, walked a short distance to the palm growing at the edge of the driving range and flipped open her cell. She tried to call her parents every day, knowing they would be concerned about her. The bar trade was heavy today, giving her no time to talk with them. It was afternoon, her first break since coming to work.

"Hi. It's me. I knew you'd be worried when I didn't call earlier." As she listened to her mother at the other end of the connection, she strolled around the palm savoring the shade and the gentle breeze blowing out of the west. Clouds drifted by throwing shadows across the driving range.

"What?" Naomi shouted into the phone. "Sorry, Mom, but that's an unpleasant surprise. Let me talk to Dad."

Her father's usually soothing voice failed to assuage her worries about her husband this time.

"He told me he'd gone into a support group for abusive spouses and now understood his problems. And he promised he wouldn't hit you again. The group leader suggested he find you and apologize for what he did. Barry sounded so miserable and so sorry for what he did. I think he's a different man. If I didn't, I wouldn't have told him where you went. Don't worry, baby. He sounded in control of himself, even said he'd stopped drinking."

"When did you tell him my location?"

"I don't remember exactly. Maybe a couple of days ago?" Her father's voice began to take on a more tentative note. "Has he been to see you? Did he behave himself, because if he didn't, I'll come out there myself and…"

Naomi wanted to scream at her father, but she also didn't want to worry her parents. She'd been through her husband's apologies, changed behavior (only temporary), and contrition before. It was part of his game to make her take him back and then begin the abuse once more. She touched the place on her face where the blow he'd landed there a few weeks ago was now almost healed. The physical pain was gone, but the shame remained etched in her mind, chiseled there by the man she'd thought she loved.

"I'm fine. I haven't seen him, but I'm sure he'll turn up. I'll keep you posted. Love ya."

She stared across the driving range into the woods beyond, certain now the feeling she was being watched was not simply paranoia. He was out there somewhere, and when he saw her at her most vulnerable, he'd attack. For now, surrounded by people, she was safe.

She dashed back into the clubhouse and closed the door behind her, leaning against it for a moment to pull herself together. Donald stood at the bar washing up glasses. The earlier rush of golfers parched after playing their round had abated, and only a few patrons sat at the bar watching CNN. Green stopped rinsing the glasses and looked at Naomi. She saw concern in his weathered face.

"Sun get to you?" he asked. "Or something else?"

You wouldn't think of him as a perceptive guy, thought Naomi, but his eyes bored into her, reading her as if she wore her worries like a sandwich board. They moved away from the TV watchers. Donald said not another word, but swabbed the bar surface while Naomi talked. She knew Emily had misgivings about this guy, yet Naomi felt comfortable with him. She spit out the story of her marriage from her first date to her present certainty her husband had found her and would extract a high price for running from him.

"It's hopeless. Even if I hid out forever, he'd hunt me for that long. The man is obsessed with controlling me."

"That man is no man," said Donald. His mouth worked as if he'd eaten a moldy piece of bread. "You need help."

"Don't suggest I go to the authorities. He's a cop and has contacts all over this state."

"I heard you and some others were out at the gun club the other day."

"Are you suggesting I pack?"

Donald picked up the container holding bar toothpicks, pulled one out and began to chew on it. Naomi watched in fascination as the cellophane end twirled around reminding her of a flower dancing in his mouth. It was an incongruous image given the craggy lines of his cheeks, the half-days' growth of beard and the fanciful whirling color at the corner of such tightly drawn lips.

He withdrew the toothpick and tossed it into the garbage. "It would be good if you had someone to watch your back."

"Are you volunteering?" she asked.

"Maybe. Meantime, you might want to find out where Emily keeps her guns."

"She doesn't have any." Unless her mother had kept the Walther, but that seemed unlikely even though Emily seemed quite fond of it.

"Doesn't she know she's living in the last settled frontier of the United States?"

"I thought that was the Wild West," Naomi said.

"Naw. The West was civilized compared to what went on around here. We've only recently taken to walking upright."

Donald's lips made some kind of motion, maybe a smile. "I'll see what I can do," he said and walked down the bar toward the TV watchers. "How 'bout another?" he asked them.

No wonder Emily was in conflict over the man, thought Naomi. I've spilled my guts, and he's offered something in return, but whether it was advice or a hired gun, she didn't know.

Naomi was still wrestling with the enigma that was Donald Green when Emily walked in the door.

"Is it three already?" asked Naomi.

"I'm early. You'll never guess what happened when I was in town. I ran into Detective Lewis, and we had coffee together."

Green's head came up with a jerk and he turned his gaze on Emily. The look said he wasn't happy to hear of the detective and Emily sharing caffeine. It said he would have preferred being the one buying the java for Emily. Maybe it was professional, the detective questioning her mother one more time about the murders, yet the excited expression on Emily's face suggested something more personal going on. Donald surely had seen the look too. He was jealous whether he knew it or not. Both she and Emily could use some help with their problems, but were men with weapons the answer?

❦

The courtroom walls were paneled in dark wood—it looked like mahogany to Emily—and the windows on the left side of the room ran from floor to ceiling, yet they were narrow and let in little light. The AC system was circa 1950, not only old but inefficient and helped little by two vintage ceiling fans that shoved hot, moist air around, blowing most of it in the faces of the people gathered beneath them. There were no seats left in the small chamber, and Emily's nose told her that many of those gathered had forgotten to bathe that morning, or perhaps anytime in the past week.

Hap sat at the table beside her, wearing his usual white suit. Emily detected no naphtha odor from the garment today, and she wondered if Hap had sent it to be dry cleaned especially for her hearing. In accordance with Hap's recommendation, Emily wore a shirtwaist dress, one of the few dresses she owned. The pattern in the material was of violets and pansies, and with her short stature, she always thought it made her look like she was playing dress-up.

She was scared. The outcome of contesting Fred's will would alter how she lived. If things did not go in her favor, she might lose her lovely park model home. It was small and not presumptuous, but it was her home for six months out of the year. The rest of the time she and Fred rented an apartment in upstate New York. That too was at stake. If she wasn't to have any of his estate, she'd have to move out of the apartment into something smaller. She sighed and glanced at Hap, in whom she'd placed her future, an old man who hadn't practiced law for years. The judge entered the room, interrupting Emily's train of negative ruminations. Everyone stood.

To most people entering Judge Howard Miller's courtroom, it would appear his brand of justice was grounded in a sense of informality. Emily watched him stride to his bench, nodding and smiling at people he knew. She heard him speak with quiet certainty, and there was no mistaking his grasp of the law, but she felt as if she was asking her father to loan her the car rather than contesting a will in a court of law. He made her feel smaller than she already was, younger, more childish and uncertain about the choices she and Fred had made in their shared life together.

He smiled at all the litigants. Emily, he called "the bereaved," which she thought was a rather sensitive way of referring to her status, yet it failed to reassure her. Although he gave Fred's ex-wife and her fancy West Palm Beach lawyer as warm a smile, Emily thought she caught a flicker of displeasure on the judge's face when Thomas Brookfield introduced himself to the court and offered a petition to dismiss the proceedings.

"Well, the way I see it," Judge Miller spoke in a smooth, unruffled, fatherly voice, "we're all here, so why don't we get on with it?"

That was good, wasn't it?

She leaned over and told Hap what she was thinking. He patted her hand and whispered to her not to be misled. Judge Miller was a by-the-book judge, and he thought of himself as a servant of the Lord as much as he did an officer of the law. He did his work, said Hap, by making everyone comfy enough to incriminate themselves.

Hap had gathered an impressive array of witnesses to testify to Emily's loyalty to Fred and the faithfulness of her love and devotion to him. As her friends told of her relationship with Fred, Emily scrutinized the judge's face for clues as to how convincing their case was to him.

Her best friend Vicki was telling the judge about Emily and Fred's relationship. "I mean, we never dreamed that the two of them weren't married. Well, maybe they were a little more lovey-dovey than most of us older couples, but I thought that was because they hadn't been married as long."

"Let me see if I get all this. Were they inappropriate in their behavior around others?" asked Judge Miller. The look on his face said he wasn't being critical, merely trying to understand the "bereaved," get a sense of her as a person.

"Oh, no. Not at all."

"What did they do that was so," he looked down at a paper on which he was scribbling notes, "as you said, 'lovey-dovey'?"

"They kissed and held hands."

"But no one else did this?"

"Ah, no," said Vicki. Emily could see perspiration beaded on her friend's upper lip.

"So their behavior was different from that of others in your small community. Out of step. A little flirty, sexy perhaps?"

Emily heard Hap groan and watched Vicki's eyes begin to jump around in their sockets. Across the aisle from her, Thomas Brookfield's chair creaked as he leaned forward in it. Emily knew she shouldn't look at him, but she did anyway. His eyes were fixed on Vicki, and they reminded her of the yellow orbs of a hunting coyote. Mrs. Ex-Fred looked like his mate, waiting for the hunter to bring home the rabbit to the cubs.

As quickly as Judge Miller skewered Vicki, he shifted posture. "You're a good and loyal friend. Our bereaved Emily is fortunate to have you here today. Let's move on, shall we?"

Several of Emily and Fred's friends from the condominium park spoke on her behalf. They gave similar stories. Fred and Emily had been a devoted couple for over ten years. The women with whom Emily played golf testified to Emily's love for her dead partner.

"Yes, yes," said Judge Miller. He sounded anxious to wrap up Emily's side of the case. "I have all the documents here. It seems you shared in expenses while you were living together. However, you did not share equally, I see."

"Well, I took an early retirement so my pension was far less than his," said Emily.

The Judge grabbed his gavel and pounded it on the bench. "Later. Your turn to testify will come after lunch." He stood and walked out of the courtroom.

Emily checked her watch. It was only ten thirty. "Lunch?" she asked Hap.

"Judge Miller likes to take late morning tea followed by a prayer break, then an early lunch."

"How do you think we're doing?" asked Emily.

"Awful," said Hap. He arose from his chair with the help of his cane and hobbled down the aisle.

"Then do something. Object or something," said Emily.

"You hired me to be your lawyer and for now we're ducking under the radar. Your side of this may appear pretty solid to a Yankee, but down here, there's community pride to consider, and appearance. Appearance is very important." He walked out the courtroom doors and wound through the gathered crowd toward the front door of the courthouse.

"What about the law?" asked Emily. She followed him through reporters, bystanders and the bored and curious folks who liked a courtroom scene better than they liked their soap operas on television.

"The law," he said as he made his way down the steps and across the wide lawn toward the shade trees that lined the street, "is a matter of interpretation. For you, the law is Judge Miller.

We must allow him room to maneuver for now." He sat down on the stone bench under a magnolia, leaned back, and closed his eyes. "I could use an egg salad sandwich and a coke from the drugstore across the street. You'd better get something for yourself too."

At the counter of the small drugstore, Emily stood in line to put in the order for Hap. She couldn't eat a thing. Not at this hour. The sound of a familiar laugh from behind her made her turn around. Lucinda Davey stood at the back of the store talking with Fred's ex-wife, Carolyn Hughes, and her city lawyer. The man behind her in line was tall and broad. She let his figure hide her. She didn't want the two women she disliked most to see her. Why were they chatting away as if they had been best buddies for years? Emily wondered what they were doing together. It couldn't be anything good. Every time she encountered Lucinda, it was like stepping into a boxing ring. She never knew when a punch would be coming her way. She had nothing to say to Carolyn, a woman Fred referred to as "high maintenance." *Fred, you jerk, why, oh why did you leave everything to that witch?*

The last time Emily saw her was five years ago at the engagement party Carolyn threw for Fred's oldest son. Since then, Carolyn had married an orthodontist and was using his money to travel and buy houses. At the party she looked gorgeous with her long, dark hair, black eyes and seductive way of carrying herself. It was bad enough the woman found money, but she also had looks. Emily sent a telepathic message toward the back of the drugstore—*gain weight, sag somewhere, lose money at the track. Experience something common like the rest of us.*

A shrill laugh cut into Emily's voodoo. She heard her name mentioned and tried to resist the temptation to sneak a look around the large man serving as her blind. *What the heck.* A tiny peek wouldn't hurt. She stuck half her face around his arm and her nose came within inches of Lucinda's breasts, clad in a stretchy lime green tank top.

"Uh, hi there Mrs. Davey," she said. She stepped back, remembering Lucinda's fondness for handling Emily's presence by physical confrontation.

"Get away from me," said Lucinda. Her voice was loud and angry. The noise level in the crowded business suddenly diminished. You could hear a toad pass gas. People craned their necks to see who was molesting the Widow Davey.

"Sorry," said Emily. She turned on her heel and fled the store, but not before she got a good look at Carolyn.

Hmm. She'd been so terrified in court that she failed to take a good look at Carolyn. And the light there was bad also. But in the bright sunlight coming through the store windows, the woman looked positively jowly. Well, perhaps

Emily's hex worked. She ought to try it more often. That's not nice, Emily, she told herself as she ran out the door.

"Where's my sandwich?" asked Hap. "And what canary did you just swallow?"

CHAPTER 20

Naomi had hugged Emily goodbye when she left for the courthouse earlier in the morning. "Good luck," she said.

Emily had convinced Naomi to stay home for the day instead of sitting in the courtroom observing the proceedings. "Go to the pool since you have the day off from the bar. Soak up some sun. Relax. My problems are not your problems."

"Maybe not," said Naomi. She walked her mother to the car. "But you've certainly gone out of your way to take on my difficulties by giving me a place to hide and getting me the job at the club. I feel guilty not being able to repay you in some way. The least I can do is be there today for moral support."

Emily hesitated before opening the car door. "I talked to Hap last night knowing you would want to go and he said no."

"Why?"

"He said you looked so much like me that people would ask questions."

Naomi turned her head and looked toward the pasture.

"I'm sorry, honey." Emily reached out and pulled the daughter she couldn't acknowledge into her arms. "He wasn't trying to be unkind. He was trying to protect me. He said you were a part of my past we shouldn't get into today. But it doesn't mean you're any less my daughter or that I don't appreciate what you're trying to do for me."

"I know. I feel so helpless." She leaned into Emily's hug.

"We all feel helpless. Everything's in the judge's hands now." Emily broke off the embrace, quickly jumped into the car and drove off. She hadn't wanted Naomi to see the tears in her eyes nor the worried look on her face.

⁂

After her mother left, Naomi trudged up the drive, head down, and contemplated the day ahead. How could she not think about what was going on in court? In the few short weeks she'd been here, Emily had come to mean more to her than a woman who had given her wonderful parents when she wasn't able to raise Naomi herself. She was like a second mother, and sometimes Naomi had to catch herself when she almost called her "Mom."

Naomi dragged her beach towel out of the dryer, took her book and headed for the lounger on the backyard patio. Maybe I'll watch the horses in the pasture today, she decided.

When the herd failed to appear after she'd spent an hour reading in the sun, a sense of foreboding stole over her. *It's too isolated back here. I need to be around people.*

She grabbed her beach bag and headed to the pool. The friends she'd made last week were already there. She threw her towel on a lounge and plopped down next to them.

"What's up for tonight?" she asked. She pushed her concern and her fears to the back of her mind as the trio of young women made plans for a night out at the Burnt Biscuit.

⟋⟍

Toby sneaked into the storage area behind the condo park and parked his car there, then walked toward the houses fronting the road. He hid in a culvert down the road from Emily's backyard and watched his target leave the lounge chair and cross the street to the pool area.

Damn. He missed her, but he'd be patient and wait. He stuck a chaw in his mouth and settled back, swatting the flies that came to bother him and nodding off every few minutes. When he fell into too deep a sleep, he could count on tobacco juice running down his chin to awaken him. Toby favored surveillance work especially when he didn't have to move too much or too fast.

As the afternoon dragged by, the sun sent rays into the concrete surround where he dozed on and off. The cement absorbed the sunlight and began to radiate its heat like an asphalt road. He removed his sport jacket and laid it down on the hard surface underneath him, making it feel only marginally softer to his butt. The three-foot-long alligator usually holing up in the culvert in the afternoon swam out of the pond and began his journey onto the grass and into his usual resting place.

"Get the hell out of here," said Toby. The reptile eyed him and retreated to the pond once more.

Still the woman didn't return, and he decided to move his hiding place to where he might be more comfortable. He walked up to the rear of the park model and tried the door. It was locked. His cell rang.

"What'd you mean, the deal's off? I got five hundred bucks coming to me. I did my bit. I followed through, and he owes me. You owe me." He listened to the caller's reply, flipped the phone closed and backed away from the building.

Another set of eyes watched him as he got into his car.

⚬

The ceiling fan whirred at a faster rate of speed, but failed to keep up with the mugginess, which descended like a punishment upon the occupants of the courtroom. As usual, the cranky air conditioning system struggled ineffectively on. A few people hadn't returned following lunch. Others seated themselves, then got up and left, deciding the show to come held less interest for them than afternoon soap operas in the comfort of their air conditioned living rooms. People shifted positions on the benches, hoping to get as far away from one another as they could.

Emily envied those who used hand fans to cool their faces. She wished she were anywhere but here. The dress Hap insisted she wear was probably a lot cooler than anything else she could have chosen from her wardrobe. Hap in his white suit began to look like a giant soft serve ice cream.

Even the judge seemed distracted by the temperature in the room. "Let's see. Where are we now? Oh, yes. It's your turn. He looked at Emily. His gaze was stern. Emily cleared her throat and nervously spoke of Fred and hers relationship. When she was finished, she returned to her seat. The judge asked no questions and neither did Mr. Brookfield.

Hap let Emily's innocent appearance and heartfelt testimony stand and concluded their case. Carolyn's hired pit bull called witnesses to testify to Emily's philandering nature. The condominium park manager along with Mrs. Wattles and Mrs. Frey, the two inveterate trouble makers, told of visits from several men over the past few months.

"As if she couldn't wait to get Fred out of her life. One was very young, too," said Mrs. Frey. She fanned herself furiously and shook her head, an offended look on her face.

Emily silently plotted revenge on the old reprobates—maybe she'd parade around the pool in a bikini or put posters up in the clubhouse inviting interested people to join the local nudist society. Or she could recommend the social committee hire a reggae band for the St. Patrick's Day dance. Wouldn't everyone be surprised when they found out what a reggae band was, Emily thought with satisfaction, imagining the shocked looks.

Hap put his hand on her shoulder and shook her. "Where are you? And get that silly look off your face. The judge will think you smoked wacky tabacky on break."

Emily brought her attention back to the present and slid lower in her chair.

Carolyn's hired legal goon called Martin Quigley to testify.

She leaned over and whispered in Hap's ear. "Good. Now we'll get the truth about whether I came on to Marcus. It's about time someone dealt with the rumors." She shot an accusing look at Hap.

He dropped his head into his hands, ran them over his face and looked up. "Don't be so certain, my dear."

Quigley looked uncomfortable, moving around in the chair throughout his testimony, keeping his eyes from Emily and Hap's and interspersing "uh" and "uhm" and long silences in what he had to say. But everyone got the gist of his statement.

One night, he maintained, after mixology class, Emily behaved flirtatiously toward Marcus, asking him to take her to a motel and she would show him a good time. Worse, he implied she had made the offer in exchange for a passing grade.

Emily jumped out of her chair. "That's a damn lie." Her reaction woke the court room out of its stupor and talk began to buzz behind her. "Restrain your client," said Judge Miller. "I will not have such outbursts in my courtroom. And no profanity, little lady."

"Perhaps a recess, your honor?" said Hap.

"No recess. I want to finish this case. Today. And pretty daggoned soon too."

And it was finished as far as Emily was concerned. Quigley had lied, but she knew the judge wanted to believe him. Her case was sunk. *Who got to him?* She looked at Hap and could tell he was thinking the same thoughts.

Judge Miller concluded the day by intoning a prayer for guidance from the Lord. Everyone bowed their heads, and for the first time, Emily earnestly prayed there was a God who was female and understood Emily's plight.

"I'll render my decision tomorrow," the judge said. He pounded his gavel, stepped down from the bench and tossed his robes at his secretary before he had even left the courtroom.

Spectators fled through the outside doors to catch any little breeze the afternoon might be offering.

"Thanks, Hap," said Emily. "I know you did your best."

Hap and Emily stood at the bottom of the courthouse steps. Not only was there no wind stirring, but a haze hung over the area, holding the suffocating air around their heads like a blanket.

A few well-wishers stopped to pat Hap on the back and wish him luck. "You're gonna need it," one said. "This is a heck of a case to come out of retirement for." Others stared at Emily, as if she wore the proverbial red letter on her chest.

Hap looked the picture of the conquered. His white suit hung on him as if he had suddenly lost weight while in the courtroom. He could have, thought Emily. With the sauna-like nature of the room, he probably did weigh pounds lighter. His head was bowed when Carolyn's ambulance chaser came over to him.

"Nice try, old man," he said. Emily knew he wasn't referring to Hap with respect.

"Go away," she said.

As he walked off, his wealthy client in tow and Lucinda Davey a few steps behind them, Hap watched them with a thoughtful expression on his face.

"Lucinda and Carolyn," said Emily. "There's a lethal combination."

"Yes, indeed," said Hap, with a hint of a twinkle in his eyes. "Justice can be slow and not so obvious."

"Give me a break, Hap. No more sagely southern wisdom. I'm beat."

❦

Emily slammed through her front door. "Naomi?" she called and got no answer. She peeled off her damp clothing and tossed it into the washer, then threw open her closet door looking for something clean to wear to the club. She was on duty tonight and that was just as well. She needed to keep busy and stop ruminating over the humiliation of her day in court. If she'd left it alone, let Carolyn take everything, she wouldn't have had to parade her past before the entire town as well as the judge. *Damn.*

She grabbed a white shirt off a hanger and noticed it had a spot of tomato juice on the front. *I'll have to get it out. All the rest of them are dirtier than this one.* Who was the idiot that established white shirts and black trousers as the appropriate wear for wait people and bartenders, she wondered. *By the time you're halfway through work, the customers can read what's on the menu by looking at your shirt front.*

Emily heard the front door open as she was scrubbing out the stain at the kitchen sink. Naomi entered looking like a lobster. "You forgot sunscreen?" She spoke with exasperation in her tone.

"I guess I shouldn't ask what happened today in court, huh?"

Emily shook her head, didn't look up and continued to scrub the spot.

"I'm going with my friends to dinner and then to the Burnt Biscuit. Want to come?"

"I have to work tonight," Emily said. Her voice filled with resignation.

Emily's tone crushed Naomi's ebullient mood. "I forgot."

Emily continued to rub at the shirt. She was wearing a blister on her finger.

"Darren and I may share an apartment," Naomi said.

Emily slapped the blouse into the suds. "Oh, that'll be great. Then when your husband finds you, you'll be living with another man. Good thinking, Naomi."

"Sorry." Naomi stood in the middle of the living room for a moment longer, then turned and rushed out the door.

Now she'd done it, taken out her anger on Naomi and added to her woes. She ran to the door to call Naomi back, but her daughter had disappeared.

⸙

"You're on alone tonight," said Clara. "Think you can handle it or do you want me to stay?"

Emily gave a dismissive wave of her hand. "It'll be slow."

Clara had listened without comment to Emily when she arrived at the bar and told her about the day in court and then about her run-in with Naomi.

"Kids're a bitch," said Clara. "Maybe I could call Donald to see if he's free to work for you."

"I asked him yesterday. I thought then I might not be in the mood to greet the drinking public with smiles tonight. He told me he had another job to do."

"So I'll stay then."

"No, go on home. Maybe you and Darren can catch a good movie on television and have a bonding experience."

Clara gave forth a sardonic laugh and repeated her earlier pronouncement on progeny. "Kids're a bitch."

After Clara left, a few customers wandered into the bar, drank a couple of beers and talked pars and bogies. Emily joined in. Once they'd replayed the entire front nine, the conversation lagged.

"That burn down near the canal seems to be moving this way. I guess they can't get it under control," said one of the men.

"Yeah, we were going to play another nine, but the air is so thick out there you can't breathe it, and you can't see your ball if it goes into the rough."

Emily had noted the smoke in the air when she drove up. Now, when she looked out the window, she couldn't see as far as the hundred-yard maker on the driving range.

She waved goodbye to the departing men, grabbed their beer glasses and washed them. The outside door to the bar opened.

"Come in quick and close it. I don't want that smell in here," she said.

"Hi, there," said a familiar voice.

"Detective Lewis." As nice as their coffee was the other day, the man still set her nerves on end. She never knew when he might depart from friendly conversation into police interrogation.

"I have some good news for you," he said. He removed his hat, set it on the next bar stool, then sat down.

"You were at the courthouse today. I caught a glimpse of you in the back."

"You looked like Little Miss Muffit in that dress."

"Hap's idea. Get to the news."

"Quigley was lying."

"Oh, big surprise. Everyone knew Quigley was lying. Even the judge, but so what? It seems only rumor, not the truth, is what counts in this place."

"You judge us too harshly. Justice here is slow and sometimes it's not obvious it's happening."

"Put that in quotes. It's Hap's line. Or did he steal it from you?" She wanted to throw the wet bar rag at him and tell him to get on his SUV and ride. She restrained herself and waited for his "good news."

"He was on his way out of town to visit his relatives in Macon, Georgia, when I pulled him over."

"For lying?"

"Lucky for me, he was speeding. And drunk. Mr. Quigley is not a happy man. He recently lost his job as general manager of the local hardware store when it closed. So he was looking for work. I guess he found it. He was carrying five thousand dollars in his pocket. Apparently someone hired him. I'm thinking the money was payoff for his testimony."

Emily dropped the bar cloth and turned wide, blue eyes on Lewis.

She gave him her full attention. "So who paid him?" she asked.

"I don't know yet, but he's down at the station, and Toby is questioning him. When we get his full story, I intend to pay a visit to the judge."

CHAPTER 21

Judge Miller opened the door to his father's room and stood gazing at the small figure lying in the bed by the window. The old man had been in the nursing facility at the Blue Heron Retirement Center for over six months. The judge didn't want him to die, but he did long for his suffering to cease.

"Dad?" he said in a low voice. "Are you awake?" The form in the bed didn't move, gave no indication he knew anyone had entered the room. He never did. Since the stroke, the judge's father lived with machines monitoring his vital functions. The doctors told Judge Miller that his father's brain continued to function, and he was breathing on his own, but they fed him through a tube in his stomach. This was his dad, who loved food and had once won an okra-eating contest in Louisiana. He was seventy at the time.

The judge took his usual seat at the window and began telling his father about the day in court. He didn't expect any reaction from him, but the doctors said his father could hear him speaking and the sound of his voice was soothing to the dying man.

"It was an unusual case." He spoke at length about the testimony. "I know Quigley's lying, but there's nothing I can do about it. For this woman to live in sin for so long. It's beyond my understanding why a woman would do that."

"She loved him," said a voice. Hap stood in the doorway, his figure backlit by the hallway illumination. "May I come in for a moment?"

"This is usually the time I spend alone with Dad. And your behavior is highly unethical, you know."

"Yes, so disbar me. This will be my last case anyway," Hap said. "Besides, I've brought a little courage, and I'd like to share it with you." Hap reached into his pocket and extracted a silver flask.

The judge hesitated only a moment, then reached out and took it, unscrewed the top and raised it to his mouth. "Sour mash." He smacked his lips in appreciation as the fierce concoction burned down his throat and spread warmth throughout his stomach.

"I gave this up when I found Jesus," he said. "I miss it." He took a second swallow and handed it back to Hap.

"I don't mean to tell you how to believe, Judge, but I don't think Jesus would mind a sip or two between old rivals."

He upturned the flask, took a long draught and handed it back to the judge, who shook his head. The figure in the bed moaned and moved a leg. Both men turned toward the sound, but it was not repeated. Only the monitors gave forth their steady bleeping.

"He has no real life." He nodded his head toward his father. "Sometimes I wish there were a plug I could pull and end it, but I guess it's up to him. He seems to want to hang on for now."

Hap chuckled. "He's waiting for his son to make a reasonable decision from the bench for once."

"You think you know what I'm going to announce tomorrow?"

"Well, you're certainly in a pickle even though you know Quigley's lying. But let's set his testimony to the side. The rest is all rumor and innuendo. You know the character of this woman, and you know she was more faithful than many wives have been."

Judge Miller's head shot up. "Let's not go there. Leave her out of this."

Hap hesitated a moment before he responded, carefully measuring his words. "I wasn't talking about anyone in particular. My only recommendation would be you use your Christian charity and forgive her."

"She was my wife, and she cheated on me. With you." The judge's words were the same as they'd ever been when he spoke of his wife to Hap, but tonight they had lost their venom. "I wonder what she saw in you, a poor, alcoholic, failure of a country lawyer."

"I was good for a laugh."

The judge held his hand out, and Hap placed the flask in it. Miller took a long pull on it.

"I can't forgive her, and I won't forgive you. As for your client, she's no better than my unfaithful wife. You've come on a fool's errand." He pocketed the flask and turned his attention back to his father.

"You're not a bad judge, but you're not as good as you could be, you know. You need a better role model than your predecessor, Judge Crawford, that broken down old bag of wind."

"And who might you recommend?" he asked without taking his eyes off his father.

"Solomon saw the truth. His decision separated the truly virtuous woman from the pretender. There's a lesson in that."

Judge Miller saw his father's eyes flip open for a second, and close again. He leaned in. A sigh escaped the old man's lips.

Hap watched the pair from the doorway. *If I were a religious man, I'd take that as a sign.* He closed the door and walked down the hallway, eager to leave the nursing care part of the facility and return to his small apartment. He knew he'd return here soon enough.

When Captain Worley left the interrogation room to get a cup of coffee, Toby leaned in toward Quigley. "Keep your mouth shut, and you'll walk out of here."

Quigley's eyes darted around the room, finally coming to rest on the small window, smudged with years of dirt.

"No I won't. You heard what Worley said. I'm looking at some serious charges here, speeding and drunk driving."

"A good lawyer can get you off those. Ask for one when Worley gets back." The name of Ignatius Palatier sprang to Toby's mind, and he laid it in Quigley's ear.

"No way. I can't afford it. I'm gonna tell the truth."

Toby sneered and grabbed his spit can off the floor. "You implicate me, and I'll say you're lying. And I'm a cop. Who's gonna believe a drunk who's out of work?" Toby circled behind Quigley's chair, then leaned down toward him again. Toby's sour breath along with the bitter reek of his chewing tobacco encircled Quigley's head.

"Tell you what. You hang tight, and I'll see if I can find the money to buy you Palatier. Deal?"

Quigley wrung his hands, then dropped his head into them. "Deal." Toby knew Quigley was afraid to be in the room alone with him, afraid Toby might do something to him and cover it by saying Quigley tried to escape or attacked him. Toby smiled, knowing Quigley was in big trouble, and it was coming at him from all sides. He knew Quigley's only hope was to implicate Toby. He couldn't let him do that. Toby had to keep him from talking with anyone else. Toby needed Ignatius, and he knew how to get him.

He left Quigley in the room alone, confident he'd covered his trail, and stepped outside into the gathering darkness, brought on earlier tonight because of the smoke-filled air. He punched a number into his cell.

"Ignatius," he said. "We have a potential problem here. Weston Quigley's been picked up with the five thousand on him, and he thinks he can talk his way out of some traffic charges by telling the truth about where he got the money. What? I know damn well he got it from me! And I got it from you. Rest assured I will use your name if he talks. Right now, he's willing to hang tough if you represent him."

"I don't want to have anything more to do with this situation. And I certainly don't want to be his lawyer," came the reply.

Toby was shocked. Ignatius was as vulnerable as he. Why wouldn't he play the game? He decided to be more cajoling. Maybe the man needed persuasion.

"That don't sound like you at all. You've got a lot to lose here, and if I don't go back in there with you on the line for Quigley, he'll name me and then you know what'll happen." He never knew if Ignatius heard his words because the lawyer had disconnected.

Something was very wrong here, and Toby wondered if Quigley's idea of getting out of town was a good one, one Toby should consider. He might run, but only after he played a few cards he still held with people who weren't so nicey, nicey about their dealings as were lawyers and out-of-work hardware managers. He punched in another number and got a better reception. By the time Detective Lewis drove into the parking lot, Toby's frame of mind was much improved.

"I think he's about to crack," said Toby to Lewis as the tall man entered the station.

"Good work, Toby. I'll go in and talk to him and we'll see what he has to say."

"He's still rolling it around in his mind. Let me have a few minutes with him, and I'll have him singing like a mocking bird."

"Go to it, man," said Lewis.

Toby walked down the hallway and found Captain Worley standing outside the room.

"Did he say anything, Captain?" asked Toby. He worried Quigley had spilled the story to the captain.

"He wants a lawyer. I told him it was damn dumb of him not to talk about the money, but he's insistent."

"I thought you had him on the run," said Lewis, walking up behind Toby.

"I do, I mean I did." Toby's eyes fixed on the closed door. "My spit bucket," he said. "I left it in there. Let me have another shot at him before we bring in the lawyer."

"You know the rules, Toby. We can't question him until the lawyer arrives," said Worley.

Toby leaned forward toward the captain, his hands held out in front of him. He looked as if he were going to drop to his knees and beg him. As Toby was about to open his mouth, the sounds of sirens from fire engines and emergency vehicles drew everyone's attention.

"Sounds like more fire fighters are needed for that blaze," said Worley. "And that sounds like my phone ringing."

Worley rushed off to his office, but returned in several minutes. "That was Quigley's lawyer. He'll be here in a few hours."

"A few hours," said Lewis. "Why so long?"

"Not a local. He's coming in from the coast. Meantime, our guest," Worley gestured toward the room where Quigley was located, "is not to be questioned. Got that, Toby?"

Toby nodded. "But can I get my spit bucket?"

Worley grimaced. "Fine, go ahead."

Toby turned to enter the room, his face hidden now from his fellow cops. It wore an expression of supreme satisfaction that his plan had worked. So pleased was he with himself, he missed the knowing look that passed between Lewis and the captain.

⁂

Emily slowed and turned onto the shoulder to allow several fire trucks to pass on her way home from the course. She wondered how far up the lake the fire had moved since this afternoon. In the distance she could see a red glow in the sky, and she worried the burn might be threatening her condo park. A steady stream of cars met her as she continued on to the park entrance and made her turn. The park manager stood at the gate and waved her to stop. Beyond the gates emergency service volunteers and designated park personnel in orange vests directed the flow of cars exiting the park.

"I got a notice from the fire chief. He's ordering everyone to evacuate from here in the next hour. So go get what you need from your place and turn around and get out of here."

Emily nodded and gunned Stan down the road. She pulled into her drive and jumped out. The smoke was heavier here, and its smell burned her eyes. The glow lit up the pasture beyond the canal. *My God, it looks as if the fire is closing in on the field. What about the horses and cattle there?* She heard the roar of several engines and watched with relief as a pickup and an all-terrain vehicle entered and herded the animals down the canal toward the safety of the far palm grove. "Naomi." She called her daughter's name as she banged through the front door. Then she remembered. Naomi was with her friends at the Burnt Biscuit. She'd grab everything of hers she could carry. It wasn't much. Naomi had arrived with only one suitcase.

She gathered together Naomi's possessions, some of her own clothes and most of Fred's. She knew it was silly to take his things, but she couldn't part with them, at least not yet, fire or no fire. She threw all the clothes in the back of Stan and returned for her picture albums.

Emily could hear the chaos outside: emergency personnel banged on doors, making certain people knew to get out. Carl, Vicki's husband, loaded their two labs into the back of the SUV.

"You coming, Emily?" Vicki shouted to her from the drive.

"Be right there. I've got another load of stuff."

The president of the park's board of directors drove by announcing the evacuation through the loud speaker, recently purchased with the park's equipment budget. He obviously thought the evacuation was a great opportunity to use it. Emily knew there were some elderly residents in this park, but she considered the sound system over-kill. Who could miss what was going on outside regardless of how deaf they might be or how involved in their primetime programs?

As if to prove her reasoning wrong, she heard Mrs. Wattles shouting at one of the board members. "I can't leave now. It's the last fifteen minutes of *CSI*, for heaven's sake. Besides, there's a canal surrounding this park. You think the fire will jump that?"

She couldn't hear the board member's reply, but on her next trip out to the car, she spotted

Mrs. Frey's car pull up in front of Mrs. Wattles' house. It was piled high with clothes and other household items, but the only thing Emily saw Mrs. Wattles take from her house was a small battery-operated television set.

Emily smiled. *Funny the kind of thing you think is important in a crisis.* Emily thought of Fred's clothes and wondered why they were of such meaning to her. As she rushed back into the house for a final load of mementos, a man wearing an orange vest with reflector stripes on it blocked her path.

"Time to get moving," he said. He gestured her toward her car.

She heard her phone ring. "That's my phone. I should answer it." He shook his head and blocked her path. She turned and got into her car, then backed out of the drive and followed the slow line of cars leaving the park. Ahead of her, all she could see through the smoke-filled air were car taillights and the blue and red flashers of official vehicles. To the east she watched the fire burn closer. Now she could make out more than a red glow. Trees with their branches ablaze shot flames into the night air. A fire this hot with the wind blowing it toward the park could jump the tiny canal. Emily despaired she had seen the last of the house. Wouldn't it be ironic if the judge announced tomorrow that the house was hers and it had burned down during the night? You're being macabre, she told herself.

The continual honking of a horn behind her made her glance in her rearview mirror. She saw women in the car waving frantically. Emily recognized them as the friends Naomi had made at the pool. She pulled over and jumped out.

"Where's Naomi?" asked the driver.

"What do you mean?"

"When the Biscuit told everyone to get on home because of the fire, she came with us while we got our stuff together. Then she said she ought to go check on you. She ran off toward your place. You must have just missed each other. She wanted to pick up her things and yours, if you didn't make it back here in time. She said she'd hitch a ride with your next-door neighbors or with you if you showed up."

Emily's heart skipped a beat, then began to pound hard against her chest. *There's no way she could have missed Naomi.* She made a dash for her car, got in and began to make a U-turn, but before she could complete it, an emergency volunteer approached and directed her toward the exit. "Move along now. Everyone needs to get out."

"But I have to go back in." Emily struggled for the right words. "My daughter is back in the house somewhere."

"We're doing a house-to-house check. What's the address?" Emily told him, and he spoke into his two-way radio. "We checked that area. There's no one there."

Okay, she said to herself shifting into gear, she must have gotten a ride with someone else, and we missed one another in all this tangle of traffic. She crept along toward the gate where the only car heading into the park had been stopped by the park manager. The driver stepped out and walked up to the manager. He was a well-built man with sandy hair and a pug nose. When he reached into his suit jacket pocket to extract something, Emily caught sight of a shoulder holster. He pulled out some kind of leather wallet and flipped it open, holding it in front of the manager's face for his inspection. Ralph nodded his head, and punched the gate code, allowing the barrier arm to raise. The brown Mercedes drove through and on down the road.

Emily gasped. She opened her window and yelled at the manager. "You've got to stop that man." Her voice was lost in the cacophony of sounds from sirens, shouting, and honking.

"Lady, I told you to move on. You're holding up traffic and endangering everyone's lives," said the volunteer who'd called on his radio for her earlier. "There's nothing you can do here."

There's a lot I can do, thought Emily as she pressed on the accelerator and headed out of the park. *And I will.*

CHAPTER 22

Naomi had helped the elderly couple living down the street load their clothes and boxes of keepsakes into their car, then headed toward Emily's. Her goodwill detour had taken more time than she originally thought it would, and she knew she'd better hurry.

Before she could enter the house, an SUV with the insignia of the city police pulled up in front.

The man in the driver's seat rolled down his window. "You Naomi?" he asked.

"Yes. Is there anything wrong?"

"Nothing except for this fire. Your mother was worried and told Detective Lewis to find you and get you out of here." He flashed his identification. "She was here but left."

"Why didn't she call me?"

"I guess she did, but you weren't home. And she couldn't get through on the cell. Detective Lewis said I should fetch you to the police station. She'll pick you up there."

"Okay, fine, but I need to go in and get some things."

"I think she got almost everything. Go ahead, but hurry. Soon they'll throw even us cops out of here."

He watched Naomi enter the house and smiled. With Quigley on ice until the lawyer got in from the coast, Toby was safe for a few hours at least. Time enough to finish business so he could collect what was due him. He chewed on his wad in contentment, occasionally spitting out the open window and leaving a dark stain on the cement.

The detective was right. Emily had cleared out the place. Most of Naomi's clothes were gone. She entered the bathroom. Her toothbrush was still in the holder. She grabbed it and headed for the door, but hesitated when she passed the guest room. She turned the knob and entered. Darren's backpack lay on the bed where he had left it when he went home with Clara.

She sat down beside it and thought about Darren's loss. The kid hadn't had a very happy life. I wonder if he wants this, she asked herself. She began to toss all the items strewn on the bed into it, but stopped when she found the birth certificate that had changed everything he thought was true about his father. She unfolded the official-looking paper and read it. Oh, my God, she said to herself. *This can't be. I have to show this to Mom right away.*

A figure in the doorway startled her. "You about ready?" asked the detective.

For a fat man, he surely was light on his feet. She hadn't heard him approach.

"Scare ya?"

"Yes. Uh, no."

"Whatcha got there?"

"Nothing. Stuff that belongs to a friend, that's all." Something about this man gave her the creeps, but she reminded herself he was Detective Lewis' partner and as much as Emily protested otherwise, Naomi knew her mother liked and trusted Lewis.

She crammed the birth certificate into the backpack and hoisted it onto her shoulder. It was surprisingly heavy. She wondered what other stuff Darren had hidden away in its pockets.

"Let's go then," she said, pushing past him, careful not to make contact. She wanted to get to Emily as soon as possible. "I'll call and let Emily know we're on our way." She reached for the kitchen phone.

"Best not to tie up the lines with other than emergency calls at this time," said Toby. Naomi hesitated, then nodded and headed out the door.

As they took their place in the line of cars exiting the park, Toby extracted his wadded-up handkerchief and swept it across his sweaty brow. He let out the breath he was holding in. She bought it, he said to himself. One step closer to his goal.

Emily pulled Stan into the Burnt Biscuit's parking lot, nearly empty of cars. She recognized the owner's Beemer at the bar room door. *Randolph's probably getting the accounts together before he leaves too.* She pulled into the sandy area across from the bar and left the car next to a huge oak tree. It couldn't be seen from the road, and she was certain the tree obscured Randolph's view also.

What she was doing was stupid, but she was certain the guy in the brown Mercedes at the gate was Naomi's husband. Emily needed to know whether he'd found Naomi somewhere in the park. She had no choice but to go and search. Getting there was the problem because it meant working her way through two miles of pasture and swamp and wading or swimming the canal that formed the back boundary of the park.

She dug through Fred's clothing and found his heaviest pair of pants, took off her clothes and put on Fred's jeans then threw on a long-sleeved flannel shirt. The advancing fire would be driving animals before it and Emily knew she had every chance of running into snakes, gators and other unhappy creatures fleeing the conflagration. She grabbed several pairs of Fred's socks, put them on and then shoved her feet into his high-top leather hiking boots. There. That would make it easier to trek through the palmetto scrub and harder for biting critters to get to her ankles and legs. If the back canal was deep enough to swim, she'd have to rethink her garb, but until then she felt somewhat protected.

She took several of Fred's work handkerchiefs and dunked them into the rain barrel at the side of the bar. It crossed her mind that she might come down with some kind of disease from the stagnant water, but she did her best Scarlet O'Hara and decided to think about that tomorrow. She tied a wet bandanna over her mouth, took the large flashlight she always carried in the glove box and set out across the fields toward her condo park.

The glow from the fire backlit the field, and she could make out movement in the long grass. To her left several coyotes fled along the fence line, then faded into the stand of oaks to the north. A snake slithered across her boot and moved quickly away from the fire. Soon the heat and smoke made walking more difficult. Despite her mouth covering, she coughed with each breath she took. Human figures moved in front of the flames, lighting the underbrush in an attempt to create an area where there would be no fuel for the advancing fire. She detoured north to avoid them and came to the canal running the length of the back of the park. It formed the tail end of a slough.

Luck's with me. Due to months of dry weather, the canal was only several feet deep. She waded through it, the mud at its bottom sucking at her boots. She looked around as she came up on the other side. It appeared that no one was left in the park, but the heat from the fire slowed her down. She could see only several feet in front of her, and the temperature was almost like sticking her head into an oven. Sweat ran in streams down her back and legs. She pushed on, thinking of what fate might await Naomi if her husband found her.

She sat down on a bench positioned in front of one of the bath houses, pulled off her clothing down to her underwear, and shucked the socks and boots from her feet. She left the clothes in a heap on the ground. She'd come back for them later. Now she could move. She ran up the deserted street to her house.

The door was locked just as she'd left it, but the house felt different somehow. She grabbed the key hidden under the sego palm next to the drive. It was her new hiding place, but not as benign as the plastic turtle. Fred would be proud she'd moved it. *Ouch, ouch.* The thorns on the damn palm stuck into her hands and arms. She congratulated herself on selecting such a good hiding place.

The living room, kitchen, bath and master bedroom looked the same as when she abandoned them earlier. *Wait. Had she left the door to the guest bedroom open?* She peeked in.

"Naomi?" No one answered. She began to walk back into the hall when she looked again at the bed. Darren's backpack was gone. *So Naomi was here, but had left.*

She looked through the large window facing the canal. The palm trees across the water were in flame and the wind generated by the fire was blowing burning limbs and fronds across the water. One flaming frond landed on Vicki and Carl's house. *There was nothing she could do about that now. She'd better hurry.* She turned on the faucet in the kitchen and wet her bandanna again, placing it over her mouth as she fled through her door and into the car port.

She locked up, but carried the key with her. Now the air was acrid with smoke so black and thick she could barely see Vicki's house.

And she certainly didn't see the man who grabbed her by the arm. "Donald," she said, once she calmed down enough to find her voice. "What are you doing here?

"Following you, of course. I was on my way out here to see if I could help when I saw your car pull into the Biscuit, so I wondered what you were up to."

"I was looking for Naomi. Her husband came into the park as I was leaving. I think she's been here, but I don't know if he took her."

"He didn't," said Green. "I saw him in his Mercedes heading back into town when I pulled into the Biscuit."

"You know about him? How?" asked Emily.

"She told me, and I've been keeping my eyes open. It's a long story, and I don't think we have time for it unless you intend for us to be the main course in a barbecue."

Emily coughed into her bandana and noticed Donald wore nothing over his nose. "Here. Take this." She handed him one of the cloths she'd wet back at the Biscuit.

"Thanks. We'd better get moving. The fire has encircled the east side and front of the park and is burning a path across the back canal. Soon we'll have no way to get out of here except to swim Nubbin Slough."

Emily shuddered. The slough was filled with alligators, most of whom liked to hunt at night. She recently read an article in the paper reporting that a young man lost his arm to a gator there when he took a 2 a.m. swim.

Emily looked at Donald and could tell he was thinking of the same incident.

"Well," she said, "State Wildlife and Fisheries killed over five gators to find the one with the kid's arm in his belly, so I guess we should look on the bright side."

"Which would be that the gators recently dined?"

"No, that there are fewer of them now."

"Let's move," said Donald. He grabbed her arm.

"Can we stop by the bath house down the road?"

"You can pee in the bushes. We don't have time."

"But I left my clothes there. Didn't you see me take them off?"

"This smoke is so thick, I can hardly see you now, and I'm holding your hand." He leaned in closer. "You only got on underwear and no shoes."

"Right." She prepared to follow him, but when she stepped outside the carport, she said, "Ugh. What's that?"

"What?"

"I stepped in a puddle of something wet and sticky. I hope it's not the carcass of some animal dead or dying because of the fire."

"Let me see that." Donald lifted up her foot while she clung to him for balance. "Nope, it's not a squished or partly burned anything." He held his finger near his nose. "It's chewing tobacco."

"Oh, God, it must be one of those old farts who's always chewing and spitting in the pool room. The woman who cleans the buildings here complains that someone misses the toilet, and she was to wipe it off the floor and the seat."

The image of the fat detective and his spit can the night she was arrested came to mind, but what would he be doing out here? There was no time to dwell on that now. She and Donald sped down the street dodging flying embers from the trees and grasses, but what she feared most met them at the end of the road. The fire had reached the back canal blocking their way out of the park. Emily grabbed her clothes and shoes, hurriedly put them on, and she and Donald ran for the slough.

⚜

Naomi rode in silence, wishing Toby would drive faster. She wasn't certain why Darren and Clara hadn't been truthful about the name on the birth certificate, but she knew the lie was somehow involved in the murders. She dug around in the backpack and extracted the paper to read it once again.

"You look worried about something," said Toby. "Maybe I can help."

"I don't think so." She tucked the certificate back into the pack. "What's the paper you got there?"

"Nothing." She glanced at him out of the corner of her eye. A thin trickle of brown liquid ran from the corner of his mouth. The car smelled of sweat and the sour smell of wet tobacco. Suddenly Naomi wanted to be out of here.

"Could we stop at the gas station up ahead? I've got to use the bathroom, and I don't think I can make it into town."

Toby nodded, turned on his blinker and pulled off. He checked his rearview mirror and spotted a Mercedes several cars behind him. It drove on by, then pulled off and parked on the other side of an abandoned bait shop.

Several minutes passed as Toby waited for Naomi to come out of the bathroom. He didn't want to have to go in and get her if somehow she figured it out and locked herself in.

Someone tapped Toby on the shoulder. Toby turned and recognized the man.

"We can make the switch here. It's probably better than closer to town where someone might see us."

"You got the money on you?"

"I got two hundred. Your work is sloppy. You promised me you'd get her this afternoon. I had to go running around the park looking for her and for you tonight."

"Two hundred! You promised me five hundred over the two hundred you already gave me. No deal."

"You're a dirty cop, Toby. I can make it hard for you." He held out the two hundred.

Toby considered his options. All his so-called part-time jobs were in jeopardy. He'd just as soon get some money than none. He grabbed the money. "Okay. Here she comes."

Naomi opened the door of the SUV, placed her backpack on the floor, and put her foot into the vehicle. The man who gave Toby the money appeared behind her. He gripped her arm and pulled her back out of the car.

Toby grabbed the backpack, extracted the paper, and scanned it. One eyebrow lifted with a look of interest.

"Well, well. This might be of some use to me." He tucked the paper in his pocket and threw the pack at Naomi.

Naomi grabbed it and whirled on the man who held her in his grip. "Get your hands off me," she said.

"Don't let's make a scene now, hear, or it'll be harder on you when I get you home." Her husband, Barry, tightened his grip on her arm and pulled her along with him as he strode toward his car.

She slapped his chest with her free arm and kicked at his legs, but her struggles were as ineffective as a cattle egret in a gator's mouth.

"I hate you. I hate you. Let me go or I'll..."

"What will you do? Call the cops? That's funny."

Toby watched the two of them from the police cruiser, saw the ugly smile on the husband's face and witnessed the young woman's desperate look of resignation. Her body went limp, and she ceased struggling, gasping for breath, tears running down her face. The big man gave her a shake and she quieted. It reminded Toby of a macabre dance, the complicated steps memorized long ago.

Toby jumped out of the SUV. "I want the rest of my money."

Her husband straightened his tie. "I don't think so. Maybe you'd like to join the little lady here in calling the authorities." A sound rumbled up from his throat, a scoffing laugh that increased in intensity until it shook his sandy curls and spittle flew from his open mouth. He yanked again at Naomi's arm. There was no way Toby wanted to make trouble for this giant. He'd take what he had and like it.

Toby watched the two of them round the corner of the building and heard the Mercedes start up. He should have been furious at losing the rest of the money, but he patted the paper in his breast pocket and thought of how he could triple the amount if he got to the right people. And Toby knew the right people.

CHAPTER 23

The glow from the fire behind them lit up the slough with dozens of glowing red balls—gator eyes. Emily hoped they weren't in the mood for hunting tonight. The fire could have riled them enough that they were off their feed. On the other hand, she worried they were so agitated that any ripple on the surface of the water would be seen as an intrusion into their territory, and the attack would be particularly vicious.

Donald and Emily exchanged wary looks.

"Roast here and be grabbed well-done by the gators or wade in and let them have us rare. What's your pleasure?" asked Donald.

"Neither. There's got to be some way around this." The roaring of the fire blasted in their ears, and the heat intensified.

Emily began to walk along the bank, parallel to the slough and the fire behind them.

"If we head this way far enough, we should come to the railroad bed. The tracks cross the slough somewhere and that means there must be a bridge."

"That's an abandoned line, and the bridge probably fell down years ago," said Donald.

"It's worth a try," she said. *And it put off making the awful choice of how to die for a few more minutes.*

They hurried along the slough, careful to keep well away from the water in case any reptiles large or small waited for prey to come rushing out of the fire.

"Look," said Emily. She pointed ahead where the supports for the railroad bridge rose before them like huge black towers guarding the entrance to a forbidden country. She ran toward them.

But there was nothing between the structures.

"You were right. The bridge is gone." Emily threw herself onto the ground at the foot of one of the trusses.

Donald scanned the area. "There aren't even any timbers around we could use as floats to get us across." He sat down beside her and pulled her into him. She leaned her head against his shoulder.

So this is the end, she thought. She'd envisioned it differently, quiet, dignified, in her own bed with those she loved near her side. And she'd be a lot older. Some kind of speech should mark the moment. She glanced up at Donald.

"You're a great bartender," she said, "and you've been a good friend. I'm sorry I've been so suspicious of you."

He looked down at her. His nose almost touched her hair. "And?"

"Oh, and you're the world's greatest bass fisherman, too."

"You are a real pain in the ass, Emily Rhodes," said Donald. He reached out and took her chin in her hand, turned her face toward his, and...

"You folks need a ride or do you think it's romantic sitting at the edge of gator-infested water with flames licking at your toes?"

Emily and Donald both jumped to their feet. Emily shone her flashlight on the water. Ahead of them, only five feet from shore, a figure stood on a flat boat, pole in hand. Several dozen pairs of eyes disappeared below the water's surface at the sound of his voice.

A large smile came slowly to Donald's face. "Well, I'll be. Merle Melnick. What're you doing out here?"

"Checking my goats. One of the kids ran off and his mommy was having a fit." They heard a bleat from the boat and could make out the form of a small animal standing in the bow.

"Not worried about the fire?" asked Donald.

"I'm on the water. But you two are about to become smores unless you climb aboard now."

They didn't need a second invitation.

❦

"You used that fat detective to help find me, right?" asked Naomi. She had moved into the corner of the passenger's seat as far from him as she could get, Darren's backpack on the seat near her hip.

"A comp between professionals," he said.

"Professionals? More like thugs. Aren't you afraid he might rat you out? You didn't pay him what you said you would."

She couldn't see the expression on his face in the darkness, but the tone of his voice told her that he was pleased and not worried. "Toby's got his own trouble."

"Like what?" She wanted to keep him talking until she could find an opportunity to make her move.

"Toby's been a bad boy for a long time. I got wind of an operation through the state attorney general's office and Toby's involved in it."

"That slug?"

"Oh, he's not one of the players, but he's been running errands for some of them." He slammed on his brakes. There was a roadblock ahead. "Damn. The highway's closed to the coast."

"I know another way."

"Oh, like I'd let you lead me out of here. I'm not stupid."

"I'm not either." She dropped her shoulders in a gesture of resignation and reached out and tapped his arm, although her entire body shuddered with disgust at the feel of his skin under her finger. "I can't run anymore. I'm willing to come home and be a wife to you if you'll control your temper and stop the hitting. Will you?"

In the light from the vehicles blocking the highway, Barry turned and looked into her eyes. "Can I trust you've learned your lesson?"

Naomi lowered her head and nodded numbly.

"Things will be different," he said. Not a promise, but a statement of what was to come.

A chill ran up her spine. This time his tone carried no note of regret for what he'd done to her. Instead she heard only threat there, and she knew he'd never let her run off again.

"Great, Babe. Let's find us a cozy little hotel where we can hole up for a few hours." He reached out and stroked her arm.

She wanted to draw back, but she knew better and kept herself very still, then looked up at him with a half-smile on her lips. She saw his shoulders relax. He checked his outside rearview mirror to make his U-turn back into town.

With his attention diverted from her to his driving, Naomi reached her hand into the backpack, extracted Darren's revolver and pointed it at him.

"What the hell?" He almost drove off the road.

"Now get out of the truck, or I'll shoot you." She cocked the revolver.

"Don't be ridiculous. You hate guns. You won't shoot me." He reached across the seat for her.

She fired. At this range she couldn't miss.

"You shot me." There was surprise in his voice and a stupid grin on his face. Barry grabbed his arm where the bullet had entered. Blood seeped through his jacket.

She was furious at him for making her shoot and appalled she had the gumption to do so. "I'll do it again if you don't get out of the car."

"And you won't get away with it."

The men on the roadblock had heard the shot and dodged behind their cars. Naomi saw one lean into his car, and she knew he was radioing for help. Or reaching for a weapon, she thought.

"Get out, Barry. This is your last warning." She cocked the revolver again. Barry hit the door handle and rolled out of the car onto the pavement.

She slid across the seat, hit the accelerator and fishtailed in reverse, narrowly missing the truck behind her. She cranked the wheel to the left and hit the brake. The car flipped around, its hood pointed back toward town. She shifted into drive and sped off.

She knew they'd pick her up, but with the authorities tied up with the fire, she figured she'd have enough time to find Emily. She settled back in the seat, surprised at how calm she'd been. She let the feel of the powerful engine take her down the road for several miles. Hmm, she thought, practice at the driving range paid off. She glanced at the gun on the seat beside her. Then she got the shakes.

When she hit the city limits sign, she saw a police cruiser up ahead parked across the road nose-to-nose with an SUV. *Could they be responding this quickly?* She had to find her mother and let her know about Toby having Darren's birth certificate. *He seemed so interested in it, and that can't be good.*

She jerked the wheel to the left, shut off her lights and turned into an abandoned strip mall. She cruised behind the building and spotted a dirt lane leading off toward a residential area, the one she was heading for. Unfortunately, a chain was strung across her exit. *Oh what the hell. The car isn't mine.* She stomped on the accelerator and gunned it through the cable, which snapped like a piece of uncooked spaghetti.

She abandoned the car on a side street and hoofed it to Clara's. When she swung open the front door, everyone looked up from the kitchen table.

"Just in time for a late dinner," she said, taking the chair at the end of the table. "Pass the spuds. I'm starved."

Emily jumped up from the table and enveloped her in a hug that seemed to go on forever, and, even though her mother smelled like a charbroiled hot dog, she didn't want her to let go. She outlined the events of her evening while she shoveled food into her mouth. She actually was starved. Shooting abusive husbands was hard work.

Emily held Naomi's hand. She couldn't seem to find her tongue. She was numb, scared for her daughter, tired. She felt defeated, but relieved. She was overjoyed. Naomi was here. And safe.

Finally, Clara spoke. "We looked everywhere for you. Emily was convinced someone had taken you, probably your husband. She sent Donald to talk with Detective Lewis. I practically had to tie Emily to the chair and force her to eat something."

"I guess I'll be needing your services, Hap, when they come to arrest me," Naomi said.

Someone knocked on the door. "Sooner than I expected," said Hap.

Clara opened the door to Detective Lewis followed by Donald Green. "If you've come to arrest her, can't you let her finish eating?"

"That can wait," said Lewis. "Donald told us a very interesting story at the station. He said he thought Toby had been at your house, Emily, and that he may have picked up Naomi. That true?"

Naomi replied before Emily could explain. "Yes, he picked me up all right. Then he delivered me into the hands of my abusive husband. Barry promised him money to do it."

"I watched Toby hang around the house earlier in the day and we," here Donald nodded toward Emily, "found evidence he'd been there later when everyone was leaving because of the fire."

"We did? What evidence?" asked Emily.

"The stuff you stepped into in the driveway. Chawed tobacco and spit."

She looked down at her foot as if she were considering ordering a new one from Sears.

"Toby's not at the station even though he's supposed to be on duty. We all are because of this fire," said Lewis.

"It seems a lot less smoky out there," said Clara. She held open the door and blocked the men's entry with her body.

"It is. The wind has kicked up and it's blowing from the west. I think it's under control for now, unless the wind shifts again," said Donald.

The men were still standing in the doorway with their hats in their hands.

"You might as well step in here. I've got some coffee on if you'd like some. And there's pie, too."

"I didn't know you baked, Clara," said Lewis.

"I don't. I bought it at Publix."

"Everybody knows everyone, I gather," said Clara. Emily knew Clara wasn't happy to see the detective, but she appeared committed to being civil.

"Aside from talking to you once on the shooting range, you've been difficult to find," said Lewis to Darren.

"He's got nothing to say to you," said Clara.

Emily thought the look on her face signaled her intent to renege on the pie offer. After the evening she'd had avoiding becoming a char-grilled entrée and knowing she had a court date tomorrow certain to leave her homeless, she was bone tired and pissed off at almost everyone.

"Oh, cut the crap, Clara," she said. So she was being nasty and insensitive. "Darren's a big boy now, and he owes the police the truth about that night at the country club. Come to think of it, I think he owes us the truth about what he saw there too."

"How dare you?" said Clara.

"Oh, stuff it. If Naomi can take a shot at her hubby to defend herself, don't you think Darren can tell the police what he was doing at the country club the night of Davey's murder?"

Emily and Clara stood toe-to-toe with each other, a stand-off between a red-headed pit bull and a blonde Chihuahua.

"Stop it, you two," said Darren. "Let's everybody sit down. Emily's right. I need to let the police know what was going on that night, and now is as good a time as any."

Emily wasn't so sure about that. A minute ago her insistence that Darren talk with the police seemed like a good idea. Now all she ached for was a final night's rest in her king-sized bed before the court wrested it from her. That along with a long soak in her tub and some "tough stuff" cleaning solution and a bucket of bleach to remove the chewing tobacco from her foot seemed a perfect ending to a troubled evening. But she'd started this ball rolling and she'd have to see it to the end.

Everybody sat down, Emily and Clara on opposite sides of the room. Clara continued to glare at her. Emily shut her eyes and hoped she wouldn't fall asleep. *This had better be a good story.*

"It's really simple," said Darren. "I was following Dad." He paused. "I mean I was following Eddie. He'd blown me off since he got out of prison this last time. I wanted us to get together, but he was always too busy. I thought something was up with him. Every time we talked he was jittery, chain smoking and drinking too much. When I mentioned it to him, he said he had a lot on his mind, a big job coming up. I didn't believe him, so I borrowed a car from one of my friends and took to following him."

Emily wiggled on the couch, opened her eyes and looked at Clara. Clara was no longer glaring at her, but had her head down. Emily couldn't tell what she was thinking or feeling.

"Eddie stopped by here, ran into the house through the back door, but only stayed for a few minutes. He came back out, drove out to the casino and pulled into the parking lot toward the back. Some guy was waiting for him there. It was too dark for me to get a good look at him. They headed back down the highway and took one of the roads leading to the country club, where they pulled around behind the clubhouse. It was late and most of the cars were gone. Except for the new bartender's." He looked at Emily who gave him a wan smile and suppressed a yawn.

"I left my car in the lot out front and slipped around the building, keeping to the shadows, but they'd walked down the path to the driving range. I heard a shot and knew I'd better get out of there. I rushed back to my car, but I was worried about Eddie, so I drove my car around behind the equipment shed and ran back to the clubhouse." Darren stopped and his eyes seemed to plead with his mother for permission to go on with his story.

"You can come down to the station and finish your statement there if you prefer, you know," said Lewis.

Emily's eyes popped open. "No, he can't. I've been waiting for too long to hear this. Get on with it. I'm tired, and I want to go home."

"She's a little distraught from outrunning the fire tonight," said Donald.

"And the gators, and the snakes, don't forget about them." Emily knew she was getting hysterical, but she didn't care. She pounded a fist on the couch. "And he tried to kiss me." She pointed at Donald who had the decency to look embarrassed. Lewis glowered and let forth a low growl.

"There, there," said Hap. He patted her hand.

Emily gathered herself together. "I'm fine now. Go ahead." She smiled one of her kindergarten teacher smiles meant for small children and parents of unruly youngsters.

Darren continued. "When I got back to the clubhouse, I heard the sound of the dumpster lid open and then close with a bang. I recognized Eddie's voice. He said, 'I thought you said we were just going to have a talk with him. You shot him.' I heard the other man say, 'He didn't want to talk. I thought he was going to pull a gun on me.'

"Dad said, 'He was drunk, and he wasn't packing.' I thought he said something else, but I couldn't hear what. Dad sounded upset. They got into the truck and left. And that's about it." Darren looked scared but relieved to get the story off his chest.

"But you called Clara from my cell phone, and I left it in the bar. How did you get in?" Emily said.

"If you're going to tell the story, tell all of it," said Clara. "You hid there until Emily came out and discovered the body."

"I went through the front door. It was unlocked. I picked up your phone from off the bar and made the call. Mom said to get the hell out of there. And I did."

"I left the damn front door open. Of course. What a dummy," said Emily. "But how did my cell and keys end up outside?"

"I didn't hear you drive off. I knew the back door was locked, so I knew you couldn't get to your keys. I didn't want anyone to see me, but I tossed the keys and cell out there. I thought you'd find them. I wasn't really thinking very clearly."

"Did you hear anything else?" asked Lewis.

"Nothing," said Darren.

"How did they leave the club, the same way they came in?"

"No, they drove out the front entrance." Darren hit his forehead with the palm of his hand. "Oh, shit, am I dumb. They saw the car parked by the shed."

The detective scratched his chin. "And someone got to wondering about the car later and figured out it didn't belong to Emily. Someone did some clever detective work, connecting the plates to your friend's car and then to you."

CHAPTER 24

"Toby," Lewis said. "Toby tracked down those plates."

"Toby's the killer," said Emily.

"Toby's a gofer," Lewis replied. "I'm not convinced he was the man with Eddie at the country club that night, but it's pretty clear Eddie stopped here to get your gun, Clara, and, for some reason, he gave it to the other man who shot Davey."

"And then someone beat up Darren, hoping they could scare him into keeping silent about that night. Right, Darren?" asked Emily.

Lewis stepped in front of her. "I think I'm supposed to ask the questions here."

"Fine, go ahead, but be quick about it. I want to hear the end of this story, but I've got only a few more minutes of being awake in me." Emily sunk into the couch, then pulled herself back up, knowing she'd fall asleep in seconds if she relaxed.

"I can't help you, Detective Lewis," said Darren. "All I know is I was taking a break out back at work. Someone came up behind me, put a gun in my back, and told me to keep my mouth shut. 'And you know what about,' the guy said. Then he shoved me from behind, and I fell onto the gravel parking lot. I never got a look at him." Darren pulled his mother to him.

Clara put her arm around her son, her head on his shoulder. Whatever animosity there had been between mother and son had disappeared. Emily still had a few questions for Clara, but thought better of asking them tonight. That could wait until another time when the two were on better footing as friends.

But before Emily could leave, Clara grabbed her arm. "In case the judge tomorrow takes a while delivering his verdict, I'll cover for you at the bar."

"Thanks. We'll talk then."

Detective Lewis told Darren to stop by headquarters the next morning to dictate a formal statement about the murder.

"I've got some more questions for you about the guy who beat you up, too," said Lewis.

"He thinks it was Toby," said Emily. Lewis shot her a look that said he wished she'd stop butting in on his case. She grinned back at him.

Before they could leave, Lewis stopped Naomi and Emily. "I'll need Darren's gun," he said to Naomi. "I'll also need you to come into the station tomorrow to give your side of the shooting. Your husband's in the hospital, but he's not saying much."

"I think I dropped it on the floor of Barry's car after I shot him. I really can't remember because I drove out of there like the devil was after me."

"We'll search the car for it."

Emily poked her daughter in the ribs, knowing she was lying about the gun.

"Toby's still out there," Naomi said low enough that only Emily heard her.

She hadn't wanted to believe him, but Hap was right. Rural Florida was still the Wild West.

"Eventually, he's going to claim you tried to kill him, you know," said Lewis.

"I don't think so, too much male ego involved for him to admit his wife shot him," said Naomi. There was a knowing smile on her face. But it was quickly replaced by a look filled with despair. "It was self-preservation. He had that slimy detective kidnap me and then he was going to have at me. Like he did so many times before. I'll never get away from him."

"Did you try to kill him?" asked Lewis.

Naomi stuck her chin out and looked Lewis in the eye. "I hit him where I aimed," she said.

"Good shot," Lewis said.

"I lied. I aimed for the other arm." She shrugged.

Lewis winked and patted her shoulder. "We'll sort this one out tomorrow then."

"Okay, kids. Enough of this shooting talk. God, I hate guns." Emily shook her head and poked her tongue out of her mouth in disgust. "I've got a court date in…," she checked her watch, "in less than eight hours and I'd like to go home for some rest and a shower. I can get back into the park, can't I?"

"I understand everything is operational. It may not smell so pretty around there, but no homes were damaged by the flames. It came close, but the fire is out for several miles beyond the area," said Lewis.

When Donald offered to follow them home, she turned him down.

Lewis, not to be outdone by Donald's offer, said, "Or you might want a police presence when you enter the house."

"We'll be fine," she said.

"Well, if you don't want a ride, I think I'll mosey on over to the hospital. See how things are going there," said Donald.

Lewis hesitated for only a minute. "I'll go with you. I assigned an officer to guard Barry's room, and he's due for a break soon. I'll spell him while you deliver our greetings to Barry."

⁂

"You're awfully quiet," Emily said to Naomi in the car.

"I'm beat. Aren't you?"

"Yes."

"But you've got something on your mind, don't you?"

"Okay, I do, but if I tell you, I want the truth from you. What do you know about Darren's father?" Emily glanced across the seat at her daughter.

Naomi looked surprised at the astuteness behind her mother's question. She tried to convert her expression into one of naiveté. "I don't...."

"Honey," said Emily, "I'm too tired and too old for games."

"I found his birth certificate in the backpack he left in the guest room. I took it with me when Toby picked me up."

"And?"

"It said that his father was someone named Morton Davey."

Emily wasn't surprised at the name. She'd guessed the truth about Darren's birth because of the picture of his father she'd found in Clara's bedroom. She understood Clara's insistence Darren not be connected to the Davey family. Emily had no difficulty believing Marcus murdered his brother and might be capable of removing a nephew who stood to inherit part of the ranch. Now, Marcus was dead. That changed things.

Naomi squirmed around in her seat and interrupted Emily's thinking. "Clara lied about Darren's father and then she lied again to cover up the first lie. I guess I don't understand, but Detective Toby sure seemed to."

"What do you mean?"

"He snatched that birth certificate like it was the winning lottery ticket."

Emily's mouth opened in shock. Lewis' words about Toby being a gofer came back to her. She twisted the steering wheel abruptly to the right. With tires spitting gravel, she pulled into a driveway, made a U- turn, and headed back into town.

Naomi grabbed the handle above the passenger's window and held on. "What are you doing?"

"I think Toby just signed Darren and Clara's death warrants. Got your cell with you?'

"No. Toby took it from me in the car. What about yours?"

"Mine needs to be recharged. Damn." She pounded on the steering wheel and pushed harder on the gas. "Tell me what we're doing."

"We've got to get back to Clara's house. I think Toby's there with his bosses. They're planning to tie up final loose ends."

Emily blew through the stop signal and skidded into a right turn at the next corner. The streets were empty.

"Here's what we're going to do," she said. She applied the brakes and hopped the curb at the Home Depot store, speeding through their parking area and exiting behind the garden shop. "I'm going to drop you at the police station. It's ahead. You run in and get some cops over to Clara's house."

"Why? What do I tell them?"

"Tell them one of their detectives is in danger. That he's being held at gun point."

"Is that true?"

"No, of course not, but it'll get their attention, more so than taking the time to explain everything."

"What're you going to do?"

"I've got to get to Clara's to make certain Toby and his friends don't leave until the cops come."

Naomi grabbed the door handle as they careened around a corner. "How are you going to do that?"

"I'm working on a plan." Emily skidded to a stop in front of the station. "Now go on."

"I think I should stay with you."

She reached across and opened the door, shoving her daughter in the direction of the building.

"Ouch. Stop it. I haven't unbuckled my seat belt." Naomi clicked the button and slid out. She then reached back into the car, extracted something from the backpack she still carried and hadn't returned to Darren and threw it on the seat. "You might need this." She slammed the door and ran up the steps.

Emily punched the accelerator and glanced at the object lying on the seat beside her. Darren's revolver. It looked huge to her in the dim illumination of passing streetlights. She wouldn't touch it. She'd outmaneuver them with a cunning plan—if she could come up with a cunning plan.

She cruised by Clara's house with her headlamps off. Only a crack of light showed through the closed drapes in the front window. Her hunch was correct. Toby's police SUV sat in the drive. She spotted another car two houses down when she turned the corner. She parked Stan behind the late model Lexus and ran through the back-yards of the houses separating her from Clara's. *Please let there be no dogs.*

The heavy night pressed down on her, the smell of burned wood and other vegetation still strong in the air, making her breathing difficult, slowing her pace when she needed to hurry. She worked her way around the house and peeked through the hibiscus bushes growing in front of the porch. She could hear the murmur of voices inside. She moved closer to the doorway and crouched below the level of the porch floor, well out of sight of her quarry but within hearing distance.

A quick peek through the screen door afforded her a sight she wanted to wipe out of her mind. Clara and Darren were trussed up like holiday gobblers ready for the oven.

"See, you don't understand. I don't do murder." She recognized Toby's voice.

"What do you call Eddie then? Didn't I see you drop him into the river?" The voice was a man's and one that Emily had heard before, but couldn't place.

"Yeah, but he was already dead. That was your doing, not mine. I seem to be cleaning up a lot of your messes," Toby said. "And I don't get your shenanigans popping him in Green's boat, then stealing it and parking it in that little gal's drive."

"Keep your voice down or you-know-who will get upset and start yelling." Emily had to lean in closer to catch the next words. "It was her idea to do in Marcus by using Eddie's wife's gun. She's plenty clever playing around with all the evidence, so don't start questioning her methods. She gets real touchy about that."

"So she sent you to do in Marcus. You didn't get twitchy and the gun go off?" asked Toby.

"Eddie was supposed to do the work, but when he found out what the real job was, he backed down, then wanted to go to the cops. So we had to get rid of him and scare the hell out of that kid, Darren, because he might have seen or heard something."

"And then you had me try to scare the hell out of his mother by shooting out the window at the club. That didn't work, and now I'm helping you tote bodies to the river. This better be the end. I'm real tired of running these errands. They get more and more messy."

The other man said something Emily couldn't hear, then Toby said in reply, "You're a real idiot, you know. You think you'll see any of the money? I, at least, get my pay ahead of time."

"Let me worry about that. Besides, you're in too deep now to back out. Tell you what. I'll help you carry these two to the SUV, and we'll follow you out to the lock by the marina. You can drop them into the water there and let the gators do their thing, or we'll shoot them first, then shove them into the lake. Think of it as feeding wildlife if it makes you feel better."

Whose voice was that?

In the darkened front yard Emily watched Toby and another man struggle to carry first Clara then Darren to the SUV, throw them in the back, and slam the rear door. She heard a low moan from one of them—she thought it might be Darren—and when she peered around the bushes she was certain she saw Clara move her feet. They were alive, for now, but she had little time left.

She'd lied to Naomi about a plan, but she'd better get one fast, or her friends would be going for their last swim ever. Her heart was pounding so fast and so hard it made it difficult to hear what her brain was thinking, if it was thinking at all.

A bubble began to make its way up her esophagus. *No! Not hiccups. Not now.* She swallowed hard and held her breath, then let it out slowly. She couldn't afford fear now. She had to act.

A woman appeared in the doorway as the men returned from the car. Emily looked up at a broad butt wrapped in coral and black striped pants, the stripes making the expanse quiver in the dim light like a hologram. It made her dizzy. Emily silently groaned to herself. That could only mean one thing.

"If I was you," said the voice above her, "I'd tie their legs together. The bitch kicked me."

Lucinda Davey.

"Already did that, honey," said the man.

Of course she'd be here. Lucinda was a hands-on kind of gal. All the pieces fell into place for Emily. Lucinda wanted her husband out of the way. So she and a lover could be together? Not likely. Lucinda was too selfish for that. More likely, knowing the kind of man Marcus was, Lucinda couldn't put up with him any longer. Emily could sympathize with not wanting the drunk around, but murder? Lucinda had gotten her way, that's for sure.

And the nerve of her, accusing me of Marcus' murder.

Emily shook with disgust at the woman, wanting to jump out of her hiding place and grab her by her long fake eyelashes. But she'd better stay hidden for now. She needed a plan, some plan, any plan to stop them.

Lucinda took a step forward and plopped her hands on her ample hips. "I kicked her back. Got her good, too."

Emily bit her lip to keep from growling out loud. Lucinda's gofers, Toby, Eddie and the other man did her work for her while she piously studied the scripture at her Bible study group. Clara was right. Everyone seemed to have underestimated Lucinda.

Emily caught a glimpse of her face when the widow stepped back into the house. Under all that curl and paint lurked someone as predatory as a gator, and single-minded in her pursuit of the Davey money.

When Toby brought the birth certificate to Lucinda—and Emily was certain that was what he did tonight—the stakes were higher. Darren could claim a part of the Davey estate, and Lucinda would have none of that. Lucinda was tying up loose ends tonight by getting rid of Darren and his mother. Emily felt like a fool, but weren't they all fools, thinking Lucinda was merely a dumb, overly made up bimbo from a strip club on the coast? That should have been a clue. If Lucinda made it from lap dancer to the wife of the most prominent rancher in the county, she certainly would have been able to engineer a life of wealth without an obnoxious drunk holding her back.

"Kick her again, honey. That'll show her," said the man.

"Don't patronize me, Lenny. I'd like to put a slug through her skull despite the noise it'll make. The bitch."

Ah, said Emily to herself, Lenny Sharples, the pro at the country club. Obviously he and Lucinda had made up. Toby and Lenny. Both wrapped around Lucinda's acrylic nailed finger. And Lenny's motive for doing Lucinda's bidding? He had gambling debts.

"No shooting around here, Ms. Davey," said Toby. "You can do what you want out at the lock where no one will hear." Toby drove off.

Emily was torn. Should she follow Toby or remain until Lucinda and Lenny left? Each thump of her heart felt like a second hand ticking off the time until Toby reached the lock. He might dump them into the lake without waiting for back-up.

Lucinda's next words brought her pounding heart to an abrupt stop. "Won't he be surprised when he ends up in the water with the two of them. Crazy Toby, the dirty cop whose career was dead-ended so he went on a killing spree, then, in a fit of despair drove his car into the lake with his latest victims in the back."

"Poor Toby. Couldn't catch a break." Lenny cackled with glee.

"Let's go. We don't want to be late for the feeding," said Lucinda.

"We've got plenty of time. It'll take Toby a while to get there and work up nerve enough to dump them. He'll probably wait for us to do the work for him. How about a little smooch?" Lenny moved closer to Lucinda.

Oh, Lenny. Do you have any idea what Lucinda has in her reptilian mind for you? Emily had heard enough. She dashed around the back of the house, ran to her car and rummaged around among the piles of clothing and other stuff she'd loaded into the back seat when she fled the fire. *It has to be here someplace.* Finally, her hand closed around the item for which she was searching. She slid it into her jacket pocket, started the car and pulled it around the corner into Clara's drive as Lenny and Lucinda ended their clinch. Their mouths dropped open in surprise.

Emily stuck her head out the driver's side window. "You'd better get a move on. The cops're coming. Hear the sirens?"

Lucinda stepped in front of the car. "You. Where'd you come from? Lenny, get rid of her."

But Lenny had heard the sirens. "We'd better get out of here. Now!"

"But our plans," Lucinda said.

"They're useless. Let's cut our losses and make a run for it." He opened the car door, grabbed Emily and tossed her out onto the lawn. "Get in," he ordered Lucinda.

"I'm not riding in that piece of junk."

"Your choice, baby, but I'm gone." Lenny shifted into reverse.

When Lucinda saw he was serious, she also jumped in. "Lenny, look what I found, a gun." She took Darren's revolver off the seat and pointed it at Emily. Emily picked herself up off the grass and looked down the wrong end of a gun barrel. *I should have come up with a better plan.*

Lucinda put her finger on the trigger and pulled. Nothing happened.

"You don't think I'd carry a loaded gun around in my car, do you?" said Emily. A lie, but she wasn't about to give Lucinda a lesson in the need to cock the weapon before pulling the trigger.

Lucinda shook the gun as if she could make it work by punishing it. "Get this sorry excuse for a car going," she said to Lenny.

"It's temperamental. It's in gear, but nothing's happening." Lenny moved the gear shift lever back and forth between drive and reverse and stomped on the accelerator, but Stan refused to budge.

"Stan hates it when you tromp on him that way." Emily wasn't happy with Lenny's treatment of her car, but she heard the sirens getting louder, nearer.

"What? It's a piece of scrap metal," said Lenny. He mashed the pedal once more.

"That's no way to talk to Stan," said Emily. *No one abused Stan the Sedan and got away with it.* She put her hand in her pocket and extracted the Walther PPK. She looked down at the weapon and shook her head, then brought it up and aimed at the driver's side window of the car. "Quit that or I'll shoot."

"Watch out. She's got a weapon," said Lucinda, but her warning ended in a laugh. "It's probably not loaded either."

Lenny banged on the dash and slammed his foot up and down on the gas pedal. "That's a chance I can't take. She's pointing it at me." He ducked his head below the window a split second before Emily fired.

The first shot missed Lenny, but flew past Lucinda and blew the glass out of the passenger side window.

Emily took careful aim again, reminding herself this time to keep her eyes open. The shot flew over Lenny's head but tore a pathway through Lucinda's big hair leaving behind a part, as if a tiny lawnmower had cut a swath through tall grass.

"She shot me," yelled Lucinda.

Suddenly, the car lurched backward for several feet then died at the end of the driveway. Emily silently apologized to Stan and shot out the left front tire. It took her only five shots to accomplish this but Stan wasn't going to move now.

A police car drove up and an officer and Lewis jumped out.

"Toby took Clara and Darren to the lock to dump them in the lake," Emily said. "He left about five minutes ago. You've got to save them."

The officer dragged Lenny out of the car and cuffed him while Lewis approached Emily. "Toby took a short cut to the police station and turned himself in."

"See, Lenny. I told you he didn't have the guts to go through with it," said Lucinda. She jumped out of the car and started a gallop across the lawn.

"You can put down the gun, Emily," Lewis said.

"Sure," she said. She handed the gun to Lewis. "Hold this, will you?" She streaked across the lawn and tackled Lucinda who was having difficulty running because her stiletto heels dug into the soft grass. Lucinda threw her off and got up.

"You lied to me. You said the gun wasn't loaded."

"I said the gun you picked up wasn't loaded. I admit I lied about that, but I never said a word about the one I was holding." She punched Lucinda on her nose. "That's for the times you attacked me, but especially for calling my friend a bitch and trying to kill her and her son."

Lucinda held her hand to her face as blood poured out of her nose.

"Lewis," said Emily.

"Yep," he replied.

"Hand me my gun, would you? I haven't finished firing, and according to Mr. Pucket, I should discharge the weapon until I know it's empty."

"That's on the shooting range."

"Can't I shoot at them again? I missed the couple of times."

Lewis looked at her. It was difficult in this light to tell if she was serious or not. She might have been, or she could have been holding back a good cry.

"Keep her away from me. She's nuts," said Lucinda. Another officer cuffed her and put her into the cruiser beside Lenny. "Look at my hair. And my scalp is burning. And my nose, my perfect nose is ruined. It cost me thousands to get it this way."

Emily looked up at Lewis who held the Walther PPK out of reach. "I think she overpaid her plastic surgeon. Can I have my gun, I mean Clara's gun back now?" she asked.

"No. Now..."

"I know. Now I have to come down to the station and provide you with a full statement and then you'll book me for discharging a weapon within the city limits."

"No, now you go home and get some sleep before court tomorrow."

Emily put her hand to her head. After the adrenaline rush of the shooting, the yelling and the punching, how could she feel any more exhausted? But she was wrong. The reminder of her appointment before the judge tomorrow made her wish she was a turtle who could sink to the bottom of the river and not come up for air for a very long time. "I almost forgot."

Another police cruiser pulled up, and Naomi jumped out.

"You okay, Mom? What happened here?" Naomi recognized the gun in Lewis' hand. "You didn't, uh, you didn't kill someone, did you?"

Emily looked at poor Stan sitting at the end of Clara's drive, his window shot out, one tire mangled, rim on the concrete. She wondered if she'd made a mistake bringing Stan into all of this.

"He wouldn't let me," she said and gestured toward Lewis. "I guess this was the night for the Rhodes women to be packing heat thanks to Clara and son." Emily and Naomi smiled at one another. Emily leaned over and pulled Naomi to her in a hug.

"Get out of your car what you'll need for a few days. I'll call to have it towed to a garage and give you both a ride back to the park." Lewis opened the passenger side door of his cruiser for Emily. "And about booking you for discharging your weapon within city limits? It's not gonna happen."

Finally something tonight was going right. "No?" The corners of her mouth turned up in hopeful grin.

"No. It's a five-hundred-dollar fine," Lewis said, turning away so she couldn't see the expression on his face.

Was he smiling, she wondered? And if so, was it because he finally got the goods on her or was he joking about the fine? She never knew Lewis to joke about anything.

CHAPTER 25

Nine o'clock came too soon for Emily. She felt as if she had just laid her head down on the pillow when her alarm rang.

Oh God, I can't face this. She slammed her hand down on the clock alarm's off button, then rolled her aching body out of bed and stood under a hot shower washing away yesterday's grime, smoke, fear and fatigue. What she couldn't soap away was the feeling that this morning would be no better than yesterday, although she was pretty proud of herself for hitting Lucinda. *The broad had it coming.*

Hap met her and Naomi on the steps of the courthouse. "Now don't expect too much," he said. As they entered the building, she wondered if having no expectations at all was too much.

As she and Hap sat down, she caught sight of Lewis, Clara, Darren and Donald taking seats at the back of the room. Vicki entered, and when she couldn't find a vacant chair, Donald offered his. *Maybe I've got little money and no home, but I've got my friends here to support me. Maybe that's enough.* Then she thought about Stan. *My poor car. I'm partly responsible for the damage, and there's no money to pay for repairs.*

Carolyn and her lawyer entered only seconds before the judge appeared. Carolyn raised her hands and smoothed back her luxuriant long black tresses much as a cat might preen itself by rubbing a paw over whiskers and ears. Emily decided she wasn't being fair, comparing Carolyn to an innocent cat. She was more like an alligator throwing his prey over his snout. *Yeah, that's it.*

The judge took the bench and banged his gavel several times, unnecessary theatrics from Emily's perspective since everyone in the courtroom was already silent and awaiting his judgment.

"This is a unique case," he said, "and while I might be tempted by the unusual circumstances of the grieving partner to grant her the entire estate of her lover," he coughed when he used the word 'lover,' especially given the wealth of the ex-wife, I must obey the law." Emily groaned silently.

Hap picked up on her despair. He reached for her hand.

The judge continued. "The estate goes to the former Mrs. Costa as stipulated in the will, but the house will go to Ms. Rhodes. There is sufficient evidence," he held up papers provided by Emily, "to support her contention that she shared in purchasing the property." He looked down at Emily from the bench. "You must, of course, continue to make the monthly mortgage payments."

"Well, I'll be darned," said Hap. "The old cur-mudgeon does have a heart. It's less than we wanted, my girl, but far more than he's ever given in such cases before."

Carolyn's mouth dropped open, and she jumped to her feet while her lawyer attempted to pull her back down.

"Your honor, that's ridiculous. I should get everything, including the house."

The judge banged his gavel. "Get your client under control. I expected you might react that way, so I've added a stipulation. If you contest this ruling, you will be required to pay all legal fees out of your ex-husband's estate. And let me tell you, there's not a lot of money there for you and your attorney to split."

Attorney Brookfield whispered in her ear while he held her arm to prevent her from rising. She shook off his hand. "But it's all mine. The will says so."

"If you want to go for all of it, you may end up with nothing," said the judge. Brookfield shook his head in agreement.

"A wise decision then," said Judge Miller. The bailiff approached the bench and whispered to the judge who looked surprised for a moment, then nodded his head. The doors of the court-room opened to let in several men wearing blue jackets with "Alcohol, Tobacco and Firearms" emblazoned in yellow letters across the back. They approached Brookfield.

"You're under arrest for trafficking in illegal drugs." They slapped cuffs on the astonished lawyer and led him from the courtroom. On his way through the doors, he struggled with the officers and glanced wildly around the room.

"Call my attorney, Ignatius Palatier." He said.

The larger of the two agents said, "I'm sorry, sir, but if you want to retain him as your legal representative, you'll have to meet with him at the jail. We'll see that the two of you share lock-up until bail is determined."

❖

"What was that all about?" asked Emily. She, Hap and all her friends gathered in front of the courthouse.

Detective Lewis strode down the steps and approached the group, overhearing her question. "The Feds have been investigating grow houses in this area for several months, trying to get at the people behind the operation. Mr. Brookfield's name came up when the Feds convinced Palatier to wear a wire in exchange for a reduction in sentence for the part he played in the operation."

Hap chuckled. "I'll bet like everything Ignatius did, his involvement was small potatoes, right, but the thought of spending even a day behind bars must have terrified him."

"Right. With so many houses in foreclosure, Brookfield purchased them for very little money, not in his own name, of course, and set them up as grow houses. Very lucrative. Very illegal. The man has an ego the size of Texas." Lewis smiled. It was the first time since they'd had coffee together that Emily had seen a real look of pleasure on his face. She was happy for him. She touched his sleeve and smiled up into his face, then blushed at her behavior. Lewis returned her look and his face reddened also.

He cleared his throat and continued. "But there was an unexpected outcome of Ignatius' cooperation. The Feds picked up Ignatius paying Toby to do dirty work for your trial, Emily, hiring Toby to dig up anything that could be used to impugn your character, even coffee with me. Brookfield leaned on Palatier to find someone to do the work, and Toby was willing. We used that information to get Toby talking about the money given to Weston Quigley to lie about you and Marcus. And about Toby's other off-the-books work."

"Did Carolyn know anything about this?" asked Emily.

"No," said Lewis.

"It appears she has lousy instincts when it comes to hiring lawyers," said Hap.

"Toby's going to be one of our best witnesses when Lucinda and Lenny come to trial for Marcus' murder. They've been pointing fingers at one another. Without Toby's testimony along with Lenny's, Lucinda might walk." Lewis chuckled. "At least she's stopped talking about suing you for assault and battery, Emily."

"And even if she did, I'd hit her all over again. She hated Marcus, didn't she?"

"I don't think she thought much about him. Marrying him gave her the ranch, which she was managing while he drank himself across the county. She considered it more expeditious to do her work with him out of the way," Lewis said.

"The woman was cold. She probably had to thermo-regulate for hours before she had enough energy to put on her make-up," said Clara.

"What do you mean?" asked Naomi.

"Like an alligator sitting in the sun so he can warm up enough to move," said Emily. "She felt right at home in these swamps."

She turned to Clara. "So, is my job at the golf course secure? I've got to remortgage the house so I can afford the monthly payments. Oh, and I almost forgot, I'll have to get Stan back on his feet. I think he needs a new shoe, er, tire."

"You may be hired as manager for the restaurant and bar. I'm going to be busy working out the legal intricacies of securing Darren's father's estate. It's safe now to declare him legally the only Davey descendent," said Clara.

"And I'll be support attorney on this," said Hap. He turned to Emily. "I know this is not all you wanted or needed, but it was the best Judge Miller could work out given his philosophy of jurisprudence."

"I know you did your best."

Hap smiled.

What little secret was Hap covering up with that smile? Something to do with Judge Miller, Emily bet.

"Got a minute?" asked Clara. She nodded toward a bench near a live oak tree.

Once Emily and Clara were away from the others, Clara said, "I think I owe you an apology."

"For what?"

"For not being more honest with you."

"You were trying to protect me like you protected Darren, or thought you did."

"I came back from the coast thinking I could get to the truth of Morton's death, but I never did. I knew I couldn't let on who Darren's father was. It was better Darren believe Eddie was his dad. Eddie did his best. He was a generous guy in some ways. He couldn't seem to find work that didn't involve stealing or doing something illegal. But he'd never kill anyone."

"I thought the picture I found looked like Marcus and for a while I thought he was Darren's father."

Clara's mouth fell open. "What?"

"Only for a minute or so. You must have loved Morton very much to leave your practice on the coast and come back here."

"I did adore that man. The best cowman in the county. He could ride, he could shoot, he could rope, and he could knock a fly off a Brahman bull's horn with his bull whip at fifty feet." Clara's face grew soft and her eyes gentle. "Best of all, he could make love like no other man I ever met. He was one hell of a man. And if you're wondering, there never was anything between Neville Landry and me." She paused.

"No, of course not," said Emily.

"Morton had his flaws, like all men." She gave Emily a significant look. "He was far too trusting of everyone, including his brother. In the end, I wasn't able to prove anything about Marcus' involvement in Morton's death."

"Marcus couldn't have chosen a better mate than Lucinda, both as deadly as a wild boar in a palmetto thicket."

"Right, but her having him killed still leaves us with the question of whether or not he killed Morton."

"You knew both of them. What do you think?"

Clara didn't hesitate to answer. "Marcus killed his brother."

"We'll have to leave it like that then."

Clara sighed, raised her eyes to the far horizon and gazed down the shady street toward the pavement's end and the beginning of pasture land with its scattering of sabal palms. "I love it here, and I surely didn't like the fast-paced life in West Palm. And it wouldn't have been good for Darren."

"We try to do what's best for our children, but it doesn't always work out that way," Emily said.

"Your daughter seems to be level-headed." Clara laughed. "Now that's she's gotten over her propensity for marrying abusive cops. Speaking of which, how about you and cops? Or is it, bass fishermen?"

Emily shot Clara a dismissive look. "Darren's doing okay, too," she said instead.

"Yeah, not bad, given his lack of parenting while growing up. I wasn't a very attentive mother, Emily."

"Me either." Emily smiled, and Clara let out the bark of a laugh, reached out and enveloped Emily in a hug.

"Anyway, I'll try to be more trusting in the future. There is one thing, however," Clara said as the two of them walked back to join the others.

"What?"

"I'll let you keep the Walther PPK if you promise to take good care of it, clean it thoroughly after you fire it and practice once in a while."

"You don't think my aim was accurate last night?"

"Desperate beginner's luck."

Hap interrupted Emily and Clara. "We were worried the two of you had some kind of a score to settle, but the smiles on your faces say otherwise. So everything's fine?" asked Hap.

"As fine as it can be given the judge's ruling. Listen, can someone give me a ride over to Stan? I need to pull out all that stuff in the back seat. I think it's about time I donated Fred's old clothes to charity," said Emily.

"I'll help," offered Naomi.

Later that day Emily and Naomi surveyed the pile of men's clothes dumped in the center of the living room floor at Emily's house.

"We could have dropped off all these clothes at Goodwill, but no. You insisted we bring them back here and go through them," said Naomi.

"There might be money in the pockets, you know. I guess I can use all the cash I can get."

They fished around in all the pockets. With only several pairs of pants and one sport jacket to go, their search yielded them a paltry ten dollars in ones and some change, mostly pennies.

"This is silly," said Emily. She picked up the jacket. "Ah, wait. It feels like there's a wad of bills in the inside pocket." But to her dismay she extracted not greenbacks, but folded papers bound by heavier stock. On it, written in Fred's hand, was a note. It read, "Happy birthday, honey. I should have done this long ago, but here you are. Love, Fred."

Emily unfolded the papers. At the top were the words, "Last Will and Testament." It was dated several months before Fred died.

"What is it?" asked Naomi.

Emily was too numb to react. "A birthday gift from Fred."

"When was your birthday?"

Emily thought back to Fred's death. The days, weeks and months after it were so filled with anxiety and uncertainty that she forgot her birthday came a mere week after Fred's funeral. She told

Naomi the date and then handed the papers to her.

Naomi scanned the document. "This is quite a present. It looks to me as if he left everything to you. And the will must be legal. It's witnessed, dated, and there's a lawyer's address in West Palm on it. We'd better get in touch with Hap and have him contact the lawyer on your behalf."

Emily found it difficult to focus on the will and what it meant for her. Instead, she thought back to when Fred was alive. "I think I remember the day Fred must have done this. He said he was going to the coast to buy me a birthday present, but I forgot all about it with his death and all. He left the document in his pocket." Emily sank down onto the couch with a blank expression on her face. She felt.... *What did she feel?*

"Oh, Fred," she said.

"Sweet of him," said Naomi. "He was thinking about your well-being after all."

Emily reached down into the feelings tumbling around in her center. "The rat! 'Sweet' is not what I'm experiencing, not after all the trouble I've gone to trying to prove my right to our house, our car, our money, the smarmy lawyer, the humiliation of having Carolyn best me in court, the degradation of having the community see me as a scarlet woman." As quickly as she condemned Fred for his forgetfulness, her anger took a U-turn.

"Why couldn't I have had my birthday before Fred died?" Emily could see Fred's eyes twinkle with joy as he handed her the will all tied up in a white box with red ribbon. Then came another jerk of the emotional steering wheel. "It was so hot the day he decided to go jogging, the idiot!" And then a yank in the other direction, "I should have stopped him."

Naomi wrapped her arms around her mother, and they sat on the couch for the next hour, Emily sobbing endlessly into the tissues Naomi handed her while the two rocked back and forth.

"You know it wasn't your fault. And it wasn't Fred's fault he died either."

"I know. I guess I pushed all those awful feelings aside. I was too busy trying to figure out how to keep the house and how to pay my bills. Everything kind of sneaked up on me. Sorry."

"Don't be. I'm glad I was here."

Emily surprised herself when she said, "Me too. It's good having someone you care about to share your most embarrassing feelings with." She reached out and touched her daughter's blonde curls. "Your parents did a terrific job raising you."

Naomi's face reddened at the compliment.

"I'll be right back," said Emily. "I've got to wash all this slobber off my face."

"How do you feel now?" asked Naomi when Emily returned from the bathroom.

"Awful. My nose and eyes are red, and I'm due at the bar in less than an hour."

"No. I meant about Fred."

"Typical Fred, I guess. I still miss him, but he did have some annoying traits. He couldn't have waited to kick off after my birthday?"

Naomi looked at her mother in astonishment.

"Just kidding. But it would have been nice if he'd stuck around to deliver the present in person, given me a cake, and we could have blown out the candles together."

"It's not too late."

Emily looked at her daughter with curiosity. "What do you mean?"

"In all of this upheaval you missed your birthday, and I'm sure Fred planned some kind of a celebration. This will proves it." Naomi waved the document back and forth in her hand. "So what do you say? Let's have a party. What would you most like to do for your birthday?"

She wanted to say, "Bring Fred back to life," but she knew she needed to move on. Emily thought for a while. The will had taken her by surprise, and she found it difficult to contemplate something as frivolous as a birthday party. But what the heck, she decided. *I know what I'd like.*

❖

Not everyone could fit into Donald's bass boat, but Emily assured Clara, Hap, Vicki and Darren that Donald promised to be back by early afternoon so everyone could partake of cake and ice cream at Clara's.

Her daughter's mood had been positively ebullient after finding that Donald and Lewis' visit to her husband in the hospital seemed to convince Barry he should avoid her at all cost.

This morning she stuck her nose into the wind and smiled widely as they sped up the river toward Donald's favorite fishing place.

"Close your mouth," said Donald, "or you'll be flossing bugs out of your teeth tonight."

Naomi laughed and waved his comments away.

The only person aboard the craft who didn't seem as happy as he might with the day off work and Emily in the boat with him was Detective Lewis. His mouth had difficulty maintaining the smile required when a man contemplated a fresh catch of speck. Emily figured he had in mind a more private celebration of her birthday, but this party was for her and Fred. Besides, she wasn't sure if she was ready for another man in her life.

And then there was the question of which man. Emily glanced at Donald who seemed sanguine about Lewis' presence, but then Donald was always hard to read.

Meantime, Emily sat in the bow of the craft and let the early morning, cool river air blow through her hair. And she determined this time to catch something other than, well, you know. She was after fish.

THE END

ABOUT THE AUTHOR

Lesley retired from her life as a professor of psychology and reclaimed her country roots by moving to a small cottage in the Butternut River Valley in upstate New York. In the winter she migrates to old Florida—cowboys, scrub palmetto and open fields of grazing cattle, a place where spurs still jingle in the post office. Back north, she devotes her afternoons to writing, and when the sun sets, relaxing on the bank of her trout stream, sipping tea or a local microbrew. In her words, "I come to the 'Big Lake' to write, hang out in cowboy bars and immerse myself in the Florida that used to be. No beaches, no bikinis, no sand. Just cows, horses and gators."

www.lesleyadiehl.com